THE
OTHER
MRS.
SAMSON

Ralph Webster

Printed in the United States of America
First Printing, 2021
ISBN-13: 9798564829403
Library of Congress Control Number: 2020923414
Independently Published
Kitty Hawk, North Carolina

In memory of Katie

Many stories beg to be told.

Whether they should be shared is an
entirely different question.

.

Introduction

2020

Perhaps it was the pandemic, because I do have a lot of time on my hands, but my search for furnace filters more likely explains how I happened upon the long-forgotten small black lacquered cabinet. It had been carefully tucked away in the corner of the attic, along with a few other items we brought back from Katie's New York apartment the week after she died.

The cabinet was curious, something others might consider an antique of some value or perhaps even a work of art. Age and travel had given it a few dents and bruises, but it seemed to have survived intact from a journey that must have been quite far.

It was not exceptionally large, little more than fourteen inches tall, sixteen inches wide, and twelve inches deep. The face and sides were inlaid with various symbols, intricate designs trimmed with silver and gold. Behind two beautifully decorated doors were seven small shallow drawers, three pairs of two with a larger single beneath.

As I recall, neither of us had any idea why Katie had kept it, where it came from, or what its use may have been. The drawers were empty when we retrieved it from her apartment, and we had no recollection of her ever speaking of the cabinet's existence. At the time, our only observation was that it was out of place. Her furniture tended to be more in the art deco style, not of Oriental origin, as the cabinet appeared. And to be perfectly honest, I am unable to remember why we saved it and didn't consider consigning it to a reputable auction house where, despite its wear, it might have fetched a good price.

When we returned from New York, it went to the attic because, like many things, there was no other place to put it and we didn't have the heart to give it away. I imagine our attic was no different from most, out of sight, out of mind, where we stored assorted things of questionable worth, objects of little use but too sentimental to part with, saved from the past with the unfounded hope that the next generation might claim them.

That afternoon, almost absentmindedly, I decided to dust it off. I must have tugged a little too hard on the bottom drawer or done something to cause its release because, when I pulled it open, the drawer slid out of the cabinet frame. That's when I was surprised to discover the hidden compartment located below the drawer and was even more amazed by its contents. Inside were batches of letters wrapped in ribbons, a small leather-bound notebook with gilded pages, and a sheaf of pages tied together with a piece of brown string.

Most stories start at the beginning. But as you can see, this one begins at its end. I was given no choice. The answers were found in that order.

One

2005 – Fifteen years earlier

After patiently waiting in line for nearly ten minutes, I found myself at the front and presented the slightly crumpled, official-looking small green form. Our usually talkative postmistress hardly muttered a word, not even bothering to look up to give me a glance. Instead, she mumbled something I failed to understand, stretched her bangled arm over to the large wooden table that sat behind her, and searched for the item sent by certified mail. Then she pointed a sparkling nail-polished finger at where I needed to sign, said a few more incoherent words, and gave me the well-taped, thick, nine-by-twelve-inch manila envelope. The return address was printed in large type. It was from a New York City law firm.

I know others enjoy conversing with neighbors and trading the latest village gossip while waiting at the post office, but not me. I'm rarely amused and mostly annoyed when I have to pick up the mail, an errand self-ishly avoided with any excuse possible. Our little community of fewer than two hundred is too small to have a full-time mailman and door-to-door delivery, so every few days, Ginger or I have to make a quick stop at the little post office two blocks north of the lighthouse to unlock our mailbox and sort through the contents.

Today was my turn, and the quick stop took much longer. Tucked in the middle of the junk mail and magazines was a little green piece of government paper, the dreaded notification that meant a visit to the postal desk, an all-too-often awkward and lengthy encounter with the postmistress, and the worry that I'm about to receive an audit notice from the IRS or something equally disconcerting.

Fortunately, today's line moved steadily, and my business with the postmistress was quickly concluded. Her mumblings were clear. She was overwhelmed and overworked, certainly not in the mood to converse. I know some of my friends in the village complain about her prickly attitude, but that's just the quirky personality most of us have come to accept. Others would argue that this temperament is a local contagion. I'm sure the summer tourists would agree. They find most of us who live here year-round to be equally peculiar.

◆

I had a million things left to do when Ginger reminded me about the post office stop. Later that day, we planned to drive to Norfolk, where we would spend the night before catching an early morning flight to Santiago. We were heading further south, near Cape Horn and the tip of South America, for several weeks of hiking in Patagonia, a welcome break from the winter quiet of our northern beaches.

This trip promised to be a complicated adventure. Snow, ice, glaciers, and mountains were all part of the itinerary. We weren't finished packing. Our hiking boots still needed to be waterproofed. We had to find someone to stop at the house every few days to make sure there was enough food on the porch for Pampas, the feral cat who has dined there for years. And I needed to drain the water lines and winterize everything. Winter nor'easters on the Outer Banks of North Carolina can be brutal, and the day's weather was miserable – cold, windy, and raining.

When I returned from the post office, I set the envelope aside on my desk. There was too much left to do in the short time remaining. The envelope would be something for later. I had a fairly good idea what was in it: nothing pressing, a few documents stored in Katie's safety deposit box at the bank.

Katie, our dear longtime friend from New York City, had passed away six weeks earlier. The last few months had been difficult and quite discouraging for all. She had been failing as she neared her ninety-fifth birthday, but any loss is a shock, even those that are expected. We had become quite close and considered Katie a member of our family. Friday nights still seemed empty without our weekly phone conversations, a cherished habit the three of us enjoyed when we could not be together.

I recognized the law firm named on the envelope. The attorney handling Katie's estate had called a few days earlier to advise us that they were sending these papers. We understood that the executor had reviewed the safety deposit box contents and removed anything of value. Katie's will specified that we were to be sent whatever remained.

Ginger and I both remembered the day when the three of us were emptying Lottie's house in New Jersey, an emotional task that Katie vowed her will would preclude. That day, she told us that all that was kept at the bank were some old papers of no use to anyone but herself – passports, Social Security cards, a few of Josef's old papers. Her advice was typical Katie: "Don't waste your time. Take a look if you wish, but you should throw it all away. There is nothing to see. I don't know why anybody would be interested in my old things. I'll leave it to you to decide. Es ist alles Müll."

Before leaving for Norfolk, I took a few minutes to open the envelope and thumb through its contents. Katie was right. There were no buried treasures. I put everything back and resealed it. Then we set out dinner on the porch for Pampas, turned off the lights, locked the doors, and departed. The envelope? The envelope would stay safely tucked away in the back of my closet. It would have to wait for another cold, rainy day.

Two

I met Katie for the first time fifty years ago, late in December of 1970. There should be no confusion. Although I was a newly minted nineteen-year-old when I was introduced to Mrs. Samson, I can assure you that this was not a Mrs. Robinson scene from *The Graduate* or anything similar.

The introduction took place during my first long-distance, on-my-own road trip, a few days past Christmas in a year still remembered for its long season of winter misery. Winter that year arrived a month too early, stayed a month too late, and was filled with never-ending snow, ice, and freezing temperatures.

The backseat of my prized, well-used, and slightly rusted yellow 1959 Dodge Coronet was loaded with all my worldly possessions, and the radio was turned up as it played Steppenwolf's *Born to be Wild,* the theme song of choice for those hitting the road that year. My clothes hung on an improvised clothesline stretching across the seat between the back windows, the much-recognized sign to passing drivers that a college student was on the way to somewhere.

Hanging the clothes across the back at first seemed like a good idea, but I soon learned that any view of the traffic behind was so obstructed that no matter how I positioned my head, it was impossible to see through the rearview mirror. That mirror was not my biggest concern. As the blinding, windblown snow continued to fall, the worn-out wiper blades in the front failed to keep up, and the view through the windshield was not any better.

I still remember my lack of cash being a constant worry. My billfold was empty, and ATMs had not yet been invented. The Texaco credit card helped but could only be used to buy gas. Finding open Texaco gas stations posed a serious problem. The further east I drove, the number of billboards advertising other upcoming gas stations increased while Texaco signs dwindled.

The solution was found in the glovebox, a slightly out-of-date map that could be used to navigate the highways. My plan was to skip the toll roads to conserve the little cash I had. What I remember are detours that were far too complicated and a journey that took much longer than necessary in those pre-GPS days. As I avoided the bypasses and searched small-town streets for open Texaco stations, the added miles only compounded the worry. My gas-guzzling old Dodge appeared to be consuming fuel at a faster rate than the miles needed to get to the next available gas pump.

The blizzard conditions didn't help, either, and my nerves were not entirely up to the challenge. I distinctly recall breathing so hard that the windows remained fogged for nearly the entire trip, a worry that required cranking open the side windows to let in cold air.

Then, with the heater set on high, hot air streaming at my face, the radio blaring, and sweat dripping across my forehead, all I could do was tightly grip the steering wheel with both hands. Those moments were intense. I remember desperately holding my breath as the threatening parade of caravanning semi-trailer trucks thundered past, splattering the windshield and blocking any remaining view of the slush-and-ice-filled road.

This unfolding itinerary would take me from the isolated comfort of college in Iowa to the relatively big-city streets of Washington, DC, my intended home for the next several months, the second semester of my junior year. This was a somewhat adventurous journey for a pretty sheltered Midwesterner who, while nervous, was still a product of the sixties and full of a less-than-deserved self-confidence.

Ohio was the first stop, actually, Cleveland, where I bunked with a distant relative. This was the first time I experienced the blizzard conditions of lake-effect snow, an unfamiliar phenomenon never seen nor heard of during my college years in Des Moines. Now, as I search my memory, I delight in recalling that 1970 was a year filled with many firsts, including experiencing sex and eating shellfish. Lake-effect snow, however, is not a memory recalled quite as fondly.

The second night, I met Mrs. Samson. I was staying in New Jersey, a stone's throw from the George

Washington Bridge, the gateway to New York City and the home of two favorites: Mom's brother, Uncle Alex, and his wife, Aunt Lotte. I had been to New Jersey once before, on a family road trip from my childhood home in Illinois. That time, I was seven, and there were no rules for child seats or seat belts. To "keep the kids from fighting," we sat in our assigned seats the entire time, Mom and my four-year-old sister in the back and Dad and me in the front seat. Whenever we traveled, I always sat up front, feigning the possibility of car sickness, a practical solution to the problem of having to sit aside my younger sister.

The car windows were kept open on that trip, too, to capture the breeze and rid the car of my parents' cigarette smoke as we drove "out East to visit relatives, see the Empire State Building, and climb the Statue of Liberty." With the exception of my sister's repeated complaints from the back, most memories of that trip have faded. What remains is the picture of my father's discomfort and pained expression when forced to drive through the crowded streets of New York City.

On my trip, I was delayed in finding my Englewood Cliffs destination because of a missed exit, the one with the sign that warned "Last Exit before Bridge," an unfortunate mistake that caused me to view the Hudson River from either direction atop the traffic-filled George Washington Bridge. This situation was resolved only after my own discomfort and an unexpected rush-hour tour of NYC as I searched for a way to turn back across.

The map? It was of no help. It only went as far as New Jersey.

Fortunately, shortly before nightfall, I managed to find my way to their house. That was when I first met Uncle Alex and Aunt Lotte's friends, the Winkels, who were visiting from upstate New York, and Mrs. Samson, who lived in the city. As for dinner conversation that evening, what I most remember are Mrs. Samson's exceptional politeness and our generational difference, which, at my age, seemed more than apparent.

Three

2006 – Corolla, North Carolina

More than a year would pass before I found that rainy day and rediscovered the thick envelope sent by the New York law firm, the one I put in the closet the day we were leaving for Patagonia. It wasn't that it hadn't rained. There had been plenty of rainy days. It's just that, as we all know, sometimes life takes over and things work out that way. I can't say I had procrastinated or forgotten. As is true all too often, I just hadn't made the time.

Again, Ginger and I were packing, but on this occasion, not for a trip, at least not one as far as South America. We were getting ready to move twenty-five miles south to Kitty Hawk, to the other side of the barrier island, trading sunrises for sunsets in a development where there were mostly full-time residents and no rental homes for tourists. This would be a big change. Both of us felt like we were moving back to the city.

10

The Outer Banks had been our home for years, ever since our son had left for college. That's when we gave up our life in the Washington suburbs and moved to the beach in North Carolina. We loved this life – waking up with the sun, long morning walks along the ocean, volunteering to ride ATVs on the beach at sunrise to search for sea turtle tracks, and staying up late to join the lifeguards and their friends for tiki-torch parties. They amplified their music using the electrical outlet behind our gazebo.

Katie enjoyed her visits here, too. Although she always referred to herself as a "big-city girl," she had discovered the wonder of life along the ocean. Even when she was well into her nineties, she found wearing a baseball cap and riding in the back of the Jeep a refreshing contrast to the life she had known first in Berlin, then in Paris, and finally New York City.

Once or twice each year, she would fly down and stay for a week, never forgetting to bring the framed photograph of her deceased husband, Josef, which would sit on the table next to her bed. She even had a designated bedroom with a closet full of clothes, like the brightly colored pantsuit she and Ginger had bought, clothes that were better left in North Carolina because "an old lady like me would never dare wear these on the sidewalks of New York," a comment always punctuated with *schrecklich*, German for terrible.

As is so often true, dreams can change. Ginger and I found ourselves becoming tired of the large numbers of tourists who arrived each summer. Age had a way of doing that. No one should misunderstand. The northern Outer Banks beaches will always be spectacular and a great place to vacation, but it's one thing to be a visitor and another to live here year-round. We will always enjoy the feeling of sand between our toes, but too many had discovered our little patch of paradise, and we were ready to move on.

The overstuffed light-brown envelope sat undisturbed on the closet shelf in the same place where I had left it. When I saw it, my first recollection was Katie's advice: "It's only rubbish. Don't waste your time. Throw it away." But then I hesitated and sat down at my desk. I was tired of packing. It was time for one last look.

◆

As I opened the envelope and removed the assortment of papers, a faded, small light-brown businesslike card dropped out and fell to the desk. I set the other documents aside and studied it carefully.

The card was for the Restaurant du Commerce and its owner, Baptiste Rey. On the back was a handwritten note scribbled in French that said: "To whom it may concern. Monsieur Josef Samson and his wife are staying in Soumoulou at my invitation." Beneath the note was the date, June 26, 1940, a signature that I couldn't make out, and an official-looking ink blotter stamp, "Maire de Soumoulou," the town hall of Soumoulou. Even I could translate these words, but I had no idea why it had been saved in Katie's safety deposit box.

A Google search for Soumoulou yielded few listings, mostly advertisements for nearby rental homes. I learned that Soumoulou is a very small village in southwestern France.

It was possible that this was the card of a friend, but more likely, it was some type of registration or identification since it had been signed and stamped at the town hall. There was no way to know for sure.

◆

Next were two sets of transit papers, one for Kaethe Samson and another for Josef Samson. Both were faded and torn, dotted with signatures, stamps, much scribbling, and various dates, all from late 1941.

On the top right corner of each was a visa signed by an official at the Portuguese consulate, with a notation of telegraphic approval from Lisbon. On the top left was a United States immigration visa signed by a vice-consul based in Marseille. On the bottom right corner was a visa granting ten-day transit through Spain, and on the left were an assortment of other stamps and signatures from various locations. On the reverse was a safe-conduct pass and an exit authorization from Vichy France, signed by the secretary general at Le Préfet des Basses-Pyrénées in Pau, a city in southwestern France. As I examined these papers, I thought about the sought-after transit documents in the movie *Casablanca*.

◆

There was a wrinkled light-yellow sheet of thin paper titled "Contrat de Mariage." Written in longhand, the
words were in French, and the handwriting was poor
and faded, making it difficult to read. Actually, there
were two sheets, not copies, but both identically handwritten and signed.

Using translation software, I learned that "German
citizens, Josef Samson, son of Wolff Wilhelm and Lina
Saloman Samson, and Kaethe Kasmund, daughter of
Franz and Agnes Schuppe Kasmund, were married on
June 24, 1940." Josef was sixty-one years old. Katie was
thirty. Both were listed as being born in Berlin but living
in Paris. Neither reported a profession, and there was no
indication of religion. There were no witnesses to the
documents, just official-looking stamps and signatures
by *L' Officier de l'Etat civil* at the town hall, the Mairie de
Préchacq-Josbaig.

Préchacq-Josbaig is a tiny village in the Basses-Pyre-
nees. Near the Spanish border, it is nearly two thousand
kilometers from Berlin and 850 kilometers from Paris.
The location is in southwestern France, not far from
Soumoulou, where Baptiste Rey and the Restaurant du
Commerce were located. Perhaps they traveled to
Soumoulou for their honeymoon after they were mar-
ried.

As for their ages, we had always known that Josef was
more than thirty years older. But what did seem odd was
the year: 1940. I tried to remember if Katie had ever told
us when she and Josef were married. Somehow I was always under the impression that their marriage had taken

place after they left Berlin and moved to Paris, which would have been sometime in the early 1930s. She never told us that they lived together for seven or eight years before they married.

◆

There was a second marriage document, quite different and more formal than the first, that bore no relation to Katie. This was written in German on a pre-printed form, with the blanks scribbled in longhand. Again, because of the handwriting and the age of the document, it was difficult to read everything clearly. Signed in Berlin, at the Rathaus Charlottenburg, it stated: "In a civil ceremony, Josef Samson, son of W. Wilhelm and Lina Saloman Samson, residents of Berlin, and Hilda Adele Samson, daughter of the deceased Rudolf Samson and wife Camilla, residents of San Francisco, California, USA, were married."

The year was 1913. Josef was listed as thirty-four years old, and his wife, Hilda, was listed as twenty-nine. The marriage certificate was witnessed by Wolff Samson, who I assumed was Josef's father, but since Josef and Hilda were shown to have the same last name, he could have been either's cousin. I was only able to read the first name of the second witness, Adele. California was listed as her residence.

We knew that Josef had been married before, that there had been a previous Mrs. Samson, but little more had been said. Since Josef was so much older and this marriage had taken place when Katie was a child of three, it was quite understandable. Still, we did not know how the marriage had ended. And there were other questions. I knew nothing about a Samson marrying a Samson or that Josef's first wife, Hilda, was from San Francisco. Katie had never chosen to share these curious details.

◆

Another official-looking paper was typed in French. The month and year were clear, June 1940, but the day had been left blank. Signed by the commandant of the Civilian Internment Camp du Bassens, Le Capitaine Gardineau, it ordered Josef Samson to be released.

The internet had only a few references to Camp du Bassens. I learned that it was located approximately twelve kilometers from Bordeaux and occupied an old powder mill built during the First World War. The mill's buildings had been modified to receive "undesirable" foreigners. Approximately eleven hundred prisoners were held there, seven hundred of them German Jews. The others were German soldiers captured by the French.

Again I was confused. I knew that at the beginning of World War II, the French had sequestered German nationals living in France into internment camps, a way to separate "enemy aliens" from the general population. This was not dissimilar from what England had done to Germans or the U.S. had done to Japanese nationals, but this document was dated nine months after the war began. Had Josef been arrested and held all that time?

And why would France imprison German Jews with captured German soldiers? That made little sense. Jews were the enemy of the Nazis. Why put both Jews and Nazis together in the same camp?

◆

As I continued to sift through the papers, a one-quarter-page form fell to the floor, a tattered, dog-eared onionskin document labeled *Camp de Gurs* and titled *Avis de Libération du Camp D'Internement de Gurs*. This time the date was clearly legible – June 22, 1940, two days before Josef and Katie signed the marriage contract at the *Mairie de Préchacq-Josbaig*.

From the light-bluish ink, it seemed that this was a carbon copy and the crooked letters were the product of a damaged manual typewriter with misaligned keys. It bore the camp commandant's stamp, an indecipherable signature, and the order to free German citizen Kaethe Martha Kasmund.

Not knowing the geography, I again turned to my computer. The Memorial du Camp de Gurs was only five kilometers from Préchacq-Josbaig, the site of their marriage. Camp du Bassens, where Josef was held, was much further away, 250 kilometers north. How long had Katie been detained?

◆

Sorting through these documents was taking more time than I had, and there were too many unanswered questions. I put everything back in the envelope and added it to an assortment of other items packed in a large box, the one labeled "old stuff."

I never expected that fourteen years later we would be housebound because of a pandemic, and I certainly had no idea that the missing answers to my questions would be found hidden in a secret compartment in an antique cabinet stored in the attic.

Four

1970 – Englewood Cliffs, New Jersey

I f memory serves me right, no one had told me there would be a dinner party at my aunt and uncle's home that evening fifty years ago. As the snow continued to fall and I nervously drove through Manhattan, I had no forewarning that other guests would be arriving within the hour.

In 1970, cell phones and texting were not words in our vocabulary. Neither was email. I was used to just rolling with it. That's what we all did. One just made plans in advance and showed up. I never considered searching for a phone booth or stopping to place a call to announce my estimated arrival time. The most important thing to do was find a place to turn around and get back on the Henry Hudson Parkway. I needed to reverse my drive across the George Washington Bridge.

Mom had made the arrangements. All I had were an address and instructions, notes scribbled while I was holding the phone in one hand and writing with the other, directions that no longer made any sense. Fortunately, just as the gas gauge reminded me to search for another Texaco station, their driveway was in sight.

When I knocked on the door, Uncle Alex met me with a big hug and his booming "Ralpheloocho," a long-forgotten nickname. As he ushered me inside, I greeted Aunt Lotte, who was busy in the kitchen with dinner preparations. That's when I first learned that other dinner guests would soon be arriving.

Through the kitchen doorway, I could see into the dining room. The table was covered with a clean, freshly ironed white linen tablecloth, and six place settings were formally arranged, with small crystal wine glasses, an assortment of sterling silverware, and layered plates of clearly good china. Silver candlesticks with slender white tapers lined the center, and polished silver serving dishes had been neatly set upon the buffet. Aunt Lotte explained that the dining table was always set for six when their "oldest friends," the Winkels, and "closest friend," Mrs. Samson, came to dinner, something the two couples and one widow did every month without fail.

They had dined together for nearly three decades, a tradition that had begun in 1942 after they had fled the war in Europe and formed their friendship in America. Their dinners had become a time to celebrate successes, share important moments, and provide comfort for one another's challenges and disappointments. Each had been robbed of years when the world should have given them more. It was a time when all one could do to survive was flee, leave all else behind, and jump into the unknown. They had been uprooted and tossed and turned by events that could not have been imagined in their youth, events that had shaped their lives, struggles that had destroyed millions of their generation, a history they shared in common.

Since five others, the two couples and the widowed Mrs. Samson, were dining that evening, I erroneously assumed that the sixth place setting, the one at the far end of the table, had been set for me. I quickly learned that I was mistaken. That seat was actually designated for its original occupant, Mrs. Samson's deceased husband, Josef, who had died nine years earlier.

After his death, the others had chosen to continue setting his place for their dinners, a way to include him in their conversations and a loving and sensitive gesture for Mrs. Samson, who had been heartbroken at her loss. It was just coincidental that their monthly dinner was scheduled for the evening I was staying with my aunt and uncle. As their houseguest, I was kindly invited to temporarily use Josef's chair.

While relieved to learn that I would not be the guest of honor, I recall an initial concern that I might be occupying the chair of a ghost or interfering with some kind of strange communication with the afterlife. However, both notions were quickly dispelled. Josef had been a big part of their worlds. Old, cherished habits and wonderful memories are hard to break, and they wanted to continue to think of themselves as three couples.

Each month, as they began dinner, they celebrated Josef's memory by raising their glasses and giving a silent toast, a moment to reflect upon their close friendship. That evening, as they turned to where I was seated and lifted their glasses, I joined them. Today, a half-century later, I understand their emotion and treasure my good fortune for being included in this wonderful tradition.

Now, as I think back upon that winter evening and begin to remember these details, I suppose one could say that dinner was when I began my lengthy acquaintance with the then-deceased Dr. Samson and started a wonderful friendship with his now-deceased wife, our dear friend Katie.

Five

J osef was the first of the three couples to die. And
since he was much older and had lived a full and complete life before he met the others, there is much
about him that remains a mystery. His death came in
1961, when he was eighty-two years old and Katie was
fifty-one. The others claimed, by the way he acted, that
it hardly seemed possible that he could have been of a
different generation. Often it was as if he was the
younger and they were the older.

His passing was not unexpected, but the end had been
difficult. He suffered in that final year, likely the price of
those months at the beginning of the war, when he
nearly starved and was left to sleep on the camp's damp
stone floor in France. The others understood. They were
all of an age where they recognized that every life must
end with death. For Katie, however, losing Josef was
much more painful. Everything in her life had revolved
around Josef. She had no other family.

After Josef's death, their monthly dinners and friendships continued uninterrupted. They were survivors and contemporaries. They lived the American dream, and when they were together, they talked about American things, like the Mets and the Yankees, the movies, and the traffic. They didn't particularly dwell on the past. It wasn't that they wished to forget their history, but they lived in the present. They were Americans. America had become their home.

As for me, Washington, DC, became my home after that winter night in 1970, and I would live there, first the city, then the suburbs, alone and then with family, for most of the next twenty-five years. Those were the years when Uncle Alex and Aunt Lotte's home in New Jersey became a place to celebrate important birthdays, a venue for family gatherings, a bedroom for theater trips to New York City, and even a driveway to leave the car when Ginger and I caught flights from Newark or JFK for a growing list of overseas adventures.

Then, late one afternoon, Aunt Lotte answered her phone and received the news that Uncle Alex had suffered a heart attack and lost control of his car on the parkway in Connecticut. One moment, he was here, and the next moment, he was gone. We were all so shocked. He added such joy and enthusiasm to everyone's lives.

How many times had he said to me, "*Ralpheloocho, ricorda che non c'è mai un giorno senza sole.* There is never a day without sunshine." Uncle Alex was the one who could make everyone forget their troubles and laugh, even in the worst of moments. He always had a good story to tell. I doubt he ever looked up to the sky and saw a cloud. Everyone agreed that their monthly dinners were never the same after Alex's accident.

It was not long after, less than a year, when the Winkels' car slid off an icy country road in upstate New York. Nina lingered in a coma for three months but never recovered, and George was never the same. He died a short time later.

In those final years, after the others were gone, when only Katie and Lotte were left to continue their tradition, they abandoned the dining room. The table was too big for just them, and it was too sad for them to look at the four empty chairs. There were too many memories, too many emotions. That's when they decided to move their dinners into the kitchen, to the small table with the vase that was always filled with fresh flowers.

Every Friday, Katie would leave the city and drive across the George Washington Bridge to New Jersey to spend the weekend with Lotte. They would never forget. At the beginning of each dinner, they would always give a silent toast to the others.

Ever since they had first met, the two had acted as if they were sisters – Lotte, short and energetic, and Katie, tall and always caring and respectful. Of course, there were times when they became angry and fought over one silly issue or another, but there was never a Monday morning when Katie returned to the city that all was not forgotten. Neither had any doubt. They were the best friends either ever had.

Then, one day, Katie called to tell us that Lotte had died. It seemed impossible. Two years older, Katie had always thought that she would be first and Lotte would be the last one left. She couldn't believe it. One moment, Katie had been holding her best friend's hand, and the next moment, Lotte was gone. That was when there were no more drives across the George Washington Bridge, when the dinners ended, and when the house in New Jersey was sold.

Six

1995

M *eine Mutter hätte es nie zugelassen.* My mother
would have never allowed it."

Suddenly, from out of nowhere, Katie said
this as we were sitting together, quietly enjoying the
warm sunshine on a park bench near the Cloisters. It was
only days after Lotte had died. Ginger and I had flown to
New Jersey to take care of arrangements and be with
Katie.

That afternoon, the weather was beautiful, and we
had decided to take some time for ourselves in the city.
Katie was insistent that Ginger and I begin spending the
nights with her in her Manhattan apartment. By now,
Lotte's house was a mess, and much of the furniture had
been removed. Katie told us she had already "moved to
the study and remade the bed."

She wanted to show us one of her favorite spots, Fort
Tryon Park in the Washington Heights section of

27

Manhattan, where the Cloisters was located. Katie loved the Cloisters, particularly the winding paths, especially in late spring, when the gardens were in bloom and people were out. After a long walk, she enjoyed resting on a bench, watching everyone who passed by. We were observing more and more about Katie, getting to know her better. People-watching was her quiet form of entertainment, a lifelong habit.

The last few days had been difficult as we had gone through Lotte's house and sorted through her possessions. We were all adjusting, and we were tired. I think others know. Anyone who has spent time cleaning out another's home – taking stock of someone's lifetime, opening the closets, looking beneath the beds, sifting through drawers, uncovering old secrets, sorting through belongings – understands the kaleidoscope of emotions the three of us shared.

Working together, we found a special closeness – the surprises, the confusion, the sadness, the memories, and the precious relief that comes with both tears and laughter. And as we sifted through Lotte's life, we came to recognize that somehow, through a remarkable set of circumstances spanning multiple generations and having little to do with bloodlines or family tree, we were destined to be linked to one another.

When we first arrived, the day after Katie called with the news about Lotte, Ginger and I were concerned about Katie's welfare, how she would fare with Lotte's absence, whether missing this important part of her life would be her undoing. We wondered how she would fill

THE OTHER MRS. SAMSON | 29

the void that had been left behind. I suppose we presumed and assumed. That week, we learned that Katie was not that fragile. She wouldn't break. At eighty-five years of age, she was stronger and more independent than we had ever imagined, insistent about her lifestyle, accustomed to her daily rhythm, and at home with the city's hustle and bustle. There was little question that she was more than able to care for herself.

That's why we were both surprised when she suddenly made this comment about her mother. It seemed out of thin air, totally out of context. Neither of us had asked a question. There had been no conversation. When Katie saw our anxious looks of concern, she paused for several moments, frowned, and stared straight ahead. Then she turned toward us, smiled, laughed, and pointed at her forehead.

"Don't worry. *Ich bin verrückt.* Sometimes I am a little crazy. Never mind me. I was just having a conversation with myself. You will see. It is something I do all the time, mostly within the four walls of my apartment when there is no one else to talk to. Don't be alarmed. There is no reason to be concerned."

Sitting on the park bench that day, we learned that Katie had been nine years old when her mother died. She added little else, only that Berlin had been overflowing with Spanish flu victims and her mother had been buried in an unmarked grave with many others. "Papa cried so much that evening. He was so sad and heartbroken."

That afternoon at the Cloisters, we began to understand that getting to know Katie would be like finding the missing pieces to an enormous jigsaw puzzle. There would be moments like these when she would suddenly tell us things that we had never known before, a little bit at a time and not in any particular order. Sometimes we would be left with incomplete sentences and questions without answers. What her mother would have never allowed was only one of the many that would remain unanswered.

Seven

It's curious how our relationship with Katie changed over those years. At first, when Uncle Alex introduced me to Mrs. Samson, I remember her as polite and friendly but noticeably quiet and reserved, a bit removed and distant. I thought of her as an older widow, almost spinster-like, who stayed very much in the background, someone who might nod approvingly but rarely offer an opinion. I'm sure Uncle Alex contributed to that impression. His larger-than-life personality could drown out most others in the room.

It was Ginger who changed this way of thinking. When Ginger entered my life, our friendship with Katie began to grow and evolve. From the moment they met, it was easy to see that the two shared a special connection, a warm, wonderful bond. That's when Mrs. Samson immediately insisted we call her Katie. Knowing both, this was not a surprising gesture. Their personalities were similar in nature. Both were quite comfortable standing together in the background, where they could enjoy one another's company. Ginger often claims that because of my loud and boisterous family, they found themselves standing together at many family get-togethers.

Each valued her privacy. Both tended to keep thoughts to themselves, content to listen and happy to let others do the talking. It was rare that either would be so impolite as to interrupt another's conversation. They would smile and observe. I know both would laugh and agree when I say this. They were "simpatico." It was as if they had known one another their entire lives. Each always seemed to know what the other was thinking.

Until Aunt Lotte died and Katie was the last of their group, what we knew of Katie was mostly through our mutual friendship with Aunt Lotte and Uncle Alex. They were the ones who always made it a point to include their "closest and dearest" friend in any celebration or gathering. Even then, as we began to think of her as a member of the family, Katie never shared too much about herself and truly little about her history. She simply preferred her privacy. She never gave the impression there was anything she wished to hide, only that she could not understand why others would be interested in her old stories.

It was only in those final years, when it was just Katie, Ginger, and me, that we began to know more about her heartbreaks and fears, beliefs and desires, and the details of her past, however incomplete. With Katie, there was always a quiet wall of separation, a personal and private space we always respected and never dared to intrude upon. She preferred to silently listen to us talk, to tell her our stories rather than answer our questions

When Aunt Lotte was still alive, she was our connection to Katie. Lotte enjoyed this role and felt possessive about our relationship. Now it had become Katie's turn. The week after Aunt Lotte died, Saturday morning phone calls with Lotte were replaced by Friday evening phone dates with Katie. We would pour ourselves a glass of wine, she in New York and Ginger and I in North Carolina, and these calls became an intimate way for us to begin to share in one another's lives.

For birthdays, we gave one another season tickets to the New York Philharmonic and tickets for Broadway shows. Then Ginger and I would enjoy frequent weekend visits to New York, and Katie would teach us about her city. She was our cheerleader, always wanting to be in our suitcase when we traveled, encouraging us as we explored the world. That was how the three of us began our own tradition. We never felt pressured or any obligation. This was something we chose. I know it may be a strange thing to say, but after Lotte died, it seemed as if Katie stepped out of the shadows and into our lives.

◆

That afternoon, after Ginger and I left the Cloisters, we drove the short distance to Katie's apartment. We had no idea where she lived. We had never been invited there before. I think we were both surprised when she told us to take the turn at 158th Street and Broadway, because the neighborhood appeared to be in decline and was not at all what we expected.

Then we followed her through the maze of darkened corridors that led from the apartment building's cavernous parking garage, past the grated and locked storage containers, wall of electric meters, and laundry room, before catching the elevator to the fourth floor. When we reached the door to her apartment, she opened her purse, brought out an assortment of keys, and quickly unlocked the three latches.

Before entering, she turned to face us, hesitating for several moments as she gathered her thoughts. Then she remarked, "After Josef died, I never wanted another soul to step through my front door, not even Alex or Lotte. They never did. You are the first to visit my apartment in more than thirty years."

All that I remember of the moment was Ginger tilting her head to the side and quizzically looking at me in amazement. We refrained from asking any questions and followed her inside.

HILDA

(Josef's first wife)

Eight

November 1914 – Berlin, Germany

Most would not characterize me as someone who dwells on the past, although I do find comfort in reliving certain moments, particularly random incidents, like an unexpected introduction, a chance meeting, watching something through an open window, the sorts of things that so often go unnoticed. I can't say I do this frequently, but it is something I do upon occasion, usually when I sit quietly by myself and sometimes late at night, when I am restless and have difficulty sleeping, which, of late, seems to be a recurring problem. Now that I'm with child, allowing my mind to wander a little has become a satisfying antidote to my nightly discomfort.

For me, these unexpected incidents are curious. They seem to solve a very confusing problem. At first, they appear isolated and unconnected. But later, when I reflect, it is as if these moments were never random, that they were always part of a much larger plan. If I follow from one to the next, I always arrive at the same destination. They lead me here, to this place at this time. Leaving my family and childhood home in San Francisco, moving to Berlin to marry Josef, and now expecting his child while Germany wages war are where these moments were always supposed to take me. I can think of no other reasonable explanation.

◆

I was just over four years old that day in 1888 when I first set eyes on Josef. He was a little more than twice my age, nearly two times my size, and according to Mama, he made a lasting impression. Mama would look at me and say, "Hilda, you are smitten." I followed Josef everywhere. He was patient and understanding and never seemed annoyed or bothered. I tried to imitate everything he did and talk the way he talked, stumbling through pronunciations, trying to make my English words sound like his German.

◆

Our unexpected meeting took place more than a quarter of a century ago in northern Germany, not far from the North Sea. It was a warm summer afternoon in early September and near the end of my family's six-month European tour, only a few days before Mama, Papa, and I began the long journey back to our home in San Francisco. Our return to New York through Liverpool was booked on a passenger ship scheduled to leave from the port in Hamburg. We had taken the day to visit Papa's relatives in Altona, the small and picturesque neighboring town perched along the cliffs on the south bank of the Elbe River.

In early spring of that year, Mama, Papa, and I rode the train from San Francisco to New York and traveled across the Atlantic for a leisurely sightseeing tour of Europe's galleries and museums. Mama loved art, music, and culture. She was a fan of the opera, always going to concerts and performances, lectures and readings, openings and exhibitions, delightful habits that I adopted as I grew older.

Others may find it remarkable that our family could afford the cost of such a trip and take the time for this lengthy European journey, but Mama and Papa had a penchant for travel and touring. This was how we lived, something they chose to do frequently. I was accustomed to these excursions. Throughout my childhood, in the 1880s and 1890s, we traveled by train between San Francisco and New York many times and made the crossing by ship to Europe every few years.

Of course, then I was much too young to understand that this type of travel for pleasure by Americans was a luxury reserved for only a wealthy few. I had no idea that our family lived differently from most. Even as I grew older, the subjects of money and wealth were never discussed in our household. I suppose, since little of consequence was ever denied, I grew up presuming that we always had more than enough.

As for the trip in 1888, I have only small traces of memories — I imagine reinforced by stories that Mama and Papa have since told me. I know that when we left San Francisco, we took the Pacific Hotel Express, a train that left on a Monday morning and arrived in New York City by Thursday evening. Mama says that the porters rearranged our cushioned seats into beds each evening. There were fresh linens every day, and the waiters in the dining car always made a big fuss, treating me like I was a little princess.

In New York, Papa attended to his business on Wall Street while Mama and I went out to lunch and spent our afternoons visiting all the big department stores on the Ladies Mile. Then we boarded the Etruria for the crossing to England. Mama said the ship reminded her of a fancy hotel with all its modern luxuries. At dinner, we dressed in evening clothes as if we were going out to a fancy restaurant in San Francisco. And once we arrived in England, we traveled by train and spent time in all the major cities, London, Paris, Vienna, and even Berlin, before finishing that year's tour in Hamburg.

◆

That afternoon in Altona, we were at a small outdoor family gathering, a backyard reunion, a chance for Papa to introduce Mama and me to many of his German relatives. Years later, I would learn that Josef was there because his grandfather's half-brother was a distant cousin of Papa's, the reason why Josef and I share the same family name.

Mama says I threw one of my tantrums when it was time to leave, throwing my coat on the floor and refusing to go. I didn't want to stop playing with my new friend. Papa lifted me into his arms and did his best to console me, but I cried and cried all the way back to the seaport.

◆

Late last evening, when Josef wrapped his arms around me and held me so close that I could feel his heart beating, we both laughed at this old story. Neither of us would admit to any recollection of that day so long ago. Josef's eyes twinkled, and in his teasing manner, he claimed that I had followed him ever since. But I am certain I know better. I will always remain convinced that he chased me.

Lying here now, in the quiet comfort of this moment, turning the pictures and stroking the pages of these memories makes me smile. I am content. I know that our life together began with that chance meeting, that totally random and disconnected moment.

Many years would pass before Josef and I would see each other again. That time, our meeting seemed as unexpected and magical as the first. I was totally unprepared and completely overwhelmed. Nothing had changed. Just as Mama once claimed, I was still smitten. It was as if we had known one another our entire lives, had never been apart, that this was always meant to be.

Then, too, when it came time to leave, I didn't want to stop being with Josef. I might have grown too old for tantrums, but just like when I was four years old, I cried and cried all the way to the seaport. That day, I was old enough to know for certain. Random footsteps might have brought us together, but Josef had stolen my heart.

Nine

No earthquakes were recorded in San Francisco on the day I was born in 1884, though the newspapers reported that only a few weeks earlier, nearly all of the city's residents were awakened by three waves of shocks damaging a number of the brick buildings along the city front not far from the Broadway Wharf. Mama says my face always brightens when Aunt Hattie tells me she didn't need to be shocked by an earthquake on the day she first saw me. All she needed to do was take one look. She claims that from head to foot, I was the scrawniest and cryingest baby she had ever seen.

Soon after my birth, the midwife wrapped me in a soft blanket and brought me to Aunt Hattie's arms so Mama could get some much-needed rest. Apparently, I had been the cause of a prolonged and difficult delivery. We all must have been pretty worn out, because Aunt Hattie contends she was never certain who suffered more that morning, Mama, Papa, or me. Anyway, Aunt Hattie and

I developed a close bond that day. Mama claims that ever since, we were like "two peas in a pod."

Aunt Hattie was Mama's older sister and as close as possible to being my godmother without actually being my godmother. While Aunt Hattie never recited a god-mother's oath, she always kept her arms tightly wrapped around me. Our family may not have been the most ob-servant in San Francisco, but we often went to the syna-gogue and respected our Jewish traditions.

◆

By all accounts, I was fortunate, certainly privileged and, according to those who know me best, more than a little spoiled. Mama's family, the Meyers, was one of the old-est and most prominent in the city, one of the dozen or so pioneer families the newspaper society pages often referred to as San Francisco's Bavarian aristocracy.

When I was born, the family's investment bank was one of the most successful in California, and I was the latest member of their rapidly expanding third Ameri-can generation. Papa's family, the Samsons, also had their own respected lineage. Their arrival in San Fran-cisco might have been more recent, but they, too, were afforded a proper place in the polite society of the city.

Of course, the day I was born, I knew none of these things. Babies never do. Crying was about all I could do. And as an only child for my first few years, I quickly learned that crying attracted attention, a technique I was to use often until shortly before my fifth birthday. Then it was my turn to be shocked. It wasn't the small earth-quake that shook us that day. It was my new brother, the scrawniest and cryingest baby I had ever seen. Until then, Mama always told me that I was the apple of Papa's eye. That day, I learned another of life's many difficult lessons. The apple would need to be shared.

Ten

As a young child, I imagine that my family's way of life was not dissimilar to most of our status and means. The fathers managed their businesses and family investments, spending most of their waking hours huddled in meetings with their associates in downtown offices or conducting their affairs in private, out of sight, behind closed doors. The mothers tended to family, home, society's demands, and, when duty called, their responsibilities with various unpaid benevolent causes.

It should be no surprise that apart from Nanny and Cook, the first faces I came to recognize and know best were the ones who stayed at home. These were the women in our family: Mama, Aunt Hattie, Papa's three sisters, and the assortment of girl cousins, of whom I was the youngest. They were all my teachers.

The boy cousins were kept apart, led a different life, and were seldom seen, always elsewhere, engaged in "boy" things. And when they grew older, they were sent away, first to private schools and then to universities. We each had our roles to perform, and they had expectations to fulfill.

As soon as I could take my first tentative, meandering steps, I was drawn to Mama's mother, my grandmother, who would beckon me with warm, welcoming arms, a loving smile, and the tempting scent of her fragrant powder. Oma was afforded an almost queenly status among the family's women. I basked in the presence of this little old woman with the wispy white hair, time-worn, wrinkled face, and curious way of speaking, who fluttered about like a tiny sparrow.

With her dark, piercing eyes and spirited gaze, I loved the way Oma would lean in close to my face, so close that it seemed our eyelids would touch. There she would listen carefully to my every word. Because we were so similar in size, I assumed only she and I shared this secret special connection. In those wonderful moments, she made me feel as if I were the single most important person in the entire world.

Oma's pet name for me was Mäuschen. I thought this was the most marvelous name and much more interesting than being called Hilda. Mäuschen was the name my favorite doll acquired and one that I hoped to bestow upon my own child someday. Oma told me that I reminded her of a little mouse because I was forever underfoot. It was the name her father had given her when she was a young child growing up in their small mountainside village alongside the Bavarian Alps.

◆

The month before my eighth birthday, Oma came to live with our family. Mama said Oma's house was sold because it was too much for her to handle, that Oma was getting older and needed our help. Since Grandfather Opa died two years before I was born, all I know of Mama's father was what others have told me and the impressions I formed from the large portrait hanging in the hallway.

After Oma moved into our household, she would enthusiastically greet me at the front door each afternoon when I came home from school. Then she would insist we sit down for a visit, just her and me. She liked to say that this was what all the important women of San Francisco did. They sat down together and discussed the day's events while they were served their afternoon tea. Having tea with Oma became a favored daily activity.

One afternoon, Oma became terribly upset with me. I fail to remember what I had done or said that day, but whatever it was, she was clearly disappointed, and I was in tears. "Mäuschen, I love you when you are good, and I love you when you are sick, but today, when you are bad, perhaps not quite so much. You are too old to be so spoiled. Life has not always been this easy. It is time for you to begin growing up." Since I always longed for Oma's approval, when she said this, I was devastated.

"You are not the first one to cry, or be unhappy, or feel hurt. You will survive. You will not always get your way in this life. There will be disappointments. When I was young and Opa came to tell me he would be leaving the next morning to join his brother in America, I was heartbroken. That day, I cried and cried. Much like you, Mäuschen, sometimes my tears come too easily and never seem to stop. I needed to learn then, and you need to learn now."

Even with tears running down my face and my small chin trembling, I was old enough to pay attention and listen, and certainly old enough to sense the emotion in Oma's words. But I'm not sure I was old enough to understand everything she told me that day. I was still accustomed to cuddling up with Mama, where everything was warm and comfortable, when we read bedtime stories with make-believe characters, stories where frightening moments passed quickly, not anything like this.

The world Oma described that afternoon was far from the world I knew, not comforting like the way we lived in San Francisco. She told me about places and events I was not familiar with, stories that had never been shared with me. I remember sniffling and nodding while Oma put her arm around me, held me close, and told me the rest of her story.

◆

"When Opa told me he was leaving, it was as if suddenly time stood still and there was nothing I could do. It didn't seem fair that Opa would leave and I would stay. No matter what he said or how long he held me, I was convinced that I would never be with him again. I just wanted him to keep his strong arms around me and never let me go. He was so certain, so confident, and so able. All the young men in our village were that way, but for me, your Opa was different. He was the most special. He would always listen patiently when I told him about my dreams. He had the kindest eyes, so clear and gentle. With Opa, I felt safe. I knew that he would watch over me.

"So many young men we knew had left and were never heard from again. I know that it may sound selfish, but when it was Opa's time to leave, I worried about what would happen to me. Remember, sometimes one needs to be a little selfish that way. It was such a terrible time in Bavaria. So many were suffering. For many in the countryside and small villages, there was barely enough food. We were young, and it should have been our turn to blossom, but the wars of the past had robbed us of our future.

"The authorities had strict rules for Jews, and for families like our own, it was especially bad. There were very few opportunities, and the Edict of 1813 allowed only a limited number of Jewish families to live in any one area. It made little difference how long our family had lived in the same village or how much good we had done for others. We were held back and denied our future. In Bavaria, after the lands were divided among the members of each new generation, all they were left with were the small patches that could barely feed a family.

"Opportunities in the trades and professions were reserved for others. The guilds and craftsmen kept these positions for their own families. If Opa wanted to pursue this kind of work, permission had to be granted. He needed a special letter from the government. And if a Jewish man sought to marry, he was required to wait and purchase a place on the community's roster, a matrikel, a registration certificate costing enormous sums, more than most had. Even then, before a marriage could actually take place, the man had to prove that he could earn a living, that he was engaged in a respectable trade or profession, but of course, this was hardly possible. We had no choice but to live by the rules set by others.

"That was the way our life was in our small village. The men would leave. The women would stay. The men would search for a future, for a place to live where they might be accepted as equals, somewhere they could be rewarded for their hard work. The women would wait. If we were sent for, we would follow. That is why I was not surprised when Opa told me he was leaving. Mäuschen, before sunrise the very next morning, Opa had left."

◆

As I grew older, I would hear this story repeated from time to time, sometimes by Oma, sometimes by Mama, sometimes by Uncle Daniel, each with a different emphasis on one part or another. But no matter who told it, the themes would vary little. They wanted me to remember. Our Jewishness was in our blood. The men in our family would lead, and when they said it was time, the women would follow. No amount of tears would change these things. This was the way life was meant to be.

Eleven

Searching for opportunity, Opa joined the thousands of others who found their way across the Atlantic during those years. Jews were not the only ones to leave, but unlike many of their Gentile neighbors, most Jewish families were rarely able to sell a homestead large enough to pay the cost of the family's journey. So, instead, they would depart one by one. The first to leave were usually single young men. Once settled and financially secure in America, they would send for their brothers, sisters, fiancés, parents, and grandparents.

Opa's older brother, twenty-year-old Daniel, was the first to depart. He left Bavaria in 1842. After arriving in New York, he tried to make his way as a peddler, learning America's customs and language by going door to door. For a brief time, he found work in a bank, sweeping floors and running errands, but when he was not satisfied with his wages, he returned to peddling. Peddling goods was an occupation many poor immigrants chose since it fit the life of a single young man and required little investment.

Opa was the next member of the Meyer family to leave. When he arrived in America five years later, he set foot in Baltimore. Both Opa and Uncle Daniel were unprepared for the world that would greet them. Like many other immigrants, they persevered, and they learned. The skills and knowledge they lacked were overcome with persistence and hard work.

Opa once told Mama there were days he would load his back with a hundred pounds of goods and walk down streets, trying to sell pots, pans, and whatever else he could carry. Despite his efforts, he never succeeded to a point where he could afford a horse and wagon. America might have been the land of opportunity, but Opa and Uncle Daniel found themselves crowded together with thousands of others, all searching for the same. Life in their new home proved to be more difficult than they had ever imagined. The rules and opportunity might have been better than in Bavaria, but despite their ambition and effort, neither met with success.

The event that changed their lives came in 1848, the year after Opa arrived. I always loved it when Uncle Daniel would tell me this story and repeat these words. James Marshall, a carpenter, found flakes of gold alongside the American River near Sutter's Mill in the California foothills. The Gold Rush began when Sam Brannan, a store owner, packed some of the precious metal into a quinine bottle and traveled the hundred miles back to San Francisco. As he stepped off the ferry, Brannan swung his hat high in the air, waved the bottle, and shouted, "Gold! Gold! Gold! Gold from the American River. There's more gold than all the people in California could take out in fifty years."

Opa and Uncle Daniel learned that San Francisco was a city teeming with possibilities for hard-working young men like themselves. Promoters claimed it was a cosmopolitan metropolis with a frontier edge. Glowing newspaper reports told of a distant land with unlimited opportunity where fortunes could be made by those willing to sacrifice and take risks. California was a place where there were no deep-seated traditions or rules to hold one back. Theirs was an easy decision. Both chose to venture west.

As the entrance to one of the Pacific's largest natural harbors, San Francisco became the central port and trading depot for the frenzied Gold Rush almost overnight. It was the jumping-off point for an invading army of prospectors. In 1848, San Francisco was a makeshift town of one thousand. Two years later, when twenty-two-year-old Opa and his twenty-seven-year-old brother Daniel arrived, the population of this city of hills, sand dunes, fog, and mild temperatures had swelled thirty times over to thirty thousand.

Their journey by sailing ship was nothing like the advertisement's promise of luxury accommodations and hours of carefree pleasure amidst gentle sea breezes. Instead, they endured a six-month trip that was met with rough storms, seasickness, and a lack of fresh water.

They ate salt-preserved meats, fish, dried beans, rice, and potatoes.

Several weeks after they rounded Cape Horn and the southernmost tip of South America, they finally set foot in California. The bustling town they entered could be described in many ways. One thing was certain. Frontier edge or not, no one who lived there would describe San Francisco as a cosmopolitan metropolis.

They found a harbor filled with abandoned ships, whose crews had deserted to head for the goldfields. San Francisco had become an uncontrolled collection of saloons and flophouses built quickly out of wood and canvas. The streets, filled with filth, mud, and stagnant water, were impassable when it rained and remained littered with old clothes and rags, broken crockery, worn-out boots, empty bottles and boxes, dead dogs and cats, and rats. Because of the constant movement between the gold mines and the city, everything was makeshift, temporary, and transient.

Men outnumbered women by seventy to one. And of the four hundred women who lived in San Francisco, it was common knowledge that more than half were prostitutes. Prostitution, gambling, drinking, shanghaiing, opium, and violence were out of control. Few laws were enforced. Their new home was clearly not a thriving community concerned about the welfare of its citizens and the safety of their property. That would change, but progress would take time.

Not everyone who flocked to California during the Gold Rush came to search for gold. Like Opa and his brother, many of the young men who followed the Gold Rush to California had been peddlers. In America, they had learned their trade and knew how to buy and sell goods. They were ambitious and anxious for success but had little interest in joining those rushing to California's hills with the dream of finding their fortune.

Instead, they hoped to make San Francisco their home, a place where they could succeed and raise families. These men used their opportunity to create storefronts that met the gold miners' demands for various things – boots, clothing, dry goods, hats, and equipment. When Opa and Uncle Daniel put up their sign, it was for a tobacco and cigar shop. Together they made a good team. Uncle Daniel, with his shrewd business sense, became the buyer. Opa, the man everyone considered a friend, became the salesman.

Twelve

Oma continued to tell me her story that afternoon after school as we sipped our tea. "In my small village of Oberallgäu, I waited and hoped. There was little else I could do. We needed money, so I sewed. Some girls I knew found jobs in larger nearby towns, like Nuremberg. One could find employment and live as a domestic in the homes of wealthy families. Others worked the land, and their fingers were raw and blistered by the end of each day.

"It was much the same throughout Bavaria's towns and villages. The women missed the men. And without the men, we missed having babies and raising children. Mäuschen, in my village, the simple truth was that the women were not happy without men. The young women worried that they would never marry and have children, that they would become unhappy and unsatisfied old spinsters.

"So many of the young men had left, and women, particularly young Jewish women, outnumbered the men.

Oberallgäu was not like San Francisco, where the women were in short supply and many men advertised or sent away for brides to join them. I really had no choice. I waited and hoped. I stayed busy and did what was needed, trying to save a few coins whenever I could. I didn't stop believing. I was always convinced that one day, your Opa would find a way to send for me.

"Four winters passed with no word. It was nearly impossible to find out anything. People were only beginning to use the telegraph, but not across the ocean. One had to rely on private means to send letters and messages. There was a mail train in Bavaria, but mail rarely came to our village. For us, word of mouth was how most information was sent. Hearing from someone in America, particularly as far away as California, and sending back a response could take months. Messages exchanged from one person to the next were seldom complete and, by the time they arrived, often less than reliable.

"I was not raised to feel sorry for myself, but truthfully, Mäuschen, this was a very unhappy and lonely time for me, and I shed many tears. No one had heard from Opa's brother, Daniel, either. Not a single word for four years. Then, one day, my brother brought exciting news. My older sister, Clara, and I should find our way to Hamburg. Opa and Uncle Daniel wanted us to join them in San Francisco. Papers were waiting at the seaport. We would take a steamship to America.

"Mäuschen, I must tell you how nervous and overwhelmed we were. All that waiting and then suddenly this news, news that would change our lives. I had never heard of San Francisco or California. All I really knew was a little of Bavaria and my village. Neither of us could speak a word of English. America had only been a distant dream. That day, our dream came true.

"I was twenty-five years old and about to begin the journey of my lifetime. I would leave my family and home behind and move to America. Always remember that there will be times in life when you must close your eyes, clench your fists tightly, and jump, hoping that your feet will go far and land on solid ground. That is exactly how I felt that day we received this news. All I could do was hope that there would be solid ground in a place called San Francisco.

"We tearfully kissed our family goodbye and left within days. Clara and I had little idea of how lengthy and difficult the journey would be. First, we had to find our way to Hamburg. We began by wagon. The nearest rail platform was in Nuremberg, twenty kilometers from our home. Can you imagine? I know you take trains for granted. You have traveled by train many times, but I had only watched them pass by and had never ridden on a train before. There were no direct trains to Hamburg from Nuremberg, so we had to take a train from one town to the next, where we would wait for another train to take us further. Hope and excitement helped. We were young, and that helped, too. I still remember sitting anxiously, trying to sleep on hard wooden benches for hours while we waited.

"With its five great churches and tall, narrow houses, Hamburg was the biggest and busiest city I had ever seen, beyond my imagination. It was still recovering from the terrible fire that had destroyed so many of its buildings, so construction scaffolds and workmen were everywhere, and the noise was nearly unbearable, not anything like the quiet calm of our village. We had been warned about the dangers of Hamburg. It was not a good city for those passing through, particularly two innocent young women like us from a small village in the mountains.

"Now you travel with many pieces of luggage, and the porters do all the lifting. All we could take then was what we could carry. We had no money to spend on porters. We carefully clung to our belongings, suspicious of everyone. We didn't know who we could trust. As the train pulled into Hamburg, I could see the landlords waiting. They were standing in line by the platform, eyeing those arriving. To me, they seemed like vultures ready to prey upon their victims. They each wanted us to stay at their inn or boarding house.

"On the train, we had heard stories about many like us who had lost much of their money, even before leaving Hamburg, by being charged extremely high prices for their lodging or being cheated by someone pretending to help. Others unknowingly spent their money on unneeded utensils for the ocean voyage. We needed every penny. One had to be careful and use common sense. I can't recall what Clara and I did, but it seemed that she knew where to find an office with people to help us, and somehow arrangements were made. We found a room we could afford in a private home and stayed in

Hamburg for a week before boarding the ship to take us to New York.

"We were fortunate. When Opa and Uncle Daniel crossed the Atlantic, the newer and faster steamships were not yet in service. They went by sailing ship and traveled in steerage, where they had to provide their own food and sleep in whatever space was available in the hold. All they ate was hard bread and salted meat. Can you imagine? They were at the mercy of the wind. Their trips across the Atlantic Ocean took nearly six weeks. Our ocean crossing took thirteen days, and at least we had somewhat fresh food. Some of the ships even kept cows penned up on their decks so passengers could receive fresh milk.

"You must understand. Crossing the Atlantic was not at all like it is today. There were no ocean liners with comfortable seats on the deck for napping in the sunshine or space for walks to stretch one's legs. There were no special rooms for dining and entertainment. There were no soft beds to sleep in or stewards to cater to your whims. Travel to America was not designed for one's comfort. Thousands were leaving Europe for America each year, and it was a lengthy, costly, and often dangerous journey.

"I remember how nervous we were when we were sent to the Castle Garden immigration building in New York after we arrived. We didn't know anyone and couldn't understand a single word, and my legs were still shaking from our voyage.

"Little did Clara and I know that our journey was only beginning. We had no idea how big a country America was or the distance we still needed to travel. From New York, we had to find our way to San Francisco, and there were only a few ways to get there. We had been told stories about the long trails, mountains, deserts, and hostile Indians, but we had never been given the choice to consider the overland routes across the United States.

"From others, we learned that those in a hurry could usually get to California in four to five weeks. They would take a steamship to Colón in Central America. Then they would hike and ride by mule or dugout canoe through the malaria-infested swamps and jungles of the Isthmus of Panama to the Pacific coast. But once they successfully crossed the peninsula, there was no guarantee of an available ship to take them to San Francisco. Some waited in Panama City for weeks.

"The other option was to avoid the shortcut across Central America and take the longer journey, sailing by steamer around South America's Cape Horn. When Clara and I arrived in New York, we learned that these arrangements had been made for us. We would follow the same route that Opa and Uncle Daniel had taken, taking the ship around Cape Horn.

"Although this was a much longer way to get to California, travel by steamer was better and safer by the time we took our journey. Mäuschen, I must tell you how happy we were to go by ship, no matter how long it would take. Neither Clara nor I were prepared to pull up our skirts and hike through the swampland of Panama.

"We arrived in San Francisco on the *Golden Gate* steamer two and a half months later, seventy-eight days after departing New York. More than four hundred passengers were on board. It seemed that all of San Francisco was there to greet our ship, but the only person I recognized was the familiar face of a handsome young man standing on a wooden barrel, madly waving his hat in the air. The very next day was our wedding, actually, a double wedding. It was a tiny affair. I married Opa, and your Aunt Clara married Uncle Daniel.

"I spent over four years waiting in Oberallgäu, and it took over four months to reach San Francisco, but Mäuschen, I have never regretted one day ever since. Aunt Clara and I followed. We did what we were always supposed to do."

Thirteen

It would take much longer to learn the history of Papa's family. I didn't have a grandmother like Oma to sit with me and tell the full story. Instead, I only heard snippets from Papa and my three aunts. Some overlapped, and there were many gaps and inconsistencies. I imagine that's true for many families. Different eyes and ears observe and interpret events differently. Often stories are left unsaid.

A decade after Mama's family, the Meyers, moved to San Francisco, Papa's family, the Samsons, began to arrive. Papa and his three sisters left Germany and their home in Altona, one after the other, and like Mama's family, they boarded passenger ships in Hamburg to take them to America.

Ten years had made an enormous difference in travel. Conditions were improved, and Papa's family was wealthier. They could afford the price of first-class tickets, allowing them to sleep in their own staterooms. Although the space was tiny, they had their own beds with mattresses and linens, a washbasin, some drawers, and even an area on the deck where they could enjoy the fresh air.

Today it is difficult to imagine how remote California was in the early 1860s when the Civil War was still underway. While California had become a state with large cities, it remained separated from the other side of the Mississippi River by vast amounts of empty land. There were over a thousand miles of mountain ranges and plains and few ways to cross them reliably. The Butterfield Overland cross-country stagecoaches and the Pony Express had cut the time considerably for important communications, but most mail continued to arrive by long-distance steamer around Cape Horn.

Despite its isolation, San Francisco was growing and gaining greater international prominence. Even then, many had begun to refer to the city as the "Paris of the Pacific," particularly after Napoleon III created a national lottery raffling off one-way trips to California, his way to eliminate nearly three thousand political opponents at the French government's expense.

By the time Papa's family began to arrive, businesses, government, schools, and charities had done much to change the face of San Francisco. Great portions of the city had been transformed. More and more streets were being improved. The flophouses of the early 1850s were displaced by larger and finer hotels, like the Russ House, Occidental, Lick, and Cosmopolitan. And fires continued to destroy old wooden structures, leading to the replacement of many of the remnants of the Gold Rush days with new and more modern buildings.

◆

Papa's older sister, Aunt Rosalie, was the first of the Samson family to cross the Atlantic and find her way to California. I was never told her story, whether there were events that caused her to leave her life in Germany or whether, like Oma, she followed her heart and was drawn. War between the German confederation and Denmark may have been one reason. Mama once hinted of a broken romance, that Aunt Rosalie was in love with a soldier who went off to war and never returned, but if that were true, it was so long ago that the story would not be remembered today.

Papa was the next to depart for San Francisco. He was eighteen years old when he arrived in the mid-1860s. By then, passenger travel from one side of America to the other had changed considerably. The war between the Northern and Southern states and Lincoln's presidency altered much of the landscape, and it was possible to travel by train and coach from New York to California in four weeks.

Both Papa and Aunt Rosalie caught the train from New York to St. Louis. Then they rode in nine-passenger, custom-built Concord coaches pulled by horses along the three-week-long overland route to San Francisco. While their trips were much quicker than Opa's and Oma's, I am not so sure that the conditions or their comfort were improved all that much. Packed tightly into small coaches with their fellow passengers, they spent sleepless days and nights, baked and frozen, bumping across the countryside. Armed guards and clouds of dust were their constant companions.

Later Papa's two younger sisters would follow. Like Mama's family, they simply followed one another and found opportunity. They were all very smart and successful. Mama says Papa pulled himself up by his bootstraps and built his business before he caught the eye of Opa and Oma. So, you can see, by the time Mama gave birth to me, not only had San Francisco undergone many changes, but there were also several generations of Meyer and Samson family members waiting anxiously to greet me.

◆

Despite their immigrant status, German language, and Jewish heritage, my impression is that the Meyers and Samsons were actually quite a bit different from one another. The Samsons could trace seven generations of history. They were a learned rabbinical family. Papa's ancestors included rabbis, scholars, teachers, physicians, and successful merchants. Records of the Samsons dated back to the mid-1600s when Altona was one of the Danish monarch's most important harbor towns with a flourishing Jewish community and many economic freedoms. Papa and his sisters were citified and accustomed to a prosperous middle-class life with comforts and conveniences. Hamburg and its surrounding towns were thriving, much older, more settled, arguably more cultured, with universities, music, and theater, and with a population larger than San Francisco.

The contrast for Opa and Uncle Daniel could not have been greater. They left a restricted village life in Bavaria that offered little. The population of the small village where they were born and raised was less than twelve hundred.

◆

When it comes to my family, there is one topic that remains unclear: our Jewishness. I am not sure that this matters, since I have never been taught to believe that anyone could be more Jewish than the next. Yet, for some reason, I've always had the impression that the Samsons were raised to be more observant than the Meyers. I imagine that this was truer when the families first arrived, especially for Papa's three sisters, who were always active in the synagogue.

Of course, the times and situations were different, and this distinction may have little meaning. I think Mama was right when she told me that much depends upon who you marry. As long as we marry within the Jewish faith, we should respect those who choose to practice and observe in different ways. Papa always says that "the God we believe in is too busy to worry about those little distinctions. Just stay true to yourself and be grateful for who you are."

Since Mama was a Meyer and Papa a Samson, it stands to reason that I am a blend of the two families and the personalities of my parents, but I will leave that for others to judge. Aunt Hattie liked to tell me that I was the thread that wove the two families together. Then she would look directly at me, and we would both laugh when she would say, "And you, Hilda? When they made you, they put the thread through a needle that you have managed to stick into both of their sides."

Fourteen

You must wonder why I choose to tell these old stories. It was Josef's idea. He encouraged me to write these pages, to tell my family's story and mail them to him with my letters. He promised to save them. "I will keep them for you to give to your children. Someday, Hilda, they will want to know. You should do the same for me."

That was how we began our correspondence. Josef made this suggestion in 1910, the second time we met. Much like the first, this unexpected moment occurred at a family gathering in Altona. It was Mama's plan. She insisted that we attend so Papa could see his family again.

Of course, by that time, Josef and I were both much older. Two decades had passed. I was twenty-five years old and no longer stumbling over the pronunciation of his words. In fact, I was quite conversant in his German language. Josef was no longer more than twice my age or two times my size, but he was still five years older and patient with me. That day, I learned he practiced medicine and led a full and interesting life in Berlin. We found that we shared many interests, passions for art and music among them.

I agreed to this suggestion, and we began to exchange letters, a correspondence that continued for the next several years, with him in Berlin and me in San Francisco. We both quickly became devoted to this exercise and, with time, began to know each other quite well. Letters were sent back and forth across the ocean every week. When we started, Josef wrote in German, and I would respond in English, but after two years, there came a day when I chose to adopt his language, a decision I've never regretted. For all the letters that followed, I, too, wrote in German. That's how I accepted Josef's marriage proposal. When I wrote back that day, I told him that Berlin would become my home, too.

◆

Throughout that time, I remember Josef's frustration with me. His constant refrain was: "Tell me about yourself." He would write: "Your letters always tell me the stories of others. What I want to know is about you – what you feel, what you think, what you believe, what you like, what you dislike. Must I be left to guess?"

I tried. I wanted to please him, but I found this difficult. I was not comfortable expressing myself. I had not been raised that way and had never been encouraged to share what I thought. I had always been taught to follow, listen, repeat, nod politely, and keep my opinions to myself. When I wrote, I wrote accounts that described events. Rarely did I choose to express my opinions or share my most private feelings. I knew my place and followed the accepted rules for women who had grown up during the Victorian era.

◆

There were times when I found Josef infuriating. My cheeks are bright red as I tell you this, but I hope someday you will understand. In one letter, Josef wrote: "I want you to remove your clothing, to undress yourself. Tell me who you are!"

Oh, I can't tell you how embarrassed I was by his words. I could not imagine what he was asking. No one had ever spoken to me like that, so direct and personal. What was he thinking? What did he want from me?

When I wrote back and told him that I had immediately destroyed his letter and would stop responding to his ridiculous questions, he only became more frustrated with me, and I angrier. Perhaps that is how I first became convinced that we loved one another. I discovered we could be absolutely honest and tell each other exactly what we thought.

One day, he wrote: "You are the most beautiful butterfly I have ever seen. Your last letter broke through the walls of your chrysalis. You have spread your wings for me." It sounds so strange to repeat his words, but I remember how pleased I was when I received this letter, how good Josef made me feel about myself in a way I had never felt before. That was how Josef was: patient, caring, thoughtful, gentle, demanding, and unrelenting. Josef pushed and pushed so much because he wanted to know me so well.

◆

Through our correspondence, those letters and pages with all their little expressions made me realize how much Josef loved me and how much I loved him. Ours was a slow dance and often a tango. It took time and patience, and I needed to learn, but once I understood, I tried and tried, and I hope I gave him all that I could in return.

As I lie here tonight in this darkness, I am amused by this thought. When we began our correspondence, I thought I was writing to Josef. Today I know that I am writing for you. Before long, we will meet. Then I will become your mother, and Josef your father. Soon I will tell Josef, but for now, we will keep this our secret. We will wait to make sure that you are really who I think you will be. Now all I can do is pray that you will remain healthy and continue to grow and I will be able to continue writing these pages so they are completed by the day you are born. Then it will be time for you to begin your journey, and perhaps someday you will add your pages to what I have written and give them to your children.

Fifteen

Three words best describe the world I grew up in –
Jewish, German, and ambitious. I am not certain
we would agree on their order of importance, but
I think every member of our family would acknowledge
that this was the heritage passed from each generation
to the next. Most would add a fourth word. They would
attach "very" to the front of each of the others. This was
the foundation that defined much of our lives.

We were not alone. Many others possessed the same
legacy. From the moment Opa and Uncle Daniel arrived
in San Francisco, they cherished the company of those
who made similar journeys, particularly the young men
from Bavaria. Opa and Uncle Daniel shared much with
their fellow countrymen – culture, language, faith, and a
strong drive to succeed. Oma once told me that the men
never seemed to suffer from loneliness. They never had
time. They were all too driven and industrious to be
lonely.

It was only natural that these men would find comfort in the familiar company of one another. With time, these friendships would grow and expand to include their families and their children's families. And even when their businesses found themselves in competition with one another, the rivalries would be spirited, but their friendships would remain. These were the people we knew, the families we spent time with, and the important relationships that would be cultivated.

Marriages between sons and daughters were expected and brought many of our families even closer together. This was our community. Above all else, these early pioneers were intent upon making San Francisco a home where their families would be safe and given the opportunity to prosper. Oma was right. I was spoiled, and I did take things for granted, but I wasn't the only one in my generation. That's how we were raised. It was the gift we were given. In so many ways, my cousins and I were the beneficiaries of our grandparents' dreams.

◆

Mama once told me that "while the men looked for gold, the women looked for God" because, for so much of her childhood, it was left to the women to practice our faith. The men were always too busy trying to be successful in their business endeavors. What I do know for certain is that rabbis and synagogues were not why the Meyers and the Samsons first set foot in San Francisco.

Opportunity came first, family came second, and if there was any time remaining, religion came third.

When Opa and Uncle Daniel arrived in the early 1850s, there was a small group of Jews, mostly men, who gathered for services in a tent behind Lewis Franklin's wood-frame store on Jackson Street. I was never told how often Opa and Uncle Daniel attended or how much they took part, but Mama always claimed that our family had some small part in that early Jewish history in San Francisco.

Although many had little interest or claimed to be too busy to practice their faith, others missed their traditions, and it wasn't long before Temple Emanu-El was established by the families of the more reform-minded Bavarian Jews. That was when our congregation moved into a newly built, large, and elegant synagogue on Sutter Street and hired San Francisco's first rabbi.

Just as San Francisco grew to become the cosmopolitan metropolis Opa and Uncle Daniel had first expected when they had arrived, Temple Emanu-El quickly became an important pillar in our family's lives. Both the Samsons and the Meyers were always active and strong supporters. For many of San Francisco's Jews, Temple Emanu-El was a cornerstone of community activity far removed from the Gold Rush days and the red-light district of the city's infamous Barbary Coast.

◆

Papa often remarked on the resiliency of those who arrived in those early years, when fires frequently terrorized the growing city, engulfing the wooden buildings, burning the shops, and destroying the merchandise. Without paid police and fire departments, courts, and other basic public services, residents were left on their own to persevere, rebuild and restock their stores, and start all over again. And for many, this would happen more than once.

Unlike Bavaria, where those in control decided who could advance and who would be held back, San Francisco's fires made no distinction between who was Jewish and who was not. If there were divisions within the community, they were of wealth and class, not religion. Nearly everyone agreed: Jewish families in San Francisco were well integrated and assimilated. Our city was a place where success was earned by hard work, persistence, and the friendships you made. It was rarely decided on the basis of one's pedigree.

◆

Soon many streets were paved, and coal gas lit the streetlights on thoroughfares. Public transportation was available through a system of horse-pulled coaches, the forerunner to San Francisco's streetcars, and water was channeled from a lake beyond the city's hills. Wooden buildings destroyed by fires were replaced with massive brick and cement buildings that brought a big-city style and a swagger of civic pride to San Francisco's center.

Opa and Uncle Daniel's cigar and tobacco business experienced both success and failure. Somehow it managed to survive, and when tobacco was in short supply and demand great, they were able to prosper. By 1858, they were ready to do more. They had learned from those who had taken to banking in the earlier days, when all that was required was a double-walled, fireproof safe in a well-protected building and the business sense to make good investment decisions. That's when they decided to add a new service under the roof of their tobacco shop. They created their own private banking venture, the Daniel Meyer Bank.

The cigar and tobacco enterprise continued until the Civil War began. Then the federal government placed an embargo on trade with the Confederacy. Fortunately, before closing their doors on tobacco, Opa and Uncle Daniel had enough stock for one last turn of profit. Then they turned their full attention to the bank. And with time and the help of other family members who joined their effort, the bank grew and brought them more success than they ever imagined.

Sixteen

I have mentioned Uncle Daniel often but have failed to tell you much about him. As soon as I was old enough to remember faces and voices, the one who stood out, who always made a distinct impression, was Uncle Daniel. While I may have been drawn to Oma's loving arms as a young child, I approached Uncle Daniel with slow and careful steps, cautiously and wary, and always with a great deal of apprehension. I was unsure about this noticeably short, strange-looking man with the peculiar tuft of hair that grew below his lower lip. I kept my distance from his strong-smelling pipe and the clouds of smoke that always surrounded him.

There was never a question as to who the elder was. Uncle Daniel was the patriarch of our family. Opa's older brother may not have been universally adored, as he had little patience for nonsensical behavior, but he was known by all and respected by everyone. For those who knew him well, he was like a fine wine, mellowing and more interesting with age. Some said it was due to his strong constitution that he managed to outlive the other men in our family. Others claimed this was the result of his cantankerous nature. In any case, I think most would agree that despite his small stature, he was an imposing figure and most definitely a striking personality few would dare to dismiss.

As long as I can remember, Uncle Daniel and Aunt Clara were central to our lives, always taking part in any family event. Mama, who seldom failed to offer an opinion, thought Aunt Clara something of a wallflower, a shrinking violet often eclipsed by the spirited nature of her younger sister, my grandmother Oma.

I can't say that I entirely agreed. Although I did regard the perfumed and dusted Aunt Clara to be quite ancient and exceedingly quiet, I also found her to be quite curious. And while we all found humor in her eccentric behavior, as she was the butt of many of our jokes, she was able to laugh at herself and was always held in high esteem. Her kindness and generosity for public causes was a source of family pride and deserving of our gratitude.

As for Uncle Daniel's kindness and generosity, he, too, shared these traits, but no one would have thought to call him a wallflower. When you were in a room with Uncle Daniel, there was never a question where he belonged. He was always the center of everyone's attention.

I know that in the polite terms of generation, both should have "great" appended to their family titles as they were my great-aunt and great-uncle. However, when I first began to speak and made several awkward attempts, it was clear that Great-Uncle Daniel contained more syllables than my small mouth could handle. Uncle Daniel didn't seem to mind. He was so pleased that I knew who he was that he told me to use whatever name I chose. We settled on Uncle Daniel, and that's what I have called him ever since.

When I was growing up, the Meyer name cast a big shadow in San Francisco. Although well known throughout the city, Uncle Daniel did his best to avoid drawing public attention. He tended to hide on the sofa in the small office kept in the rear of his building, where there was always a procession of visitors vying for his attention. Despite his best efforts, Uncle Daniel's name would appear in the newspapers frequently. He was a civic leader, an investor, a patron of the arts, a member of boards and commissions, a generous benefactor to many causes, and very influential in financial circles.

The *Overland Monthly* referred to him once as "the greatest Jewish financier on the Pacific Coast, universally regarded as a financial genius." I suppose those accolades explain why it was impossible for him to be all these things without, from time to time, also becoming the center of controversy, which did happen on more than one occasion, often to the embarrassment of others in the family.

Whenever a family member married or achieved any notoriety, the *Chronicle* and *Examiner* would typically begin their articles with "Daniel Meyer's niece" or "Daniel Meyer's nephew." His coattails were long. Perhaps, had Opa lived a longer life, he would have taken on a larger role in our extended family matters, but I am pretty certain both Oma and Mama would agree that Uncle Daniel would have retained his patriarchal status. It was the nature of his person, the gravitas of his personality.

Mama once described Opa as "everyone's friend." Then she smiled, laughed, and said, "But Uncle Daniel was one of a kind. Anyone who knew him well was convinced he was their very finest friend." When it came to friendship, Uncle Daniel was ferocious with his loyalty.

There are so many stories to share about Uncle Daniel that I hardly know where to begin. He and Aunt Clara had no children of their own. I suppose that's why Mama, Aunt Hattie, and their two brothers became the heirs to the Meyer fortune. As for the members of my generation, Uncle Daniel and Aunt Clara were delighted to become our adopted grandparents, and they cherished the idea that we had become their adopted grandchildren.

Their massive four-floor Victorian home was filled with antiques and marvelous collections obtained from throughout the world. On Uncle Daniel's birthday, we would all be invited to join him there, and he would present each of us with a velvet bag of silver dollars, one for each year of his life. And since he lived to be nearly ninety years old, the coin-filled bags became a heavy weight for a child to carry and a great deal of money. Actually, because he was a leap-year child, born on February 29, he often boasted he was one-quarter of his age. I remember my twenty-first birthday. That year, despite his eighty-four years, he claimed we were both exactly the same age.

Uncle Daniel always laughed when articles were written that stated he had extensive training in banking before he arrived in San Francisco. "All I did was sweep their floors and deliver their messages. I guess that's what bankers do if you live on the East Coast." And one day, when I asked him to explain the difference between his work at the bank and Papa's work as a broker, he told me, "The banker sits at the end of the table and makes important decisions. The broker must always sit in the middle and do what the banker tells him to do." The newspapers quoted him saying things like this all the time.

Uncle Daniel was the last of the family men of his generation to die, and the news of his death was widely reported. In 1911, the San Francisco newspapers wrote that because of his enormous wealth, Mama, Aunt Hattie, and their brothers had paid the second-largest inheritance tax from any estate in California's history. Uncle Daniel may have died a very wealthy man, one of the wealthiest of his generation, but what I liked best was the description I read several days after his death: "His busy life as a banker and man of affairs did not prevent him from acquiring a fount of knowledge and education that stamped him as a man of culture to an unusual degree.

Seventeen

Oh, what fun,
Oh, what fun,
To be in the class of naughty-one.

Cheer of the Girl's High School Class of 1901

I am proud to be called a "naughty one." We all were. Everyone graduating that June day agreed. I've been lucky to have been given two pet names in my lifetime, "Mäuschen" and "naughty one," and I can't think of any two that could be better.

All forty-eight girls in my 1901 graduating class cheered loudly and whooped and hollered when Republican Congressman Julius Kahn stood at the podium and referred to us this way in his congratulatory commencement address. My high school, the Girl's High School of San Francisco, the four-story red brick building at the corner of Geary and Scott Streets, may have had a celebrated history dating back to 1864 when the high school girls were separated from the boys, but my graduating class had the unique distinction of ushering in the twentieth century.

I remember how disturbed Principal Brooks became because of our behavior that afternoon and how everyone's eyes were glued to our favorite Miss Stark, the Latin and Greek instructor. She struggled so hard to keep her mouth tightly closed, holding her breath as she tried to keep a solemn and straight face. Then we watched as her cheeks expanded and turned bright red, and it seemed she might explode. Finally, she couldn't contain herself and burst out laughing. We all cheered when she joined in our celebration.

A more than sixty-year era ended with Queen Victoria's death that year, and all of us sitting on the stage that day knew it. We were more than ready to welcome a new and exciting time. As a class, we had successfully weathered one last remnant of the Victorian Age, the Anti-Flirtation League promoted by the school's most senior teacher and head of the history department, Mrs. Prag, a name that fit her quite well. During the winter term, she boasted that she would "put the boys out of business" when she overheard a boy say that the "Girl's High School girls were easy." Then everyone in our class had no choice but to enthusiastically sign a pledge to abstain from any form of flirtatious behavior.

By April, we all must have caught a whiff of spring fever because, by then, most of our initial enthusiasm to abstain had waned. Graduation meant that we had fulfilled this prudish and old-fashioned obligation and were free to set our own standards. We were no longer required to save our sister students from going down this perilous path or obliged to recover any GHS pins that we might spot worn on the front of boys' shirts. You can be sure that by the day we received our diplomas, Mrs. Prag had made certain that each of us was well versed on high moral standards and aware of the grave dangers that would result from any form of needless flirtation.

◆

Public schooling has a way of teaching much more than subject matter and required curriculum. For me, it was more than mastering the German language, reading the preferred books, or learning about world history. School had been an eye-opening experience, an opportunity to take tiny steps beyond the walls of my sheltered cocoon, to test a few limits, something I did very slowly and with a great amount of caution.

I was most comfortable staying within my own small circle. I wouldn't say that I was the ugly duckling of my class, but I certainly was not the social butterfly. Perhaps I was a little more introverted than others since my world revolved mostly around family, the synagogue, and proper societal obligations.

When I first began school, I was surprised to learn that not everyone was afforded the same privileges and opportunities as me. I received important early lessons on humility and modesty, and know that I stumbled on more than one occasion. By the time I graduated, I had been given many other lessons. While I was a good student and did well in my subjects, always receiving high marks, I also became aware of the distinctions and responsibilities associated with wealth, social class, and gender.

And although our mothers might never have spoken about their bodies or childbirth, my generation was mildly curious and felt a certain freedom to discuss these topics amongst ourselves. I believe that the end result was a full and balanced education, one that prepared me for the world I was about to enter. Like the rest of the "naughty ones" who sat in those chairs on graduation day, my biggest challenge would be understanding what this twentieth-century world wanted. I needed to come to terms with what was expected of me.

◆

The new century unveiled many contrasts. At midnight on December 31, San Franciscans from all parts of the city joined the pandemonium and celebrations on the streets. With horns, trumpets, bells, and whistles, the thoughts of one century suddenly passed into history, and another, with all of its hopes and dreams, was born. The San Francisco I knew and enjoyed could not have been more different than the San Francisco Oma and Opa had experienced when they first arrived in the 1850s or the San Francisco Mama had known when she and her classmates attended the Girl's High School in 1870.

Some say the speed of progress doubles or triples with each new generation, and that was certainly true for the final decades of the nineteenth century. I may have been raised as a product of the Victorian Era, mindful of my family's history and taught all the social graces, yet my classmates and I were teetering on the edge of a new era, one that would question many accepted behaviors and ways of the past.

We wouldn't dress the same. We wouldn't act the same. We wouldn't dance the same. We dismissed the old ways. The past could not define us, and neither would its teachings. I sometimes wonder whether our thinking was not all that different from how previous generations might have felt as they set out to make their mark. We considered ourselves quite modern and knowing in every possible way and were anxious and ready to test and embrace the new norms of the next century.

Cars, motorcycles, light bulbs, electric irons, radios, ballpoint pens, jukeboxes, escalators, cash registers, telephones, sewing machines, typewriters, vacuum cleaners, roller coasters, gramophones, and motion picture cameras had become commonplace during my generation. But it was not only these comforts and conveniences that changed everyone's lives. The city of San Francisco had changed, too.

San Francisco had grown to become one of the largest and most sophisticated cities in the country, with its own culture, which was becoming known throughout the world. The massive, strong-looking, utilitarian structures built after the fires had been replaced again, this time by buildings of a more elegant style. We had neighborhoods like the Western Addition, Haight-Ashbury, Eureka Valley, and the Mission District. There were Golden Gate Park and the Sutro Baths. San Francisco had hospitals, medical schools, colleges, thriving businesses, a stock exchange, and mills that produced iron for bridges, railroads, and steamers. Nearly all the cable cars had been replaced. Now we used electric streetcars to take us nearly anywhere we needed to go.

Famous authors and musicians had walked our streets and performed and lectured in our concert halls. Mark Twain, Rudyard Kipling, Robert Louis Stevenson, and Oscar Wilde had given San Francisco cultural prominence. And while we had been taught to stay away from the dance halls, bars, jazz clubs, and variety shows along Pacific Street and Broadway, we were all more than aware and curious about the many temptations San Francisco had to offer. Well before O. Henry repeated these words, Californians had taught us that "East is East, but West is San Francisco."

Eighteen

Although the matter took place quite some time ago, it still pains me today to speak about Martin, not because I loved him, as today I don't believe I really ever did. But I always felt a sense of disappointment, that I had let down those who loved me, that I failed to fulfill their expectations. I think Mama and Papa always assumed that I would marry Martin. Most of our family assumed this, too. I know for certain that Aunt Hattie, Aunt Rosalie, and my other aunts did. And I imagine Martin's family thought the same. Everyone did. Why wouldn't they? It was as if this was meant to be.

I suppose there are many ways to describe our match – expected, presumed, anticipated, planned, assumed – and each description would begin with one word: "always." This was a pact that had been made for as long as I can remember. Love had not played a part in any of these descriptions. It was not a consideration. Ours was a pairing of two families, an economic endeavor.

I know Mama had convinced herself that Martin was a suitable match. He was six years older and met the right requirements. All the boxes could be checked: Jewish, wealthy, intelligent, family, predictable. Papa agreed and also considered Martin to be worthy. For Papa, being worthy was the most critical measure, an approval that was necessary, the standard he struggled to meet when he asked Opa for Mama's hand in marriage.

I can't remember anyone asking for my opinion or thinking my feelings really mattered. To be perfectly honest, if they had asked what I thought, I am uncertain whether I had an opinion to give. I am sure I would have said that I was thrilled with having this issue settled, as it did seem to be a solution to what others considered a pressing problem.

When it came to matters of family function and responsibility, I had always been dutiful. And as was so often true for members of my generation, other than the occasional passing comments of a few school classmates, no one had ever encouraged me to consider the obvious benefits of passion. The women in our family never discussed this topic.

Martin's much older brother had married my first cousin, Julia, and ever since, I think the others concluded that Martin and I were destined to be together, too. Neither Martin nor I were indifferent to the promised certainty of financial security and family blessing, so we both went along willingly, the result being that, to my knowledge, neither of us chose to pursue any others. There seemed little reason to do so, and for much the same reason, there seemed little point in exploring any interest we might have had in one another.

When we were together, we remained polite, respectful, and, above all else, chaste. Mrs. Prag and the Anti-Flirtation League would have been proud of this behavior. Of course, now I can see we were destined to become quite proper and settled in marriage without having enjoyed the experimentation of courtship or satisfying the curiosity and romance of newlyweds.

Neither of us felt any particular hurry or urgency to further our relationship. Since there was no need or desire and our comfortable life was presumed, there were no other expectations to fulfill. We could take our time and wait as long as needed. After graduating from the university, Martin traveled east, to New York, to attend to his medical education and training while I stayed home and pursued my interest in art by enrolling in classes.

The San Francisco Art Association had established the California School of Design in the Mark Hopkins Mansion. The palatial and elaborate Victorian mansion on Nob Hill had been converted into classrooms and studios for emerging artists. I could not claim to be an emerging artist, but I was quite interested in drawing, painting, and art history. It didn't take long to conclude that interest and talent are not always closely connected. But, as long as I was able to afford the price of tuition, which I was, I was invited to attend lectures, participate in classes, and assist the curators when they scheduled special exhibitions.

My life was full, and my calendar complete. I had my courses and volunteer work, family responsibilities, social engagements, and charities to attend to. I was living the comfortable, cultured life I had been raised to live, perhaps not that of a charming socialite, like some of my more daring cousins, but I had certainly adopted the habits of a responsible young member of San Francisco's upper class. Martin's life was full, too, with the demands of his medical training. As long as we both felt fulfilled and pursued our interests, we could postpone our presumed nuptials for years – which is what we chose to do. Perhaps I had been lulled into a false sense of complacency and assuredness, because I was not prepared for the letter that arrived by post one day announcing that Martin had fallen in love with another.

I'm not certain that anyone can prepare for such a disappointment, at least anyone like me, who has lived such a protected existence. Disappointment is rarely a slow occurrence. By its very nature, it is something that takes place suddenly. One moment, you can be happy, and the next moment, you are not. I believe that disappointment is a reflection of desire: the more you want something or someone, the greater the disappointment when your expectations are crushed.

Perhaps that was what made Martin's decision to marry someone else so confusing. There had never been as much as a spark between us, not a moment of trial and error. We had never succumbed to temptation or expressed any hint of desire, yet I still found myself deeply disappointed and hurt. What I felt was an overwhelming sense of rejection, the sense that I had been given a task and had failed. Others would say that I mostly felt sorry for myself. I felt that I had been aggrieved.

And once again, it took Oma to remind me that I remained spoiled and had some growing up to do. She held me close, wiped away my tears, looked straight into my eyes, and offered this advice: "Mäuschen, you need to wait patiently. You won't always get your way. You know that life has disappointments and you should not be confused by what others expect. There will come a time when the right person asks you to follow. And when you are asked, you will know what your heart tells you. You will not be confused. You will know what you should do."

Nineteen

Most generations have their defining moments, those events always remembered as reference points, punctuated by expressions of before and after. Papa liked to claim that in his lifetime, these moments occurred more frequently, that my life had been more protected and that I had been spared. I didn't know if that was true, as his life seemed to be much the same as mine. But perhaps I had been more sheltered. My world seemed quite tame when compared to the lives of my grandparents.

I suppose that the bubonic plague scare of 1902 could have become one of these moments, as it had the potential and was frightening when it appeared, but somehow the plague was contained and passed quickly, and now it seems mild by comparison. Then those in charge made us wonder whether the illness was even real. At first, they led us to believe that buried corpses contributed. Motivated by the opportunity for profitable land speculation, the politicians banned all burials within San

Francisco and moved the cemeteries to an undeveloped area just south of the city's border.

◆

This time, there was no question. Our lives all changed on April 18, 1906. Everyone who lived in San Francisco on that day will remember the date for the rest of their lives. The day before was a Tuesday and was remarkable for reasons having little to do with that evening's plans.

The morning began when I accompanied Oma to a benefit luncheon for the Golden Gate Kindergarten Association, an organization Oma and her sister, Aunt Clara, had strongly supported. At the luncheon, they presented an emotional posthumous award to Aunt Clara for her many years of financial support and annual donations of warm clothing and shoes for the children at the Jackson Street Kindergarten. We all missed Aunt Clara terribly and it was a wonderful, touching tribute. I know that Oma was glad to be there in Aunt Clara's stead.

Later we were looking forward to attending an evening performance of the opera. As long as I can remember, our family members were patrons of the San Francisco Opera Society. We always subscribed to season tickets, and for many years, we had much-sought-after seats in the dress circle. When the Opera Society discontinued the dress circle seating, we were moved to the orchestra section. Mama and Aunt Hattie always made a big fuss about this. Each year, they would search for their names in the newspaper society pages since the paper would list all the season ticket holders and where their seats were located.

I loved to go to the Grand Opera House on Mission Street. Evenings at the opera always promised to be a wonderful spectacle, with several thousand in their seats, elegant surroundings, and everyone dressed up, a gathering of San Francisco society. Following every performance, the critics at the *San Francisco Call* would write long articles describing the evening's scene, gossiping about who had been holding court, who had been with whom, and who had been wearing what.

The year before, we had attended Olive Fremstad's triumphant performance as Kundry in Wagner's *Parsifal*. The entire company of the New York Metropolitan Opera House performed under the direction of Heinrich Conried. What a fabulous evening that was, a night everyone remembered because of the sensuous kiss in the second act, quite an unexpected and outrageous moment.

Mama and Aunt Hattie were still blushing when they talked about it as we took our seats this year. The papers said that Fremstad's night set the box office record, the biggest draw the Grand Opera House had ever had. Yet no one was surprised when this year's performance broke the record again.

Five of us attended – Papa, Mama, Aunt Hattie, Aunt Rosalie's daughter Adele, and me. Oma was unable to join us, and I know how disappointed she was. Ever since she had taken a fall, getting to and from the aisle and seats had become too difficult.

The evening program was the season-opener, and like every year, it promised to be more splendid than the last. Enrico Caruso was the star and had been the talk of the city for weeks. Articles had been written about him in all the newspapers. The music critics referred to him as the greatest operatic tenor of all time.

This season, Caruso was engaged to perform in a series of five different operas during his San Francisco stay. The first, Bizet's *Carmen*, had been sold out for months, all the seats and even standing room only. It was an absolutely delightful evening, and Caruso, with his tremendous voice and marvelous stage presence, was magnificent.

When it was over, the applause continued for several minutes, and he was called back to the stage for bows a number of times. I can't remember ever seeing so many bouquets of flowers thrown onto the stage from the upper levels. Everyone was raving about him as we walked out through the doors of the Opera House and into the late-night air. I think the evening's spectacular success made what happened the very next day all the more sudden and devastating.

That night, when we left, the Grand Opera House, breathtaking with all its glittering lights and elegant beauty, was still standing. By the next morning, it was nowhere to be seen. It no longer existed.

Nearly every San Francisco resident was awakened at 5:12 a.m. by the forty-eight-second earthquake shock that killed and injured many. Two hours later, when the second major shock struck, much of what was left of downtown San Francisco was destroyed.

Within hours, U.S. Army troops from Fort Mason had reported to the Hall of Justice, and Mayor Schmitz called for the enforcement of a dusk-to-dawn curfew. Soldiers were authorized to shoot to kill anyone found looting. By evening, President Roosevelt had placed the city under martial law. Thousands, carrying their blankets and provisions, were making their way to shelter in the refugee camps at Golden Gate Park and Ocean Beach.

The earthquakes had ruptured water mains throughout the city. Without an adequate water supply, the fire companies were unable to fight the flames, and the fires sparked by the earthquakes burned out of control for days. Firefighters dynamited entire city blocks, hoping to create firewalls and stop the spreading fires from causing even more destruction. Unfortunately, some of these explosions inadvertently resulted in even more devastation.

Death and suffering were everywhere. Hundreds were killed or injured, crushed, burned, and struck by debris falling from crumbling buildings. Even San Francisco's fire chief was mortally wounded when the California Theatre dome and the adjacent hotel fell upon the fire station where he lived.

The entire city was in shock. Nothing felt real. Downtown San Francisco resembled a war zone. Buildings that had managed to survive the earthquakes in the morning were consumed by the fires that blazed across the city before nightfall. Initially four hundred deaths were reported. Then, within days, we were told that hundreds of fatalities in Chinatown had been ignored, some said because of a government cover-up to downplay the quake's real damage.

Only when it was over and the authorities could fully survey and reveal the extent of the devastation did we learn that as many as three thousand people might have been killed, one-quarter of San Francisco's buildings destroyed, and more than two hundred thousand people left homeless. The newspapers told us we would never know the actual numbers.

Twenty

The city was in chaos for those first days following the earthquake. Telephone and telegraph communications were disrupted. Food was in short supply, and the homeless stood in long lines at improvised soup kitchens. Transportation was nonexistent. Search parties scoured the rubble, hoping to find anyone trapped. Then, as rescue efforts ceased and recovery efforts began, searchers turned to finding and identifying the remains of those lost in the disaster.

We mourned for the loss of lives, prayed for those who were being treated for injuries, and worried about who might be next affected by the spread of the fires, which were rapidly devouring block after block of the city. We all volunteered to help those in need, offering shelter, distributing food, and providing clothing and support.

For four consecutive days and nights, the city endured hundreds of aftershocks, each threatening more nightmares. I think every San Francisco resident shared the fear that another significant earthquake could occur and destroy any part of the city that had remained standing.

Our family was extremely fortunate. We quickly learned that family members had been spared much of the devastation. We suffered no injuries. Our Pacific Heights homes were beyond the fires' reach and received only minor damage from the earthquake shocks. While we did receive the news that fires had destroyed Uncle Daniel's bank building and Papa's office, both buildings had been vacated, and these losses seemed minor compared to what others had sustained.

By the following Monday, the fires were out, and the rebuilding process was already beginning. Despite the devastating loss of life and destruction, San Francisco would recover quickly. We lived in a city that knew how to rebuild.

◆

I wish I knew more to tell you about the earthquake, but despite the horror and tragedy and many stories of heroism, my attention was centered elsewhere. Only months before the earthquakes occurred, Oma had taken a nasty fall, and her injury prevented her from joining us at the Caruso performance the preceding evening. She hadn't recovered well, and we could all see that her health was deteriorating. I wanted to spend as much time as I could by her side.

104 | RALPH WEBSTER

Oma's sister, Clara, had succumbed to old age four years earlier, and now it seemed clear that Oma was beginning to suffer the same fate. Mama and I took turns sitting with her since she spent most days confined to her bed. Even our trip to the Kindergarten Association luncheon took its toll and left her quite tired.

There was little else we could do but stay close and keep her company. Sometimes we read to her, but much of the time, she kept her eyes closed and slept. Oma never complained of pain, but we all know that old age has a way of catching up with everyone, even the most spirited. Papa said that the heart had only so many beats to give, and the doctors claimed to have no cure.

One day, as I was fluffing her pillow and tucking in the sheets, Oma motioned me close and reminded me of how much she enjoyed our afternoon teas, how she would greet me each day when I arrived home from school and we would sit down together like all the important women of San Francisco do. Then she looked into my eyes and whispered, "I think today we should do this again. We must have another tea. There are some things I would like to tell you."

◆

The early fall day was beautiful. The leaves had started to turn, and they glowed with a palette of yellow, gold, chestnut, copper, ginger, and cinnamon. That warm, sunny afternoon, as we sat outdoors in our chairs and slowly sipped our tea, Oma handed me a sealed envelope. She had printed my name on it. "Mäuschen, remember when I told you that sometimes in life, you must close your eyes, clench your fists tightly, and jump, hoping that your feet will go far and land on solid ground? This is what I want you to promise me you will do. Save this for a day when you feel ready to make that jump. That's when you should open this."

◆

Oma's eyes remained closed, and her heart stopped beating later that evening, as if she had orchestrated the events that had occurred throughout the day. Mama held her hand as she took her last breath. She died peacefully, surrounded by our family.

Days later, the San Francisco newspapers referred to my grandmother as a "pioneer of San Francisco and one of the best-known women in the city." I knew her as Oma from a small village in the Bavarian Alps who always beckoned me with warm, open arms and a loving smile. I knew her as the person who always spoke her mind and wanted what was best for me.

◆

I followed Oma's advice and waited many months before I opened the envelope. When I did, I found a scribbled note that read: "Mäuschen, now it is your turn to fly like a sparrow." Attached was a check with my name on it for ten thousand dollars. I couldn't stop crying. Choosing to wait or deciding when to follow was a choice I could now make for myself. I wouldn't have to depend on others. It was 1906. I was twenty-two years old, and Oma had given me something she had never received: the gift of independence.

Twenty-One

I t's curious how certain little events can give direction to one's life. One of my favorite memories was my ninth birthday in 1893. I unwrapped Uncle Daniel's gift to find a book. On the first page, his inscription read:

Dear Hilda,
You are a bright little girl with a big imagination, and your room has a light to read by into the night. I think you are ready for an incredibly good book to keep you company.
Love, Uncle Daniel

I love to read and was always encouraged. It didn't matter if it was day or night. I could sit absolutely still, undisturbed for hours with my legs tucked under me, a book in one hand and my face glued to the pages. Papa said that when I was reading, I would not even blink. All that would move from time to time would be the tip of my index finger when I turned from one page to the next or the tears that might run down my face when a story tugged at my emotions.

As a child and a young adult, I spent as many hours as I could reading, living within my imagination, dreaming of faraway places. Everyone said Oma was right to name me Mäuschen. When I was reading, I stayed as quiet as a church mouse.

Uncle Daniel deserves much of the credit. He was the first to recognize that I was old enough to read a hardbound book on my own, without Mama's or Papa's help. That year, he presented me with Jules Verne's *Around the World in Eighty Days*, and for my birthdays in the years that followed, he helped me build an extensive library of good works. Each year, Uncle Daniel would add several books to my growing collection: *One Thousand and One Nights*, *Gulliver's Travels*, *The Count of Monte Cristo*, *David Copperfield*, *Treasure Island*, *Great Expectations*, each with his handwritten inscription and a brief note of encouragement.

Uncle Daniel wanted me to see what the world looked like across the oceans and beyond the walls of my home. These gifts required my promise to visit him in his office and discuss the book after I had finished, a task I took quite seriously. Reading good books was his hobby, too, and we had many wonderful visits.

Many things shape our lives. For me, reading *Around the World in Eighty Days* made a lasting impression. What particularly caught my imagination were the vivid images of Yokohama and Japan. It seemed such a faraway, enchanting place. I still remember how Phineas Fogg reunited with Passeparout at the Yokohama circus before they boarded the steamer bound for San Francisco.

Years later, when I was taking art classes at the Mark Hopkins mansion, Yokohama and Japan caught my imagination again when the San Francisco Sketch Club sponsored a series of art lectures at the First Unitarian Church on Franklin Street. One thing led to the next, and soon I became active in the Japan Society art programs, which were organized at the Palace Hotel. Then, when Mrs. Stanford acquired rare Oriental art treasures from the Ikeda collection, I jumped at the opportunity to help the curators prepare the exhibit at the Stanford Museum.

Since Mama and Papa knew of my interest, I don't think it was that much of a surprise when, one evening, after supper, I announced that I would use some of Oma's gift to travel to Japan for six months and study art. Phineas Fogg's trip on the steamer *General Grant* might have been fictional, but my journey would be real. Surprise or not, Mama and Papa both looked at me in amazement. They were encouraging and pleased with my growing independence.

◆

I had thought long and hard about my windfall. I listened carefully to Oma's advice and, as she suggested, didn't open the envelope until I was ready to jump. I was never prepared to receive such a gift and wanted to honor

Oma's wishes. While I made a donation in Oma's name to the Hospital for Children and Training School for Nurses, deep down, I knew that this time, Oma intended her charity to be me. I think she would have been pleased with my decision.

◆

I had crossed the Atlantic ocean many times, but never the Pacific, and I certainly had never ventured this far on a trip on my own. Traveling to Japan as a single young woman in 1908 was an extraordinary journey and a marvelous personal experience, challenging and inspiring. I spent the first month in Tokyo, visiting and studying at the second annual Bunten Exhibit, the government-sponsored contemporary art forum patterned after the public art exhibitions of the Académie des Beaux-Arts and Société des Artistes in Paris.

For the remainder of my trip, I traveled twenty miles south to the port city of Yokohama and stayed in the home of a family. There I studied the magnificent artwork crafted in the small villages of the surrounding area. I devoted my time to visiting many of the artisans' tiny workshops, where I could observe the techniques that had come into fashion when Japan had returned to direct imperial rule under Emperor Meiji.

When I began my voyage to Japan, I carried four pieces of luggage filled with all my necessities. By the time I returned, I had added several crates of artifacts and the beginning of a small collection of Meiji artwork with the plan to make a gift to the Sketch Club. They had lost most of their collection to the San Francisco earthquake and fires.

◆

I chose to keep a few items as my own treasures – an inlaid, signed Nogawa vase, a silver bowl, and a bronze usubata for ikebana flower arrangements. My favorite was a small black lacquered chest decorated with scenes of tiny chrysanthemums made of gold and silver inlay. Behind two elaborately decorated doors were seven drawers that were perfect for storing jewelry.

The chest was a curious object, well-constructed and a very fine work of art, certainly of value. What made it most special was that concealed beneath the seven drawers was a secret chamber, a three-inch-deep hiding place only visible when the inlay on the left side of the cabinet was pressed and the bottom drawer removed.

Twenty-Two

I never asked, but I am almost certain that Mama was secretly relieved when Martin and I did not marry. I always thought that she might have been troubled by her choice, unconvinced of her own matchmaking skills, perhaps concerned that she might have made a miscalculation. She never appeared terribly disappointed when Martin announced his engagement.

Of course, her reaction might have been much different if our wedding arrangements had been planned and invitations mailed. I cannot imagine the fuss she would have made then. What I never considered is that she might have had another suitor in mind. With the encouragement of Papa's three sisters, Mama regained her enthusiasm. Then, without my knowledge, she made a second attempt.

Often I thought Mama was of two minds on the matter of Martin. "Hilda, wait until you have a child. You will be confused, too. There will be times when you never know for certain what you want for your children.

Mostly you hope that they will remain healthy and find happiness."

On the one hand, Mama wanted to be certain that I would be taken care of by someone, that I would become settled and secure and live a life without worry. On the other, she encouraged me to go my own way, find my independence, and do something different. I know she was proud when I ventured on my own to Japan to pursue my interest in art.

Mama was fond of saying, "We each need to cut our own cloth," one of many phrases she seemed to invent out of thin air. She had many strange sayings to offer – I'm sure the result of being raised in a home where German maxims were often translated into English advice.

I was not the only one trying to find my balance on the edge of a new era. While Mama was ferociously proud of her family's prominence and generosity, a side of her wanted to embrace the idea of "cutting her own cloth." I suppose that Mama was no different than most of us at the turn of the century. She wanted to put her own stamp on life. One could argue that Mama succeeded when she chose to marry Papa.

Everyone in our family agreed that Papa's family, the Samsons, approached life differently than the Meyers, particularly the earlier generations. The Samsons were more accustomed and at ease with privilege, and they earned the incomes necessary to support their lifestyle in a much different way. Perhaps that's what Uncle Daniel meant when he joked about the difference between a banker and a broker: the idea that the banker makes studied investments and waits patiently for his return, while the broker collects his profits on each and every transaction regardless of its outcome.

Unlike Papa, I know that few Meyer family men ever chose to take a day for themselves away from their work. In that regard, Papa was different. He always felt that there was more to life. He enjoyed his avocations more than his vocation. And while my generation did spawn a few exceptions, as a rule, the Meyer men were more generous in their giving than the Samsons. Many chose to pledge much of their fortunes to benevolent causes. They gave what they made. By contrast, the Samsons tended to keep their money and use it for themselves. Others would say they were self-indulgent.

Mama and Papa appeared to have adopted this latter view. Instead of giving what they made, they spent what they had – primarily on themselves. They felt it was their responsibility to enjoy the finer things in life. Given the choice, rather than work, they took time to travel. Others would argue that some of this thinking rubbed off on me, too. Although there were times I was uncertain and occasionally self-conscious, I admit to taking our upper-class extravagance for granted. Oma was right when she said I was spoiled.

As I consider this, I can only offer that the difference between the end of Victorian ways and the norms of a new century was not only a divide that affected my generation. It was confusing for my parents' generation, too. Everyone, including Mama, was searching to find their way to balance the pull of the old with the push of the new.

◆

I soon learned that I wasn't the only family member to receive a windfall from Oma. After she died, Mama and Papa received a substantial inheritance, an amount that was never disclosed but certainly changed their lives. And once the estate was settled, they decided to enjoy a small part of it.

I had finally finished my studies, and Papa had faithfully completed his civic duty as a juror in the infamous Calhoun graft trial, a lengthy saga that had occupied the attention of the San Francisco newspapers for weeks. That's when Mama made her announcement. We would leave San Francisco and move to Europe for eighteen months. Through a business acquaintance, Papa leased a spacious and elegant apartment in Paris's 16th arrondissement as a base for our travels throughout Europe. The apartment had enough room for Aunt Hattie to join us, too.

I could not imagine a more delightful idea. I could spend my days exploring the museums and galleries throughout Europe's grand cities: Paris, London, Rome, Berlin, Vienna, and Prague. As for my evenings, I would be kept busy. They would be filled with the beauty of music and theater, the gatherings of society, and the salons of Europe. Mama knew people everywhere.

◆

Those eighteen months were eventful. Among a host of marvelous undertakings, we also experienced the 1910 Great Flood of Paris, an enormous catastrophe that occurred when the Seine River, carrying winter rains from its tributaries, rose eight meters above the ordinary level and flooded the entire city. And later that year, in May, our trip to London coincided with the death of King Edward VII, the "Uncle of Europe." There we joined the millions of spectators who lined the streets from Buckingham Palace to Westminster Hall to watch the funeral procession of the nine kings who rode on horseback, accompanied by their heirs apparent, royal highnesses, and queens.

◆

Before returning to America, Mama informed us that there was one other city we would visit. She claimed it was Papa's sisters' request. We traveled to Hamburg and spent several days with the Samson family in Altona. Another family gathering was planned. Apparently, Mama and my aunts knew that a certain young gentleman would be there, the perfect opportunity for me to be reintroduced. As for me, I had not been advised. I had no idea until we arrived at the party. That day, Josef suggested we begin our overseas correspondence.

Twenty-Three

I n January of 1913, two and a half years after we began sending our letters back and forth across the Atlantic, Josef and I were married in one of Berlin's most elegant buildings, the recently rebuilt Charlottenburg Town Hall, with its lavish interior, richly decorated façade, and enormous tower that dwarfed all the other buildings around the palace. Neither of us professed any interest or felt any purpose would be served by planning anything more elaborate than a simple civil affair, and we were quite pleased with the small wedding attended by our immediate family.

On the matter of a religious ceremony, we agreed. While we both embraced our heritage, neither of us felt bound by its traditions. Our wishes were fulfilled by being surrounded by close family. We were joined by Josef's parents, who were gracious and welcoming and, as a gesture to their impression of American familiarity, insisted that I call them Wolff and Lina. Both sides of my family, the Meyers and the Samsons, were there to support me: Mama, Aunt Hattie, and my cousin Adele, Aunt Rosalie's daughter. Adele and Josef's father, Wolff, signed the documents as witnesses to our marriage.

I am afraid that my emotions got the best of me that morning. Until then, I had been so overwhelmed by the move to Berlin and excitement of my wedding that I had failed to stop and consider all that I would soon miss. I would not return to America. When Mama and the others departed, I would stay. Berlin would become my new home. I was about to leave all that I had ever known behind and wave farewell to my San Francisco family.

As Mama helped me dress, I thought about the many faces who would not be with us that day: Papa, his sisters, Uncle Daniel, and the others. We were all still in mourning for Papa. His illness had been sudden and had taken him quickly. There had been so little time to say goodbye. What I did know was that he thought the world of Josef. He would have been pleased with my choice and considered him worthy. As for Oma? It was her face I missed most. She could always lean in close, look into my eyes, and somehow find those things that I could never see for myself.

I hoped I was like Oma. I had waited and then followed. Wasn't that the way she said life was to be? Of course, now I was old enough to know that I had been mistaken at first and confused for no reason. When I was eight years old and heard her words, I was too young to understand. Oma was never constrained by the notion that men are to lead and women are to follow. She always knew this was a choice she could make. She chose to wait, and when she chose to leave Bavaria and follow Opa, she found happiness by following her own heart.

As Mama and the others helped me dress that morning, I could still hear her say, "Mäuschen, sometimes in life, you must close your eyes, clench your fists tightly, and jump, hoping that your feet will go far and land on solid ground." And that's what I chose to do when I accepted Josef's marriage proposal. I had waited long enough. It was the right decision. I chose to follow my heart.

For me, everything was perfect that day. If the number of tears defines the success of a wedding, then we certainly more than succeeded. After completing the ceremony and signing the official documents, Josef treated the wedding party to a delightful luncheon. We dined at the famous restaurant in the Hotel Excelsior on Potsdamer Platz, the social hub of Berlin, where Charlie Chaplin and the kaiser were often seen in the early evening hours.

Then, quite suddenly, after we had finished our meal, the various toasts had been recited, and all the bottles of Champagne had been emptied, it was as if a magician tapped his wand and made everyone vanish. They all departed on cue, and Josef and I remained to begin our new life together as husband and wife.

◆

While the celebration might have been wonderful, the others in my traveling wedding party might have found the trip from San Francisco to Berlin a bit more tedious than first anticipated. As might be true for any lengthy journey, there were moments when I was not certain whether my companions agreed that the brief town hall ceremony warranted the distance and time taken for their travels.

Nevertheless, our small entourage must have been a sight to behold: four well-dressed ladies with enough luggage and baggage to require the assistance of three, and sometimes four, porters, with Mama leading the way, Aunt Hattie close behind, and Cousin Adele and me following in order like a family of small ducklings.

Mama and Aunt Hattie made certain that we traveled in style. Pullman sleepers took us to Chicago, where we spent two entertaining nights at the fabulous Palmer House before boarding the overnight train to New York. When we arrived in the city, the new Beaux Arts-style Grand Central Terminal straddling Park Avenue was just as magnificent as the newspapers claimed. We were treated like royalty at the newly opened Vanderbilt Hotel, with its fluted fans, painted panels, and delicate plaster ceiling ornaments. Our time there was a delight.

Before crossing the Atlantic, we lunched with my cousin Charles, Adele's brother, who had moved to New York to embark upon a writing career under the curious pseudonym of James Madison. That afternoon, we joined the procession of elegantly dressed women visiting New York City's glorious department stores. And the evening before we boarded the ship, Aunt Hattie surprised us with tickets to a wonderful performance of

Hamlet featuring Sir Johnston Forbes-Robertson at the Shubert Theatre.

By the time we reached Berlin and sent a cable to the San Francisco newspapers formally announcing my engagement, you can be certain that my trousseau was complete, our conversations were exhausted, and I had received enough marital advice to last a lifetime.

Twenty-Four

We were both anxious to begin this next chapter of our lives together. Before I arrived in Berlin, Josef had found the perfect home, a spacious and grand twelve-room apartment filled with large spaces, vaulted ceilings, and sunlit windows in a quiet area on Martin-Luther Straße. And having been tutored by Mama, Oma, and my aunts since I was a young girl, I was ready to join him there. I had spent my life training for this new role as Josef's wife.

I suppose that our experiences were not altogether different from many new marriages. Most would agree that marriage requires a period of adjustment. After the initial excitement begins to wane, there comes the morning when one stares glassy-eyed at the ceiling, at a loss to know what exactly has transpired. I found Josef to be worldly, practiced, and experienced at a variety of marital functions and duties, many of which were previously unknown to me and not ever imagined. He may have found me to be a bit awkward and fumbling, curious and enthusiastic, and, at times, distraught and more than a little confused.

As for most other aspects of our marriage, I know he would agree with this assessment. My life had been more uprooted and upended. Perhaps it was as Oma once said: the women follow. While I traveled thousands of miles and crossed an ocean to be with Josef, he took few steps, hardly finding it necessary to even venture across the Spree or any other of Berlin's rivers and canals. Most of his life remained unchanged, and I had been invited to join it.

Nevertheless, Mama always said that most of marriage is give and take, and in that regard, I voice no regrets, at least none that might be considered serious. So, with a great deal of shared patience and an equal amount of perseverance, it was not long before we settled into a satisfying and comfortable daily rhythm, one we were able to both enthusiastically embrace.

I would be less than truthful if I didn't admit that there were troublesome moments, particularly at the onset. Perhaps I had unrealistic expectations. And, I was quick to learn that, being new to Berlin, I had no one else to talk to. There were days when, like many new brides, I shed more than my share of tears, and I imagine Josef was at his wit's end, not knowing what to do with me. What quickly became apparent was that we had spent fewer than two full days in one another's company before my arrival.

Since our marriage had grown from a distant overseas romance and two chance meetings, Josef was known to me more by his letters than his person. No matter how well composed, written words do not replace the subtle expressions of give-and-take conversation or the glimpse of emotion reflected in another's eyes. Letters, by their very nature, suffer from a lack of spontaneity. Now, in one another's presence, we had to learn and understand each other.

Josef and I were not the first to face these realities of romance. There were discoveries to be made, him of me and me of him, and we needed to respect and appreciate each other's peculiar habits and be mindful of one another's sensitivities. Was either of us disappointed? I don't believe so. Were we surprised? Every day. Were we required to be patient and compromise? Absolutely. Did we express our emotions? Often.

I imagine, in one regard, we were no different from many other newlyweds. The marriages we had witnessed, the ones we knew best, were those of our parents. While I had no knowledge of any secrets Mama and Papa might have had in their private moments, I was accustomed to how they treated one another, how they acted together, how they spent their waking hours in their home. Josef had observed the same.

Because we were a little older than most young couples, we were a bit accustomed to our own ways, and we both had been raised to be a little self-centered and selfish. We quickly discovered that blending our two lives required each of us to give a little more of ourselves than we might have first expected or were prepared to give. It takes time to change one's habits. Marital bliss requires a certain amount of initiative and unselfish behavior. One cannot always wait for the other. I can see Mama's smile when I write these words.

For me, one of the most worrisome struggles was that, despite my wishes to the contrary, Josef would not entirely be mine. I was required to share him with his profession, and I soon learned that he could not be with me day and night. I was not entitled to be possessive, nor could I be jealous. He was very serious and intense about his work, very studied and committed to the care of his patients. I had to adjust to becoming a physician's wife, a lesson many others had learned. His cases came first. I came in second and oftentimes third.

Perhaps I should have known, but Josef had never advised me of this requirement, and sharing was not something I have ever excelled at. Of course, this worked both ways. Despite the demands and importance of his schedule, it was necessary for him to understand that I had not married him only to do his bidding. While I was anxious to please, I had my own interests and expectations to be acknowledged and treated with respect.

What quickly became clear was that I needed to build a relationship with my new in-laws. I was the family addition, and it was my responsibility to understand how I fit in. When I married Josef, I made no vow to marry his parents, particularly his mother, although I soon formed the opinion that she might have thought otherwise. On this matter, I was at a loss for what to do. Other than Oma, who had never appeared a burden for Papa, these family complications never became an issue in my San Francisco household.

To his credit, Josef was a dutiful and loving son. Being an only child, he felt a deep responsibility for the care and well-being of his parents. However, his mother had very specific expectations, which I soon began to view through the lens of obligation and infringement.

I never had any issue with Josef's father. It was his mother, Lina, who, while often kind and generous, I found increasingly difficult and, at times, overbearing and manipulative. She possessed a sense of entitlement and was always first with her opinions. While I was expected to accommodate her requirements, she saw no need for adjustment or compromise, none at all. One requirement was that Sunday afternoons, regardless of circumstances, were to be spent in her home. Another was that she expected to hear from her son by telephone or in person at least every other day so she could inquire about his happiness. These conversations were theirs alone, and I was not invited to join.

So, you can see that our differences quickly became territorial. With Lina, I found it necessary to clearly mark my territory, often with an obstinance that made this a less-than-satisfying exercise for Josef. He frequently found himself in the middle, torn between the expectations of his wife and the strong will of his mother.

Josef was just as intense and passionate about his hobbies and other interests as he was about his medicine. On these other matters, he was a perfect joy. He shared enthusiastically, and I could not have asked for more. We spent many Saturday afternoons with our easels and paints in the Tiergarten, uncovering all of its mysterious nooks and magical places. And on those days when the weather cooperated, we often rented one of the park's small boats. Then I would sit comfortably beneath the shade of an umbrella and watch Josef row about the Neuen See.

Frequently, in late afternoon, we indulged ourselves with long walks along the expansive Unter den Linden, beneath the watchful eyes of the statue of Frederick the Great as we passed the enormous state buildings that line the path from the City Palace to the Brandenburg Gate, walks that often led to amazing discoveries. If friends were about, we would stop for drinks at the crowded bar in the Hotel Bristol or for an early dinner at Kempinski's on Leipziger Straße.

We preferred to spend at least one hour each evening practicing our music, him on the piano and me accompanying him on the flute. We were both serious students of music and quite accomplished, and we loved our practice time together.

I also learned that Josef was a habitual collector, a hobby he had relished since childhood. It didn't seem to matter the subject – stamps, art, photographs, coins, or books – Josef was devoted to his collections. Our afternoons were often spent visiting various shops hidden on the marvelous streets of Berlin as we hunted for the missing item in one of Josef's collections. And on those occasions when we could think of little else we would rather do, we found great pleasure in silently reading our books and sharing the gentle warmth of being close, within arm's reach of one another.

With regard to his friendships, I quickly discovered that Josef was passionate and had many. He was gregarious by nature and curious by personality. He was a true Berliner and had collected friendships from all walks of life. His friends were artists, musicians, physicists, physicians, and a variety of opinionated politicians, both seasoned and rising. Josef readily shared his friends with me. I admit, I found some a little pretentious and off-putting, but Josef insisted that his friends were to become my friends, and I was quickly invited to join their lively debates and discussions.

So, I was presented with an intense, expansive, and energetic way of living in wonderful surroundings. Berlin had much to offer and was full of many new experiences. Although the German spoken was not always the German I knew, and from time to time, I suffered the pangs of homesickness, I can think of nothing important denied that I might have wanted. Just as Mama had always hoped, in Berlin, I was taken care of and able to continue my life of leisure and civility. I moved from one prosperous household to another, from the cultured lifestyle of San Francisco to the even more cultured lifestyle of Berlin. My upbringing had prepared me well for this new life as Herr Doktor Samson's wife, and I embraced it with excitement and enthusiasm.

Twenty-Five

I fell in love with Berlin's magnetic appeal during those first months of our marriage. The city was remarkable, a kaleidoscope, a cultural capital, far bigger, bolder, and more cosmopolitan than anything I had expected. With nearly four million residents, greater Berlin was a frenzy of continuous construction, eight times the size of San Francisco and with a population that rivaled New York. Josef would often boast, "Whatever it is, if you find one in San Francisco, then you can be certain that Berlin will have many and they will all be better and definitely more entertaining."

Day and night, Berlin's streets were crowded, a curious mix of tradition and modernity. Well-dressed ladies wearing grand hats and outfitted in the latest styles paraded arm in arm on the sidewalks. A sense of unfiltered permissiveness oozed from its streets. The seats in bars, restaurants, and concert halls were filled with artists, intellectuals, and adventurers from throughout Europe. At night, searchlights filled the sky and shone on the new

Zeppelin that flew high overhead, illuminating the advertisements on its sides. There were tramways, underground railways, smokestacks, concert halls, cafes, and massive buildings made of stone. People were always out and about. Businesses were booming, and the department stores, with their marvelous large window displays, were full of shoppers. At first, I had trouble crossing the busy streets. There were so many cars on the roads that the police had to stand at major intersections and direct traffic.

There was so much new to learn, and Josef was my teacher. He had lived in Berlin all his life and seemed to know every neighborhood, street, and building. I never felt that he took the city for granted. He shared my enthusiasm and amazement. Every day we were delighted by new surprises.

Josef often claimed that Berliners were unlike other Germans. He would tell me that one should never be confused. One must think of Berlin in the way one might consider New York City or even San Francisco in relation to the rest of America. The people of Berlin viewed life in their own distinct terms and curious outrageous manner. Berliners took pride in being different from the rest of Central Europe.

The reason the German spoken in Berlin seemed so strange to me was that the city had its own dialect, one that I had never been taught, the result of a population that had grown so quickly. The Berlin Hauptbahnhof was a crossroads for the trains carrying those leaving their homes throughout Europe and made the city a melting pot of dialects and nationalities. So many residents were born elsewhere that Berlin had found its own peculiar way to speak the language. Berlin was a city where differences were accepted. It was far too big and busy to be concerned with whether everyone was exactly like the other.

More than anything, I learned how immensely proud Josef and his friends were of their home. They told me I should not be distracted or swayed by the glamour, magnificence, or history of the great capitals of Europe: London, Paris, or Vienna. Berlin was more than their equal. Every Berliner I met agreed. They were convinced that Berlin would soon reach its heights and be afforded the respect and recognition that was long overdue.

◆

Each day was a joy. I remember one evening when we met the most interesting young man, someone I am convinced the world will one day discover. Josef's close childhood friend Georg Lewin, whose wife, Else, oddly insisted everyone else refer to as Herwath Walden, invited us to an opening for a one-man show he had curated at his well-known Galerie Der Sturm, beneath *Der Sturm* magazine's offices on Potsdamer Straße. Georg, a left-wing German art critic whose magazine had rapidly become the mouthpiece for modern art in Berlin, was quite an entertaining and talented character himself. That day, his gallery featured a promising upcoming young artist, someone he had met at the Salon des Indé-pendants in Paris. I must say that I was quite taken.

The artist, Moïche Shagalov, was a modernist who was trained in St. Petersburg. I felt that I had a well-trained eye for art, and his pieces were different from anything I had ever seen, a mixture of style and splendid color based on Eastern European Jewish folk culture, a personal style that defied classification.

Late that afternoon, after the exhibit closed for the day, Georg insisted we join Moïche and a few others for drinks at the Esplanade. We talked well into the evening. Although he and I were close in age to one another, I could not help but be struck by the paths we had each taken, how entirely different Moïche's life was from my own.

He had grown up in Belarus, part of the Russian Empire. The eldest of nine, his father was a herring merchant, and his mother sold vegetables from their garden. He told me that his father would be up before sunrise each day to pray at the synagogue before beginning his work. I learned about his struggle to become an artist. In his village, he practiced by copying pictures found in books before his father could afford to send him to St. Petersburg. Later, when he moved to Paris, he spent his days and nights refining his craft. I was unable to imagine the road Moïche must have traveled to have his works exhibited in Berlin.

As Josef and I walked back to the apartment that evening, I thought about how small the world is and how marvelous my Berlin life was becoming. With Josef, I was discovering all these new experiences. Later that night, I wrote to Mama to tell her about Moïche and to beg her to have the bank send funds so I could purchase one of his works. I knew it would be a wonderful addition to Josef's collection.

Twenty-Six

While Josef saw patients in his office and at the hospital, I devoted my time and attention to decorating and furnishing our apartment. Mama and Aunt Hattie had overwhelmed us with gifts: silverware, table linens, china, serving dishes, crystal, and much more. Even with the cartloads of luggage that followed us from San Francisco, I have no idea how they managed to pack so many things in their suitcases and still find room for their clothes. It was as if they had purchased the entire contents of Shreve and Company and, before carrying their purchases to Berlin, managed to have every item monogrammed.

As her special wedding gift, Mama gave us an extraordinary seven-piece silver tea service in Shreve's most coveted pattern. With so much silver to polish, I was certain that Elena, our housekeeper, would be busy for days. I had no idea how we would possibly make use of all these things. We had twenty-four of every dish, fork, knife, and spoon, far too many wine and cocktail glasses, and serving dishes for more dinner courses than I could possibly imagine. If Josef wished to entertain his friends and put all this to use, we would need a much larger table in the dining room, and the food and drink required would severely deplete his savings.

◆

As a single young man, Josef had accumulated an assortment of very ordinary furniture, most of which I found less than appealing. Apart from the walls, which were covered with the wonderful works of many of Berlin's young, upcoming artists, I wanted to start over again and decorate the apartment to suit my own style and taste. The apartment was quite deserving, and we had been given so many wonderful gifts to display in interesting places.

At first, Josef was reluctant. He found the prospect wasteful and the time required unnecessary. He only became enthusiastic after I explained that I was prepared to use my own funds and devote my time to this purpose. On only one matter was there minor disagreement – his refusal to part with the round piano seat, which he claimed was a much-adored possession dating back to his childhood. As the seat was his alone to sit on, I acquiesced when he agreed that I could find an upholsterer to replace its worn fabric.

And that was how my treasure hunt began. I had never lived in a home where I could test my decorating skills and had the most fun searching the streets of Berlin for art deco furnishings: tables, chairs, cabinets, and the like, not only furniture but lamps and chandeliers. This became my personal adventure, and although there were times when Josef found himself confused by the purpose of certain purchases or how a certain chandelier might hang, I believe that when the day came to announce the completion of my masterpiece, he was quite pleased and took great pride in showing our guests the result.

◆

That day, I had a second announcement to make. I had waited for this moment long enough to know for certain. It was no longer the art deco furnishings or the chandeliers that would leave Josef confused. That evening, I took hold of his hands, looked straight into his eyes, and told him that our apartment would soon have one additional treasure. That's when he learned I was carrying his child.

Twenty-Seven

I must tell you. While I find comfort, solace, and great joy in the knowledge that so many others have shared this experience, I did not anticipate being so overcome by the conflicting emotions of exuberance and anxiety when I first understood that I was with child. That summer in 1914, before I announced this news to Josef, I found myself quite shaken by the very thought of impending motherhood. It was not a sense of dread or foreboding; in fact, it was quite the opposite. I was of an age where I felt it was time.

Yet I also had a sense of uncertainty. I was unsure if I was prepared for this new arrival. Berlin might have become my new adopted city, but many days I could not help but feel that my old home in San Francisco was far too distant. This was a time when I longed for the loving arms of Mama and Aunt Hattie. I needed both to tell me how this all should be.

Josef was thrilled by this news. I wish you could have seen his smile and his tears. He can't wait to meet you.

Isn't that marvelous? Now that I have told him that he is about to be your father, it won't be long before you begin to refer to him that way. On that matter, we will wait for your arrival. I will continue to call him Josef and leave it to you to decide what you wish to call him whenever you are ready. As for what we should call you, there is a name I once was given. For now, we will call you Mäuschen. You are perfectly suited. Soon you will be underfoot, but at least for this moment, you remain as quiet as a church mouse.

Twenty-Eight

I n those first eighteen months, before the assassination of Archduke Franz Ferdinand and the start of the Great War, I found Berlin to be a city pulsing with its own energy, always abuzz with a dizzying air of excitement and newness. Then, as I explored its streets, I had no idea that Germany's generals had spent nearly two decades crafting their war plans or that after the country's leaders had convinced themselves of war's necessity, they had amassed the weapons and prepared their military.

In those early days, I was not aware of Germany's ambitions. I did not know that the Fatherland was poised and ready, waiting for the opportune moment to strike and stake its claim to the empire. I had no knowledge of Europe's web of secret treaties and alliances that would soon foretell such a calamitous outcome. And I most certainly would have been unable to predict that within a short time, Josef and I would join the crowd of thousands milling in the streets and massed in front of the

Berliner Schloss on the first of August when we anxiously awaited Germany's response to the answer Russia
had given to Kaiser Wilhelm II's ultimatum. That afternoon, at five o'clock, we listened soberly and in hushed
silence to the official announcement that war was about
to begin, and we recognized that our lives were about to
be turned upside down.

◆

Before the heir to the Austro-Hungarian Empire and his
wife, Sophie, were shot to death in Sarajevo by a Serbian
assassin in June of 1914, no one had told me about the
delicate balance or the hidden dalliances of the various
powers of Europe. I knew even less about Kaiser Wilhelm II's lofty but so often inconsistent and frequently
changing desires. My life in San Francisco had been a
world away, far from this unimagined madness. Before
moving to Berlin to be with Josef, I had paid scant attention to the tensions brewing in Europe and certainly less
to anything concerning the Balkans.

Why would I? I knew no one in San Francisco who
did. To me, the kaiser seemed only a pompous figure
with a hooked mustache, known to be chauffeured
through the boulevards and broad, swept streets of Berlin in his Daimler, his horn clearing the way by playing
the thunder theme from *Das Rheingold*.

Later, as Germany gathered its armies for war, I
would become more educated on these matters. I would
sit up until the darkest hours of the night and listen

carefully to Josef and his friends as they expressed their points of view. After the war broke out, I could hardly believe they were the same people I had heard once before. They all became enthusiastic, brimming with patriotism and passionately engaged, so unlike the opinions they had expressed before the war began.

Before the war, they had said little, certainly nothing that could have prepared me. Then they were disciples of Norman Angell's *The Great Illusion*. They could see no reason. What would be gained? There would be no point. No country would win. Everyone would lose. Why, in this day and age, with all the advancements in weaponry, would anyone be so vain or so foolish?

◆

So, I hope you can see. When I first moved to Berlin, I had no reason to be concerned. I was given no forewarning and had no clue. There was no worry, our lives were untouched, and I gave no thought to the prospect of war. Then everything changed, and my eyes were opened.

Twenty-Nine

That August, when the war began, no one really knew what might be next. There were myths and realities, rumors and facts, and confusing interpretations. One day the newspaper might tell one story, and the next day a different paper another. It was an uncertain and troubling time. In the month before war was declared, it was quite apparent that Berlin's citizens were divided. Then we thought that the only ones who wanted war were the nationalists and imperialists.

At first, the desire for war was not a view shared by Germany's working class or members of the Social Democratic Party. In July, Josef joined the more than one hundred thousand who took to the streets in protest. But then the events that began in Sarajevo escalated into an unimagined international crisis, and while many of us were unable to understand the real cause and wondered whether certain actions had been contrived, little else seemed to matter.

We were told we were hemmed in on the continent, surrounded by hostile powers, and that Germany was left with no choice but to defend itself against Tsarist Russia. After Austria-Hungary declared war on Serbia, it was not long before Russia, France, Great Britain, and Serbia joined together on one side and Germany and Austria-Hungary on the other. Suddenly the Great War was underway. That's when those who had been against the war were quick to change their minds. Newspapers, speeches, and songs stoked this sentiment. They called for national unity, and they cried for war.

When I first heard these words, I couldn't help but remember our late-night discussions, the times Josef and his friends had argued that war, no matter how quickly decided, would be folly, that no leader would be so preposterous or foolhardy.

How abruptly they forgot these views and switched their devotion. Now they agreed with Friedrich von Bernhardi, who claimed that war was a biological necessity, that it was Darwinlike and reflected man's struggle for existence. They argued that Germany had the right and bore the responsibility to wage war, to be the aggressors, to become the invaders, to take whatever actions were necessary to gain the power it deserved.

In August, after war was declared, the anti-war protests were replaced with demonstrations urging the government to stand firm and defend Germany against its enemies. It was clear that Berlin was willing to make the sacrifice, that Germany's men were prepared to take part in the fight and ready to march to war. And in those early months, as the armies in the west made their victorious advance into neutral Belgium and those in the east defeated the two Russian armies who had threatened East Prussia, the euphoria of victory only grew day by day.

Every afternoon great crowds of excited people would parade through the streets, waving their flags and singing "Deutschland Uber Alles." Giant flags hung from buildings. Church bells rang. Patriotic speeches called for solidarity. Newsboys would stand on the corners and distribute their free "extras" announcing the army's latest successes. Huge rallies were held throughout the city. Those who had criticized the kaiser in the past now stood by his side, locked in arms. His cries for war made him the most popular man in Germany.

So many things changed. Led by the police chief of Berlin, words of foreign origin were expunged from the German language. Countless self-interested hotels and cafes throughout the city adopted this sense of national pride, and many adopted new patriotic names. The Piccadilly Cafe was renamed the Kaffeehaus Vaterland, the Cafe Windsor became the Kaffee Winzer, and the sign for the Hotel Bristol on the Unter den Linden disappeared. The Hotel Westminster became the Lindenhof, and a nearby confectioner was told to stop using the word "bonbon" to sell his candy. German cigarette manufacturers changed many of their products' names. The Berlin-based company Manoli replaced the popular Gibson Girl with Wimpel. Even *adieu* was discarded and replaced with *auf wiedersehen*.

◆

During those early days, when the war first began, Germany's leaders promised it would end quickly, that the battle would be a brief skirmish and the soldiers would be home before Christmas. The kaiser was confident in his generals. Hadn't it taken his grandfather Wilhelm I only six weeks to defeat France in the Franco-Prussian War of 1870? This time the outcome would be the same. Germany would overpower and outgun its enemies.

On the war's first day, Kaiser Wilhelm II stood on the palace balcony and told the crowds of men assembled before him that "before the leaves have fallen from the trees, you will be back in your homes." He assured us that Great Britain would remain neutral and Paris would be taken in days. Germany's armies would then remobilize and strike a quick blow at Russia before she had time to gather her armies and position her resources. Germany's years of war preparation would finally bear fruit. That's when Gottlieb von Jagow, the foreign minister, proclaimed that war would give the Fatherland the chance to finally secure "its place under the sun."

◆

But by year's end, we began to understand that Germany's generals had not planned for a lengthy war. In Berlin, most provisions were used up within the first few months. Even before Christmas, the newspapers began publishing housekeeping tips on the use of potatoes and suggestions on how to feed a family for two weeks on less than two marks. A weekly menu consisted of potato soup (twice), potato pancakes, baked potatoes, potatoes with onions, and potatoes and fat – with a bit of cabbage and rice.

As the war dragged on and everyone's lives were affected, it became apparent that those in charge might have been so overly confident that they had dramatically underestimated the deadly power of new weapons. This was a new era and an industrialized war, one with tanks, machine guns, poison gas, and artillery. And by then, we had learned of Great Britain's resolve.

That's when we heard people say that the kaiser must have been confused when he had made his promise, that he might have been mistaken, that he knew little about trees. Others said he must have been talking about pine trees. Even at the earliest age, schoolchildren are taught that pine trees have no leaves.

Thirty

G reat Britain made its decision to enter the war quickly, only days after the kaiser stood on his balcony and made his promise. While Great Britain's Liberal Party cabinet was staunchly anti-war, the conservatives threatened a parliamentary election, and a majority voted to declare war on Germany. They claimed they were protecting Belgium, that Germany's armies had violated the terms of neutrality when they had used Belgium as the stepping stone to begin the attack on France. Most agreed that defending Belgium was not reason enough for Great Britain to declare war. Great Britain was intent on preventing France's defeat and declared war to stop Germany's advance and taking control of much of Europe.

Both Josef and I understood that we also had decisions to make. Although it seemed that the war would be fought elsewhere and there were few reasons to fear that Berlin might come under attack, we recognized that the war would bring many changes. Now we had an unborn child to consider. The casualties could be great, and Germany's armies would need many physicians. Josef had been called to serve before and was uncertain whether he would be called to serve again. He never said whether he might find this to be his patriotic duty, and I never considered whether he might enlist. And I had no idea what dangers war might bring or what any of this might mean for our family.

When Great Britain joined the war, our concerns were only heightened. The "English" became Germany's enemy. It didn't seem to matter that Americans wanted no part or that America remained neutral and hoped to conduct business with all sides.

Immediately there was much talk about spies and internal security. All foreigners, including Americans, were in an increasingly dangerous situation. My safety became an immediate issue, and Josef was reluctant to allow me to leave the apartment, even with my promise to never speak English.

Few Berliners were able to distinguish the difference between an American or British accent, but they certainly could recognize who spoke German with an English accent. As soon as the war began, we heard stories about Americans who were chased and attacked by crowds on the streets. Others had been arrested. The U.S. embassy quickly issued warnings.

◆

My first impulse was for Josef and me to leave Germany, to move to America, where we would be safe, secure, and far from the war. I wanted to put all of this behind us. Money would not be an issue, and I was sure Mama could pull strings. I knew Mama and Aunt Hattie would be more than willing to help us get settled. They would be thrilled, and we would be surrounded by family. Josef would be able to resume his profession, and we could live a peaceful and prosperous life in San Francisco.

Josef refused to consider leaving. His refusal was complete. He would not be a traitor. He would not abandon his country in time of war. He would not give up his life in Germany. He would not leave his parents. He was a German. He wanted his children to be German. Germany was his ancestral home. It was where he belonged.

Then he took me in his arms and told me that no matter what I chose, he would always love me. He was concerned for my safety and the safety of our child. He did not want me to leave, but if that is what I felt I must do, even if only for the duration of the war, he would understand and accept my decision and beg for my return.

When Josef refused to leave, I refused to leave. I could not bear the thought. He was my husband. I could never leave him. Being with him was all I wanted. We would stay here forever. That day, I told him there was no reason to ever have this discussion again.

◆

During those first few days, the U.S. embassy was over-run with Americans, who crowded in front of the Wil-helmPlatz complex. Thousands of American citizens were in Berlin. Before the war, passports were not re-quired for travel within Europe. Crossing borders be-tween countries was not complicated. But now stamped passports became a necessity for those trying to return home. Many Americans were without passports, and the line for applications became lengthy.

◆

I thought long and hard about my decision and began to have second thoughts. I would not leave but would make sure I was prepared to do so. I couldn't bring myself to tell Josef, but I registered our names in the embassy's card index and answered their questions. I made certain my documents were in good order and marked "recom-mended for transportation to America." This was not a time to be selfish. I had another responsibility. Mäu-schen, no matter what, I promise to always keep you safe.

Thirty-One

Dear Mama,

I trust you are well and that Aunt Hattie is recovering from her winter cold, with no lingering ill effects. I know how much she hates to be under the weather. And please give my fondest regards to Aunt Rosalie and the others. Tell them all I am well and I now know that Mäuschen is becoming anxious to meet them.

I may be mistaken, but it seems I am reminded nearly every day. I find my current state agreeable and believe I have weathered these moments quite well. The war continues to be a worry, but to relieve that burden, I spend many of my waking hours having lengthy conversations with Mäuschen, whom I am convinced now knows the sound of my voice.

There are so many things that have changed here. The worst news came in the last few weeks when Josef received his notice from the army. He remains out of danger, but yes, he is now an army physician, and there is nothing we can do to change this. All the men are being called, even those who served before. I know he feels that this is his duty, but I am not of the same mind. I pray for the war to end quickly and for the men to come home.

As I know you do, we all want Germany to defeat its enemies and emerge victorious, but now, every day I hold my breath with worry and concern. The war has already lasted much longer than the politicians promised. At least Josef has not been sent to the front, where we hear reports that men are being injured and killed in great numbers. But we have no way to predict the future and no idea what it may bring. Tell me, what do San Franciscans say? Do they even know that there is a war?

The stories are tragic. Fortunately, Josef has been assigned to the Berlin district and is kept quite busy. He frequently spends his days treating patients at the Am Urban Hospital in Kreuzberg but mostly spends his nights at Beelitz-Heilstätten, which has been converted into a hospital for the growing number of war casualties who have returned to Berlin. He rides the train between the two. I see him rarely, only if he is permitted to be home or when I visit him briefly. Though allowed, Josef discourages me and wishes I would stay within the walls of the apartment. I pray he can be with me for Mäuschen's birth, but that is still two months away, and I am afraid that will not be in our hands to decide.

When I last saw him in Kreuzberg, he asked me to send you his love. I worry, as he seems to have aged overnight. He has lost weight and appears exhausted. But you know how Josef can be when it comes to his medical matters, and he refuses to tell me if there is any cause for my concern. He is troubled by the numbers of young, untrained volunteer soldiers being sent to the front. He says they are being used as cannon fodder. Their injuries are severe, not like the soldiers who can be quickly patched up and returned to the battles. Sometimes he wonders whether these men are truly fortunate to have survived.

Mama, I have no understanding of this war. Many men will never leave the hospital. Some have lost their sight and parts of their faces. Others suffer from severe brain injuries and are unable to think or speak. Even the most fortunate remain crippled. They have lost limbs and will be severely disfigured for life. Josef says that these soldiers went into battle unprepared, that the weapons of this new war are much more destructive, not like wars of the past. Their commanders continue to throw waves of our boys into the face of artillery, poison gas, and machine guns – hordes of volunteers who are only trained to run towards the enemy.

Each day, when I peer through our front windows, I count my blessings. So many children have taken to the streets in search of food, and people stand in lines at the butcher and markets for hours. I know how troubled you would be to watch this. It would break your heart, but there is little one can do. We are all on our own these days, especially those without livelihoods or enough money.

So many are suffering and are beginning to feel the effects of Great Britain's sea blockade. The newspapers remind us that we must feed the soldiers first and can only depend on what the farmers can grow. People are hoarding supplies, and the shelves in many shops are empty. At first, the bakers were using potato flour for their bread, but now they seem to be using other substitutes. I heard some claim that even sawdust is being used. The shortages have led to bread, meat, potatoes, and milk all being rationed, and the government gives us cards with little stamps that must be used for this purpose.

At least we are fortunate. You should not worry about food for us. I have enough to eat for two, and Josef has access to the food he needs. But I do worry for others. I know that this may not sound fair, but we must all watch out for ourselves first, and I must be particularly careful for myself at this time. As long as our funds last (thank you – the bank helped me, and I was finally given access), we can afford the high prices of those items that are not rationed, and we have the means to purchase whatever else is needed.

The past few weeks, the temperatures have turned very cold, and there are coal shortages. Those of us who use electricity are told to use less, which I think is good because, rather than use the coal to create electricity, people need enough to keep their homes heated. Any outside apartment house lights are to be turned off by nine o'clock, and stores are forbidden to illuminate their shop windows. Theatres (which still seem to be well attended) must close by ten pm. At night, only every other electric streetlight is lit, and if there are many lights in a lamp in one's home, only one bulb may be used.

There is another rather remarkable thing. As all the men are being called into the army, women are filling the jobs they used to hold. The new underground road is being built largely by women. I am told that this is not as difficult a matter in Berlin as it would be in the cities of America. Berlin is built upon a bed of sand, so there is no need for heavy rock excavation. Women are also employed by the railroads, working with pickaxes on the roadbeds. And when I am outside the apartment, I often see women driving the great yellow postal trucks that deliver the mail. There are even women conductors on the tramways and motor-women driving the tramcars. I think if I were not in my current state, I would do one of those things. I know that is what Oma would have done, although I cannot imagine her ever driving a great yellow postal truck!

There remains much concern about spies, although that seems to have settled down a bit, and I don't think there is as much danger as there once was, particularly towards Americans. Germans know that America remains neutral, but I am not sure they always trust us. Some say that America is more interested in profiting from the war than choosing sides. They say that America is more engrossed in the hunt for the dollar than producing a strong army. At least I am somewhat known in our neighborhood, which I do think helps.

My German continues to improve, and I seem to have mastered Berlin's way of speaking. The authorities have prohibited the use of English in public places, and when *speaking on the telephone, one does have to be in the habit of always speaking German. As for the spies, there have been terrible stories, but one does not always know what is true. At least Josef has come to understand that I do need to get out from time to time, if nothing more than for some fresh air. (I always wear an American badge on my coat so I am not thought to be British.) As for the marketing and the other outdoor tasks, Elena continues to handle these errands.*

Oh, I failed to mention this in my last letter. After a lengthy conversation, we did decide to keep her, and she is still with us. Given my situation, Josef felt better spending the money to keep her employed. Otherwise, her room would be empty, and having her in the house gives me some companionship since she is always hovering about. She does watch me carefully. I know you would caution me to not be this way, but I think of her less and less as a housekeeper and more as a companion. We seldom talk about things other than the weather. I long for friends to talk to and know there is only so much that can be said to Elena.

Finally, before I finish, because I am sure you are tired of reading and I have put you to sleep with my troubles, I must tell you what they are doing to retrieve gold coins for the Imperial Bank. There are signs on the underground cars which read, "Whoever keeps back a gold coin injures the Fatherland." Josef told me that he heard that if a soldier presents his superior with a twenty-mark gold piece, he receives twenty marks in paper money and two days' leave. (I think I should give Josef some gold pieces and encourage him to do this!) He was also told that if a schoolboy turns in ten marks in gold, he receives ten marks in paper and a half-day holiday from classes. At the cinema, if a patron pays in gold, they get an extra ticket, good for another day. And there has been a story circulating that an American woman was awakened early one morning by the Berlin police, who had been told that she had gold coins. They threatened to search her apartment if she did not turn them over. Apparently, the American ambassador interceded and was successful in returning what was taken. Rest assured, the only gold I have here is on my finger – which is now too swollen for the ring to be removed. I just hope they don't start looking for any silver, because you have surely given us too much!

I know how much you want us to move back to San Francisco, and I beg you to understand my decision to remain in Berlin. Please stay well and know that Josef, Mäuschen, and I think about you and Aunt Hattie all the time and love you very much. Do not worry! We will stay safe. I am sure that Germany will succeed, Josef will be home soon, and all this madness will be over. Then I promise we will visit and introduce Mäuschen to all of you in San Francisco.

Your loving daughter,
Hilda

Thirty-Two

I received the handwritten invitation in the post on a snowy morning in early February. It was from Mrs. Gerard, the wife of the American ambassador. Her husband had been a New York Supreme Court justice before President Wilson appointed him to his current post.

There had been no forewarning, so the invitation was not expected, and I was quite surprised, particularly since I couldn't recall ever being introduced to Mrs. Gerard and only knew her by name. I was invited to join her for a private lunch later that week. The only explanation I could think of was that if I searched carefully, Mama's or Aunt Hattie's fingerprints would likely be hidden somewhere on the envelope before it was sealed.

I had only been to the Esplanade Hotel one previous time, before the war had begun, the evening that Josef's friend Georg Lewin had invited us to join him for drinks at the bar when we had visited with Moïche Shagalov. When I arrived and the doorman opened the door, I was overwhelmed by what greeted me. I had forgotten that the hotel was always intended to be a gathering place for the great world of Berlin in times of peace, somewhere where royalty, statesmen, diplomats, military officers, financiers, and other important officials could rub shoulders.

As I entered the lobby, it was as if I had stepped into a portrait of a time gone by, a peaceful and opulent time that seemed so at odds with all the misery outside its doors. Inside the hotel, one would never know that the world was at war, particularly not Germany.

Under the watchful eyes of silent but attentive and immaculately groomed hotel staff wearing brocaded attire, the floors of the spacious lounge were covered with luxurious carpets and huge cushioned armchairs that appeared to reach out, begging one to sit. The vast reception area was filled with groupings of flowers and plants.

Scattered throughout the hall were quiet corners screened by sheltering palms, discreet private areas intended for important matters of state or perhaps occasional affairs of a lighter nature. A wide flight of stone steps led to the dining room and its pillars of veined gray marble, flowered ornaments, and crystal chandeliers, all in the style of Louis XVI.

It didn't take long before I understood the invitation's purpose. As I was greeted by the maître d' and escorted to Mrs. Gerard's table, everything became perfectly clear. I was being sent a message and reminded that I belonged in these surroundings, that this was what I was accustomed to, that this was how I was raised and where

I was meant to be. I understood the secret code. Mama was telling me that it was time to return home.

◆

Our conversation was friendly, polite, and entirely in English, which seemed strange yet exciting, as it had been several months since I had conversed in my native tongue. Mrs. Gerard was delightful and gracious, and she made few attempts to be overly persuasive.

There was no question that she cared for my safety. She was aware of my condition and circumstances and expressed concern for my health, but mostly she wanted to tell me about her travels throughout the countryside of Germany, to the small villages and towns, and of all the suffering and misery she had witnessed. I suppose she wanted to make sure that I recognized the dangers.

She reminded me of the enormous burdens that had been placed on the shoulders of Germany's women, how they had been left to do men's work but must still do their own, how the little that they earned went into the pockets of those who sold them food at enormous prices. She seemed quite concerned about these things.

We talked about many topics, and she was very interested in hearing what I had to say. She asked questions and shared her opinions. "Why should the women work, starve, and send their men out to fight? What does this bring them? More work, more poverty, their men as cripples, and their families destroyed. And what is it all for? A little more land? A few more riches? What will the

Fatherland really gain? After the war, how much wealth will be shared with these women and their children? How will their lives change?"

She spoke of the man whose face she had seen pressed against the glass windows of the hotel and his expression of disgust when he had seen the elegance inside. How could this be amidst the horrors of war? And she told of her American friend who came to her, crying and distraught. She couldn't understand the distrust that some Germans were beginning to show toward those Americans who once had been their friends. It was not what they said about Americans, but it was the look of scorn on their faces.

As we had our coffee, she began to ask the more important questions, the ones I was dreading. She failed to understand. "Why do you stay? Will your child be in danger? What will you do if there is not enough food? What will you do if something happens to Josef?"

She reminded me that America had no enemy in this war. America had not chosen one side or the other, but then she looked at me carefully and said, "But you, Hilda, you do have an enemy, and that enemy is war. I beg you. Please consider your child. Don't take the risk. Go while you can. I am afraid that soon it will be too late. Enjoy all that your family has worked so hard to achieve. You deserve something better, not this. Your child deserves better. Go home to San Francisco."

◆

When it was time to leave, I thanked Mrs. Gerard. Then I slowly walked home and watched the suffering around me – all the enthusiasm when the war had first begun and now hunger and misery, children without their fathers. I spent that night in tears. I was all alone in Berlin. There was no one to talk to, no one like Oma, who could always tell me what to do. Josef was not there to hold me. We were on our own.

There was so much to think about and only you, Mäuschen, to talk to. What do you want? What should we do? If we choose to leave, we must act quickly. The trip will be lengthy, but in the end, we will be safe. I am certain the embassy can help, but there are no guarantees, certainly not any for our condition. But staying? If we stay, there are no guarantees, either. No one can say how long the war will last or how it will end. And if America enters the war, who knows what that might mean?

All night long, I kept asking myself, "What should we do? How long should we wait? How will I know? How can we leave Josef?"

Thirty-Three

It was in mid-February of 1915 that the Berliner Zeitung Ammittag published the headline in their extra edition: "Wilson Sends Berlin Ultimatum." I read the article after Elena returned from the market and brought me a copy. Disputes between the United States and Germany were increasingly troubling. They had been brewing for days since the German admiralty had warned that the waters surrounding Britain and Ireland were considered a war zone. Germany had declared that all ships would be subject to attack by submarines, issuing a threat to America's neutral ships and Germany's intent to violate international treaties.

In response, President Wilson had made it clear. The U.S. would not give up this right. His response was not a declaration of war, but a thinly veiled warning and the first indication that America might be prepared to enter the war at any time. "If there is a sinking of an American ship by a German vessel, America will be constrained to hold the German government to strict account."

Later that same day, I received a courtesy telephone call from the embassy to advise me that there were ships in Denmark and Norway available to return Americans to the United States. Someone was watching out for me. Should I choose to leave, the embassy could help me. No one knew if America would actually declare war, but it was obvious that this news was spreading like wildfire throughout Berlin. Josef telephoned in the evening to tell me he would be at the hospital in Kreuzberg. He was concerned about my health and wanted to be sure that I understood the danger.

Thirty-Four

This morning in the post, I received a very chatty and cheerful letter from Aunt Hattie. She seems to have included all the news that is fit to print without one word about the war: Harry Houdini has performed an amazing straitjacket escape performance that no one is able to figure out; the U.S. Congress has rejected a proposal to give women the right to vote; Ernest Shackleton and his ship, the *Endurance*, are exploring the glaciers in the polar regions along the Antarctic coast; a train in Mexico derailed and plunged into a canyon, killing six hundred passengers; Alexander Graham Bell and his San Francisco-based assistant successfully completed the first coast-to-coast telephone call.

◆

At midday, I telephoned for a taxi and went to see Josef at the Am Urban Hospital. It was time to discuss our plans. On the way, we passed by the plaza in front of the

Brandenburg Gate, where there was the most bewildering sight. Workers had constructed a web of scaffolding, and the outlines of what was within were perfectly clear. It was a figure of a man almost twenty feet high. I learned that it is the likeness of General Paul von Hindenburg, the general who gave Germany its first great triumph on the Eastern Front.

Similar statues made out of Russian wood are being built throughout Germany and will be used to help raise funds for the armies. Soon patriotic Berliners will be able to purchase nails of iron, silver, or gold for one, five, or a hundred marks apiece. Then, rich or poor, they will climb up a tall ladder and hammer nails into the statue – a way to share the glory of one battle while making a contribution to the war effort so Germany can continue the fight.

◆

At the hospital, the waiting room was full of patients. Josef was very busy, and our visit was brief, less than five minutes. Mäuschen, how I hoped it could have been longer. There was so much I wanted to say, but there was only time to tell him a little more about you and to explain my decision. I can tell you one secret. Josef hopes that one day soon you will decide to call him Papa. I agree. I think that would be an exceptionally fine name.

JOSEF

Thirty-Five

It was late in the afternoon when I received the urgent telephone call in my office at the hospital. Elena, our housekeeper, was on the line. I will never forget her words. "Herr Doktor Samson, you must hurry home at once. Frau Samson must have taken a fall. I heard her call for me and ran to the bedroom to see what was wrong. I found her on the floor. Herr Doktor Samson, you must hurry home quickly. I will telephone the rescue corps for an ambulance. I don't know what else I can do."

◆

When I arrived, the rescue corps workers were there, and Elena was in the kitchen, crying. I immediately ran up the steps to the bedroom. That was when I saw the blood, and it was clear that when Hilda had fallen, we had lost our child. But then, when I kneeled on the floor to examine her more closely, I knew what else had happened. I had lost Hilda, too.

Thirty-Six

I don't think one can ever prepare for or imagine the suddenness, the emptiness, the deep sense of help-lessness, the loss and despair I felt in those moments. I wanted to scream at the top of my lungs, to shake some-one, to make someone listen and hear me. But I knew. There was nothing that could change this. I had nothing to hold on to, nothing to cling to, and I felt totally con-sumed by my grief. I was alone, devastated, and para-lyzed, wanting it to be my heart that had stopped, that I had taken my last breath, that it was my life that was lost. How could this be? Why did this happen?

Perhaps I was too clinical. I have always known that bearing a child is one of the most dangerous things a woman can do, and my profession has trained me to be a bit insulated from death and sorrow. But now I could not comprehend. I failed to understand. What I felt was beyond my reach. When I saw Hilda lying there with my unborn child, all I saw was nothingness, the terrifying darkness of nothingness, the forever of nothingness. All

I ever wanted was truly gone, and there was nothing I could do.

I have seen and witnessed loss. I was not the first to lose a wife and child, and I certainly will not be the last to be confronted with such a loss, but there is no comfort, no relief, only sympathy given in that knowledge. All I wanted was for my world to end, to suddenly stop so I could join them. I wanted to be wherever their souls might be. There is nothing left for me to say.

◆

Late that evening, as I sat alone, I reread our letters and all the many pages Hilda had written for Mäuschen. I tried and tried to relive these memories – our joy, our hopes, our expectations and dreams. But as much as I tried, I was unable to bear the pain. My instinct is to destroy everything that was written, to take a match and burn it all. Instead, I will do what Hilda would have wanted me to do. I remembered the promise we had once made to one another to keep these for our children. That was when I added the words written here.

When I am finished, I will wrap the letters and pages together in string and place them in the hidden compartment of the black lacquer cabinet that Hilda cherished. She always said that is where difficult memories should go, to a place where they can be forgotten.

◆

Today I was given the death certificate. It is clinical and emotionless, and I am left with only this final piece of paper to add to the others. The death certificate states that the cause of death was eclampsia – an eclamptic seizure, a fall, and massive bleeding – a condition that could not be diagnosed and is sudden, a death that ended the life of our child and could not have been prevented, a mystery that kills at the cruelest of moments.

All the arrangements have been taken care of, and there is little left for me to do. I cannot stare at these walls or sit here any longer. After I write to Hilda's mother in San Francisco and explain what has happened, I will pack my bags and return to the barracks. Then I will ask the commanding officer to send me off to the war.

KATIE

Thirty-Seven

I choose to believe there was one moment when our eyes met, a passing moment, the few seconds it takes for someone to walk through one door and out another. The date is certain, and the memory refuses to fade. Even though I was at a young age, I clearly remember the smallest details of all else that occurred on that day.

What remains uncertain is that one single moment. Still blurred, so brief and so sudden, even now I am unconvinced whether it was imagined or actually did occur. Once, when I asked Josef if he recalled the afternoon or could confirm or deny the instance, he gave me no answer. He seemed terribly anguished and was unable to respond. On most matters, Josef would willingly offer opinions. On matters involving Hilda, he remained silent and reflective. I've always thought he preferred to forget.

That moment took place in Berlin. It was in late winter of 1915, a little more than six months after the war began. The snow and ice were beginning to thaw, and I was not much more than five years old the morning I accompanied Mutti and my fifteen-year-old-brother, Fritz, to Am Urban, the old Kreuzberg municipal hospital that sat at the end of the street near where the two roads crossed. It was a short distance, only a few paces from our house on DieffenbachStraße, not far from the Landwehr Canal and close enough for Fritz to walk, even as fatigued and weak as he was.

Fritz had been ill for several days, unable to sleep and suffering from unrelenting coughs and terrible night sweats. We were taking him to meet with the doctor. As we were leaving the house, my other brother, Karl, gently pulled me aside and whispered the frightening words Mutti had told him that morning. Mutti feared that Fritz might have *schwindsucht*, a word I only knew because it sounded so harsh and was repeated so often. That day, as we walked through the slushy ice and snow, I was much too young. I had only a vague notion of what this word really meant.

War was extracting its toll on Berlin, sapping our energy and already lasting far longer than anyone had expected, certainly much longer than the kaiser had promised. Throughout the city, food was in short supply. There were many days when, after I stood with Mutti, waiting our turn at the markets, there would not be enough to fill our shopping basket. We would return home with less than half of what the stamps on the ration card entitled our family to receive. Soup and potatoes were quickly becoming our everyday meal.

Nearly every family on DieffenbachStraße was suffering from the terrible misery that accompanies hunger and the worry that illness would not be far behind. There had been reports of more and more cases of tuberculosis, the dreaded disease the doctors were unable to cure, the sickness that resigned those afflicted to spending their lives as outcasts. Even at my young age, I was beginning to understand. I had seen the large warning notices posted on the front doors of the houses. Others in our neighborhood were already victims.

That day when we walked with Fritz to the hospital, I did not meet the doctor. There was little time and no need for introductions. Our visit was not a social call, and the room was crowded with patients, all waiting their turn to see him. I was told to sit quietly outside the office door and mind my manners while Mutti and Fritz conferred with the doctor.

As we waited for the nurse to call Fritz for his examination, the doctor's office door opened, and a well-dressed woman close in age to Mutti stepped out. I watched her walk quickly across the small room to the door that led to the hospital corridor. As she passed, she turned her head toward me, and it seemed our eyes met for that one brief instant. Then, as she opened the exit door and disappeared into the hallway, I am almost certain I heard the nurse say, "*Auf wiedersehen*, Frau Samson."

A short while later, as Mutti and I retraced our steps back up DieffenbachStraße, she explained that Fritz needed to stay behind so he could be seen by other doctors. I remember the dark circles under Mutti's eyes and the worried look on her face as she pulled me close and said these words. When I woke the next morning, Mutti told me that Fritz had been sent north of Berlin to the Hohenlychen Sanatorium, where he could be away from the city and get fresh air and recover. Beelitz-Heilstätten, the sixty-building park-like complex to the south of the city, was no longer available for tuberculosis patients. It had been converted into a hospital for the growing number of war casualties sent home from the front.

After we left him, I never saw my brother again. Fritz never recovered from his illness. All I would be left with is this memory, one that I can never forget.

Thirty-Eight

There are few pleasant memories from my childhood. I would rather not share them. Why should anyone know of these things or hear these stories? What good would that do? I was the product of a distressful and dark time in the world and have since attempted to put what I do remember in a little box hidden in a secret place that has long been forgotten. Those years are so difficult and painful to recall that even when Josef asked, I told him I would much rather leave them that way. He asked often. He was like that, always digging and pushing, unrelenting, always wanting more from me. Of course, I know he meant well. But these memories? No. These memories should be forgotten. They are too private and sad. They are better left behind.

◆

After Fritz was sent away to the sanatorium, our home became empty and neglected. Laughter and caring were replaced with the cruel loneliness that so often accompanies disappearance and then silence. That late winter day when we left the hospital and retraced our steps, Mutti must have already been convinced that we would never see Fritz again.

I don't believe she ever recovered from the loss of her eldest. She was never the same. I remember waiting and waiting for Fritz to come home. I wanted him to reappear as if he had never left. Every night I would pray for him to return. He was always so kind to me, always laughing, always patient and considerate, always looking out for me. At five years of age, I was old enough to be told what had happened but much too young to understand what it really meant.

Losing Fritz weighed heavily on Papa. He struggled to fight his depression. When he returned from the war, dear Papa tried and tried until he became too tired. Mutti had already given up trying, and if she did try, it was rarely with me.

Somehow she and I were unable to find our balance. I have always believed that I loved her more than she could love me, that I was a weight she had no choice but to carry. I think that she was resigned to her fate, that her losses destroyed any reason to continue, that they were more than she could handle. And then one day, Papa, Karl, and I stood together and watched helplessly as Mutti slowly withered away.

When Fritz suddenly vanished from our lives, I was too young to have known that there had been another story, that it had taken place years earlier, that Fritz was not the first child my parents had lost. I did not understand that before I was born, the portrait of the Kasmund family had been complete, with Mutti, Papa, and their three children. First Fritz, then Liesbeth, then Karl, one for each year, beginning with the turn of the century. My arrival would not take place until 1910, a decade later, after they had become accustomed to their lives with one another and all the seats at the family table had been taken.

I have often wondered whether, in Mutti's eyes, I may have been more of a trespasser than an accepted substitute for the daughter she had lost. By the time I was born, my six-year-old sister, Liesbeth, was already a memory, one that was spoken of but could no longer be touched. I could never be her replacement. I tried to be strong like Papa. I tried and tried, but Mutti was rarely satisfied. It seemed that for Mutti, no matter how high I jumped, I could never jump high enough.

◆

As for my brother Karl, together we survived our childhood and the war's difficult times, but we were left with lingering scars, ones that would never heal. Our parting would come years later, after he moved to Munich. Then it became clear that our differences could not be reconciled, that neither of us approved of or even accepted the other.

Karl was a year too young to join the army and go to war. After the war, when he left home and began searching for work, the armies were returning, and the jobs were all taken. Karl joined with those who were angry and bitter and took to the streets, shouting. He needed someone to blame.

He was drawn to the voices of the German Workers' Party when it was in its earliest days, when they met in Munich at the Bürgerbräukeller. This small group of twenty-five raging and dissatisfied men blamed the Jews for profiting from the war and taking the jobs that should have been filled by those they considered true Germans, the Aryans.

That's when it was apparent that we would follow opposite paths. The reasons Karl vanished from my life might have been different from either Mutti or Fritz, but the result was the same. Then I was left with more memories to be hidden, too painful and private. Why should I remember? What good would that do?

Thirty-Nine

I n August of 1914, seven months before Mutti and I accompanied Fritz to the Am Urban Hospital, three million German men between the ages of seventeen and forty-five were suddenly called into service. This was a massive military mobilization, and Papa was among the first of those ordered to report. He had served in the German army before, when all young men who turned twenty years of age fulfilled their requirement. Then it had been peacetime, and he had not been in danger.

When Germany mobilized its troops for the Great War, Papa was a *Landwehr*, a reservist and eligible to be re-drafted. Within two weeks of receiving his notice, he was assigned to Germany's Second Army and sent to the Western Front to join General Karl von Bulow's troops in the Battle of the Marne. It would be more than four years before the defeated German army would withdraw from France and the worn and weary troops would come home. That day, when Papa left our home and was sent off to war, he had no way of knowing that by the time he returned, Fritz would have vanished from our lives.

During the war, there was no fighting or destruction in Berlin and very little in Germany, only in East Prussia during the earliest months. Germany's battles were carried out elsewhere, in France and Belgium in the west and Russia and Eastern European countries in the east. In Berlin, we felt safe from any invasion and cheered the army's successes. Our worry was for our fathers, brothers, sons, and husbands. They were sent away to join in the fight.

In Berlin, our biggest danger was hunger, our biggest enemy was the naval blockade, and our biggest fear was that the war would continue until we starved to death. Great Britain's Royal Navy blocked the entrances to the English Channel and North Sea, and France and Italy maintained their tight grip on access to the Adriatic.

Slowly Central Europe would weaken and lose enthusiasm for the war, and without fertilizer, Germany was unable to grow enough food to meet the requirements of its armies and feed the stomachs of its people. The authorities responded by raising prices at the markets, hoping this would reduce the public's demand. When that failed to solve the problem, the government chose to control distribution and ration what was left. If one had sufficient money, there was always the black market, where everything could be found for a price. But for the rest of us, there was no choice but to scrounge. We became known as hamsters, always scrounging for food.

Some families took trains to nearby rural villages where they could barter directly with farmers. The authorities turned a blind eye, allowing the railroads to add extra cars to their trains to handle the demand. Others stayed in Berlin and spent their nights waiting at the markets, hoping to be first in line. There they would sit on stools, knitting or sleeping on straw mattresses. In some neighborhoods, children would skip classes and join gangs, searching for anything that could be exchanged for food.

To help support Karl and me, Mutti found work, and I was sent to stay with a neighbor. Extra rations were given to the women who worked in the munitions plants. And before the war was over, Karl quit school and searched for the occasional odd job to give Mutti some relief. As for me, my elementary school made its contribution, too. I joined my classmates as we marched through the streets of Berlin, carrying our flags, waving our posters, and encouraging Berliners to buy war bonds.

I know that everyone who lived in Berlin at the time has their own memories of that war. Mine are through the eyes of a child. What I remember was that at first, when the war began, everyone came out to show support for the troops. How exciting that was. As they passed, the streets would fill and line with people. All the church bells would ring. We held banners and waved flags. We shouted and cheered. I remember the parades, marches, rallies, and long speeches. Black, white, and red German flags were hung in front of shops and buildings.

At school one day, we were told about the glorious victory at the Battle of Langemarck, when German forces captured the Flemish town from its Belgian and British defenders. We were so proud of our soldiers. We stood at attention each morning and sang the words to "Deutschland über alles."

We were all taught to support the kaiser, that our national pride was at stake and there was no sacrifice too great to be made for the Fatherland. We listened carefully to our teachers and believed what they told us. We were taught that we were the greatest people to walk on this earth, that this was a war of necessity, and that we were fighting for our due. But this support would not last.

As time wore on, people grew tired and weary and lost their enthusiasm for the war. By that first Christmas, Berlin had become a city of dark shadows. On the streets, we saw more and more women dressed in black. Karl said that so many men had been killed that the government stopped displaying the lists of fallen soldiers for public viewing in front of the city palace. He claimed we were being misled, that the government was not telling the truth, giving the illusion of victory, censoring the newspapers, not wanting people to know the enormous toll the war was taking.

Then, when Mutti and I stood in line at the market, one could hear the women complain that the rules were different for the privileged, that the wealthy were eating at restaurants, going to the theater, cinema, and music halls, and acting like they had few worries. For the rest of us, there was no flour on weekends, no meat on Tuesdays and Fridays, and no fats on Mondays and Thursdays.

I remember the butter riots, when the women filled the streets and marched and Mutti let me carry the sign protesting the high cost of food and the Hindenburg program, when everything was needed for the war and the government collected church bells from steeples, copper roofs from buildings, and even the chandeliers and pots and pans from people's homes.

The worst was the winter between 1916 and 1917, when throngs of hungry shivered on the cold, snow-filled streets and coal to heat the houses was nowhere to be found. They called that the turnip winter because the potato harvest was so bad. Instead of potatoes, all we had to eat were turnips: turnip bread, turnip jam, turnip soup, turnip cakes, even coffee from dried turnips. I will never forget the foul taste.

In the spring of 1918, we were told that the great German victory was finally in sight. Once again flags reappeared on all the buildings. Newspaper headlines claimed that the great offensive had begun and Paris would soon fall. But in August, the French and British armies launched their Hundred Days Offensive – a counterattack that pushed the German armies back. Soon there were over a million American troops in France, and following a series of crushing defeats on the Western Front, Germany's war efforts collapsed. That was when our armies began to retreat and withdraw and Kaiser Wilhelm II was forced to abdicate, bringing an end to the Hohenzollern dynasty's three-hundred-year rule. Germany's back had been broken. We no longer had the will or the resources to win the war.

That December Papa was among the defeated and broken armies of men who marched up Unter den Linden to the Brandenburg Gate. That day we stood on the streets and watched as the armies disintegrated and the men returned to their homes. We knew we were fortunate. Although tired and worn, Papa had survived. Many of my schoolmates had fathers and brothers who never returned. Others lived with terrible injuries.

Germany had endured a devastating loss. Half of the men sent to war were casualties. Nearly two million of our soldiers had been killed, and over four million more were wounded. And throughout the world, a generation of young men had been sacrificed.

◆

Weakened by the war, many of the men returning from the front suffered from illnesses. Papa was one of them. Mutti nursed him, and with rest, he recovered. But then one day Mutti complained that she must have caught the three-day flu from Papa. She had no appetite and a dry, hacking cough. I remember Papa tried to feed her beef broth and had her chew on cinnamon. He thought that this was supposed to be the cure. The next day she couldn't stop shivering and sweating and refused to leave the bed. By the third day, she looked gray and pale and could hardly breathe. That evening we watched as she gave up trying and took her last breath.

Mutti was one of more than two thousand Berliners who died that week from the outbreak of the Spanish flu, the epidemic that spread rapidly and killed indiscriminately. It had been carried from the cramped, dirty, and damp conditions of the German trenches, when two million malnourished and exhausted men returned from the battlefields and were dispersed into the streets. She was buried in an unmarked grave with many others. Young and old, their names were forever lost.

It was not long after Mutti died when Karl decided that our house had become too small. It carried too many bad memories. He was seventeen, and it was his time to move on. By then, I was nine years old and in my fourth year of school. The war had consumed nearly one-half of my life and most of what I could remember. Millions had lost more, but I had endured the pain of being without a father and losing my mother and a brother.

I had no idea that in a few short years, the Nazis would claim the allegiance of my only other sibling. And without any recollection of what it was like to live before the war began, I had little reason to believe that my life would be any different now that the war was over. All I had left to cling to was Papa, and all he had left was me.

Forty

I was told that in 1910, on the day I was born, Papa brought home a Hofuhrmacher mantel clock, which he placed next to my cradle. Then he silenced the chime so the steady cadence of the ticking clock and swing of its pendulum would become my comforting companions. The clock would help me sleep through the night. From that day forward, the mahogany, rounded-arch clock was one of my favorite possessions and never kept far from my sight. Throughout my life, I have found it to be a steady hand in a sea of uncertainty, always a source of comfort kept close by my side.

Four years later, on the evening before Papa left to go to war, he came to my bed, held me close, and whispered that he had something serious to discuss, that I was old enough for an important responsibility. While he was away, I was to promise to open the back, take the brass key, and ever so carefully wind the clock every eight days so it would never stop ticking. Then he adjusted the chime so it would be just loud enough that I would be the only one in the house to hear its sound. This was to be our special secret, a solemn promise we made to one another. Papa told me that the chime would be his way of knowing I would never forget him, that I should never lose faith, and that he would return someday. When I listened to the chime, I should always remember that every evening he would be listening and thinking of me, too.

When the war was over, after Mutti died, Karl left home, and Papa and I were alone, he came to my room one evening and offered to silence the chime again as he had on the day of my birth. Now that he was home, I would no longer need the chime as his reminder, but he thought that I still might need the steady cadence of the ticking and swing of the pendulum. I might have been older, but Papa understood that I needed to mend and heal, that the war had left me unsettled, that my person was less than complete. He knew that the clock would help me sleep through the night once again.

Papa was always like that: sweet, caring, considerate, and patient. He was willing to listen, and most of all, he was understanding and unselfish. When he came home from the war, he was everything I wanted and exactly what I needed. He never failed me, not once that I can remember. And years later, when he came by train to visit and whisper his final goodbye, he refused to leave until he was convinced that I would be cared for. He wanted to be certain that I would be secure and protected. That's how Papa was. I can't say that we always agreed with one another, but I can say that he always understood. He always kept his arms tightly wrapped around me.

Not having known my grandparents, I have often wondered if they were the ones who made him this way. I know little of Papa's family. I suppose this is because mothers are usually the ones to tell their children about these matters. Whatever her reasons, Mutti chose not to share this information, and when Papa returned from the war, he was more interested in how I would live my life than in reciting the stories of his past.

I have always thought that the war, losing Mutti and Fritz, and seeing how angry Karl became made Papa want to erase his memories. I don't know how, but he was a man who managed to remember the good and forget the bad, a habit that is not easy but one I would always try to follow. All I learned about Papa's history was that he had grown up in Berlin and his two younger brothers didn't survive the war. In any event, I choose to believe that my grandparents must have been wonderful parents because they raised a good, caring son.

I have no recollection of Mutti's parents, either, and have always had the impression that they died before I was born. After Mutti's death, there was no one left who could tell me. I do know that her family was close-knit and that she came from a farm village not far from Berlin. During the war, we often took the train to visit her sisters, and I remember spending time with my cousins, at least those who were closest in age. But when the war was over, I was still too young to know the name of the village, and after Mutti died, these connections were lost. I know that there were cousins somewhere in Germany, but Papa had little interest in them, and I never saw them again.

What I remember most about those years that followed were our long walks. Papa would often say, "There is nothing better than being lost in a long walk." At first, I was concerned that we might actually get lost, but before long, I understood that he was talking about clearing the cobwebs out of one's head.

Taking long walks became a cherished habit, one that I have enjoyed wherever I have lived. No matter the weather, every Sunday, Papa and I would go for a long walk, the longer the better. Papa worked six days a week as a tramway motorman, but Sundays were reserved for us, just Papa and me. We would spend the entire day together, and soon I felt like I knew every square inch and every street in Berlin and could never get lost.

Each Sunday we would pick a new destination, a new place to explore. Berlin had so many to choose from, each to be appreciated in its own special way: Potsdamer Platz, Alexandra Platz, the Tiergarten, FriedrichStraße, the River Spree, the aquarium, the zoo, the botanical gardens, the Old and New Museums, the Charlottenburg Palace, the National Gallery, the Emperor Frederick Museum, Exhibition Park, and the Palace of Emperor William I. And on those Sundays when there wasn't something new to add, we were happy to sit quietly in a park and watch people. Papa always enjoyed watching people.

Sundays were about far more than the destination. These excursions were our discoveries. Together we learned and watched as Berlin recovered from the losses of the war. After years of difficult stumbles and falls, we marveled as it regained its footing, filling the air with hope and promise.

As we walked arm in arm, Papa taught me that it is not always where you go that matters; often it is how you arrive. There were days we would walk in silence, days we would engage in conversation, days we would take the most direct path, and days our steps were misguided and slow. The best part, and the one I remember most, was that we always took these steps together.

Forty-One

Those first few years after the war was over were not easy for Berliners, nor the rest of Germany. We were a country that had lost its patience and a great deal of its pride. Germans were exhausted and disillusioned, and nowhere were the voices expressed more vigorously than on the streets of Berlin. Despite the government's enthusiastic claims and pronouncements, the armies had failed in their mission, and the German people had said enough is enough.

The war's aftermath was not about rebuilding. Germany had little need to do so because the battles had taken place elsewhere. Instead, it was about death and despair because Germany had suffered so much and lost so many young men. And since the war had not ended with victory, fingers were pointed, and Germans were angry. Many felt betrayed. They were searching for answers, wanting to place blame.

Eventually Germany would recover. Then the streets would fill with a frenzy of activity and excitement, and

Berlin would once again enchant the world with its passions: art, music, literature, and science. But in those first few months, when the Spartakists and the Social Democrats bloodied Berlin's streets with their snipers and fighting, it seemed that the war had not stopped, that too many had been left behind, that it would never end.

Germany's problems took years to resolve and were fraught with miscalculation. After the troops came home, Germany struggled with jobs, inflation, hopelessness, and the inability of those who led to convince enough of their faithful to follow. There were no simple solutions, at least none that succeeded. Even those who celebrated when the war had ended soon found their misplaced exuberance quickly erased.

The war left Germany with a steep price to pay, a burden that made us beg and dragged us down to our knees. The blockades and hunger continued until the victors were satisfied, and the negotiations moved slowly because their demands were relentless.

Many thought this unfair. The kaiser and his supporters had been the ones who had chosen to lead Germany to war, but throughout the war and later, in its peace, it was not the wealthy or the monarchists who were called upon to make the great sacrifices.

It was the people caught in the middle: the workers in the factories, the tramway motormen, the men who mined the ore, the teachers in the classrooms, and the farmers who toiled the land. First, we fielded the armies, and our men gave their lives. Then we shouldered the burden of the war's cost and were left to pay its enormous bills.

I know few details about the Treaty of Versailles. I can only tell you that the streets of Berlin remained in turmoil for months and years to follow. The toll it extracted left voids. Seeds were planted that would one day grow into reasons for another war, one which would tragically claim the lives of many millions more. Marches and demonstrations continued, and the shouting did not stop.

Papa showed absolutely no interest and wanted no part. He ventured little opinion, only that he was glad to be home. When the unions demanded that the workers protest, Papa would remark, "Why should I spend my time worrying about these things when there are so many better things to do?"

On these matters, he and Josef were worlds apart. When it came to voicing opinions, Papa stayed quiet and preferred to go about his business. He kept his opinions to himself and his views private. Josef could not have been more different. He always remained impassioned, ready to right what was wrong. While quiet when I asked about Hilda, he became vocal and animated when expressing his thoughts on most other topics.

◆

Papa often worried that I was forced to grow up too quickly, but I knew that I wasn't alone. I was a product of these times. So many of us in Berlin shared that same

198 | RALPH WEBSTER

story. We had survived the same years. The truth was that there was little one could do. The war had changed the lives of most families. All we could do was shrug and do what needed to be done.

After Mutti died, I was left with many of her chores and responsibilities. Daily visits to the market, cooking, laundering, and cleaning became my tasks. With only the two of us, I never thought these responsibilities too difficult a burden, but they did rob me of the remainder of my childhood and much of my adolescence. While Papa worked and supported us, it became my job to take care of the household.

Others may say the age of nine is too young to assume the role of *hausfrau*, but there was no choice. We had not come from privilege, and there was no one else to care for us. There was no money to pay for a maid or a cook, no one to launder our clothes or mop our floors. We were left on our own.

When the government printed massive amounts of money to pay off the war debts, the little money Papa had saved was eaten away by the ravages of hyperinflation. Everyone struggled in these absurd conditions, when waiters needed to stand on tables and shout menu prices because they increased as each hour passed.

My other responsibility was to go to school. Papa was insistent that I receive a good education, and I took my schooling seriously. The new government in Berlin had lofty requirements for children. Attendance was mandatory until one reached eighteen years of age. Because of my home situation, I might not have had the time that others did to pursue friendships and participate in activities outside the classroom, but I was a fair student and proud to receive my diploma.

◆

In 1928, I celebrated my eighteenth birthday. Then I found myself tempted and pulled by the lure and glamour of Berlin. Our cosmopolitan city was alive with excitement. This was the golden era, and somehow I had suddenly grown up. I was mature, capable, and complete. I am not sure that I would characterize myself as brimming with self-confidence, because the world's events had made me too realistic and, due to our financial limitations, I had never enjoyed the opportunities given to some. Yet I felt perfectly able to care for myself, and I possessed the skills of an accomplished homemaker.

Papa had taught me well. I had learned to listen and observe, was able to distinguish good from bad, and certainly had developed a strong sense of like and dislike. I think living in a big city like Berlin during the war years did much to shape me. My life had not been innocent or simple, and I was certainly grounded enough to take little for granted. While I might have missed many important parts of my childhood, what I had gained was the maturity that one expects to accompany adulthood.

Growing up, like countless others, I had been shielded from little and exposed to too much. And by spending Sundays exploring Berlin with Papa, I had witnessed the rawness and richness of its streets and viewed nearly everything else that occurs in its hidden alleys and darkened corners. Big cities have a unique way of doing that. They cause one to develop a certain wariness and toughness, perhaps even a chip on one's shoulder.

That's the way I think of Berlin and my childhood: full of experiences, little that was hidden, unafraid, prideful, a sense of big-city sophistication. I suppose I had grown up to become a bit hardened and resistant to emotion. My tears refused to come easily. As for those early memories, I have no wish to relive them, nor do I wish them on anyone else. They are to be forgotten. I would never want them repeated.

At eighteen, I had blossomed into a grown woman. I had few doubts. I knew I was a Berliner, that I belonged to the city and was ready to tackle its streets. Yet there was one question that loomed, a question I was unable to answer. I wasn't alone. For women, it was an especially confusing time. I had no idea what might be next.

Forty-Two

Papa and I both knew it was time. Nearly a decade had passed since the war had ended, and now Berlin beckoned. The post-war rules had changed many things for my generation. Before the war, German boys would leave home when they were required to join the army. German girls would leave when a match was made, a dowry agreed upon, and it was time to marry.

The end of the war altered this way of thinking. For young men, the draft was abolished, as it was a requirement imposed upon Germany by the Treaty of Versailles. As for young women, many traditions had been broken. Inflation meant that most families no longer had funds for dowries. The war had opened the doorway to the workplace for women. The Weimar Constitution called for equality, and nowhere in Germany was this truer than in Berlin.

But knowing it is time and doing something about it are two different things. Leaving home was one of the most difficult and emotional decisions I ever made. I was cautious by nature and had been raised to be careful by habit. And in many respects, my responsibilities at home had kept me quite sheltered. Were I to leave my life with Papa, my skills were limited. There were few things I was trained to do. Whatever I chose would have to be made to fit me.

I was very attached to Papa and would have stayed had he made it easier, but he chose not to. He gave me a push and taught me that oftentimes pushing is what parents must do. Years had passed since he had come home from the war, Mutti had died, and Karl had chosen his path, even longer since Fritz had disappeared from our lives. Throughout, Papa and my relationship remained simple and comfortable. There was no interruption. He watched over me, and I took care of him. We would rarely argue or disagree; neither were in our makeup. We were polite and respectful and accustomed to living together in this quiet, predictable way.

On the matter of my leaving home, our opinions were oddly contradictory. Papa would often remark that for his own selfish reasons, I should stay, but because he loved me and wanted what was best, I should leave and experience my own life. I would respond that for my own selfish reasons, I knew I should leave, but because I loved him and wanted to care for him, I would stay. Then we would laugh and agree that most generations are faced with this difficulty. What I do know for certain is that had it not been for Papa's encouragement, very little in my life would have changed.

One evening, Papa arrived home, excited about an opportunity. He had learned of an elderly woman who was in need of a full-time companion, not so much a housekeeper as someone to share her apartment and be of general assistance. There would be light cleaning and some cooking, but this was a woman of means. Her husband had died recently and left her sufficient funds. She could afford to hire help for any serious work that might be necessary. What she required was someone to keep her company, to accompany her on walks, to sit with her in the park, to join her for meals, to go with her to the theater, and to make sure she was safe and secure.

I called and made an appointment. When we met and discussed the responsibilities and she learned of my background, I was hired on the spot. We agreed that I would stay with her full time six days a week and be paid a modest sum. She would pay for any additional expenses, such as when I accompanied her to the theater or a restaurant. And since her son always stayed with her on Sundays, that could be my day off. The position was ideal. I could continue to spend my Sundays with Papa.

Forty-Three

Coincidences, by their very nature, are infrequent, and I am not sure that this incident would qualify. Only when I look in the mirror and reflect am I able to acknowledge that the possibility exists, and even then, the event seems rather ordinary. Clearly, at the time it occurred, there was no reason to give our introduction any further consideration. The memories of that long-ago day were much more heartbreaking and significant for entirely different reasons. Why would I recollect the never-since-mentioned name of a doctor whom I had never met?

Thirteen years had passed – enough time for Germany to wage war, a country to recover, and me to grow up. I was five years of age that late winter day Mutti and I had taken Fritz to see the doctor at the Am Urban Hospital. That day, no one had spoken his name, and I had not seen his face, so when Herr Doktor Samson came to the apartment late on that first Wednesday afternoon to visit his mother and I was introduced as the young girl who had been hired to be Frau Samson's companion, I had no reason to give him another moment's thought.

The day we first met, apart from my employment by his mother, Josef and I had no connection and certainly found nothing that could be even remotely construed as being in common. In social class, culture, education, and age, we could not have been more different. We were exact opposites. He was a physician, and I had no occupation other than the position of sitting with his parent. At first glance, he appeared to be as old as my father and, in the old German way, quite stiff and perhaps a bit stuffy.

To be perfectly honest, I found both him and the moment rather unremarkable and mostly quite forgettable, and I am certain he felt the same. As I recall, after the briefest of introductions, I took my leave and quietly returned to my room. There had been no hint of an invitation to join them in conversation.

As unremarkable as I found Herr Doktor Samson, I found his mother, Frau Samson, quite the opposite. I had never met anyone like her, certainly not anyone living near my childhood home on DieffenbachStraße. Nearly eighty years old, she was cheerful, urbane, and witty, a woman with opinions about everything and expectations about anything. She was curious, asked many questions, and had a delightful sense of humor. I suppose one could describe her as spry as she had much spring in her step. She had an abundance of energy and enthusiasm. I did take note of her impatience with listening and disdain for interruptions, both known to be frequent habits of those inclined to hearing the sound of their own voice.

To my surprise, I was informed at the outset that she had no desire for our relationship to be strictly one of "matron and maid." Despite the differences in our respective roles and ages, we could bend the rules of formality a little. She expected me to be her companion, not her housekeeper, and pledged to treat me as such. She had spent her entire life as a *hausfrau* and took great pride in being capable of preparing dinner or doing the laundry or any other chore.

Until her husband died, she had been very devoted. He had been the center of her universe. Now she had turned her attention and remained extremely close to her only child, an adult son who was very occupied with his medical profession and passionate about his other interests. There was no other family in Berlin, and she had never taken the time nor had the desire to develop close personal friendships. She was alone. Her apartment was too quiet and empty. She needed to hear footsteps and missed having someone to spend her days with.

I must tell you that soon I found spending my days and nights with Frau Samson terribly exhausting. Her energy left me dizzy. I was accustomed to my quiet life with Papa. He and I could spend hours within the same four walls in silence. If there was no reason to speak, we wouldn't. Neither of us was entertained by or felt the need for continuous conversation. The contrast could not have been greater. For Frau Samson, silence was very unappealing, a large blank canvas begging to be painted. I quickly learned that her conversations demanded my full attention, particularly as she expected informed answers to her many and frequent questions. Her need for a companion was obvious. Finding someone like me had been her son's suggestion, and it wasn't long before I understood his reasoning. As Frau Samson remarked, I was the "relief" to Herr Doktor Samson's "burden."

Please do not misunderstand. I must be more kind in my comments. Despite having to adjust to the habits of my new employer, within the first few weeks, I began to find Frau Samson, while quite certain of her opinions, very kind and generous. She filled a void for me, too, one that I had not realized had been empty for quite a long time.

From Frau Samson, I was encouraged to learn about a different way of life, things that may have been missed or skipped in my adolescent education, like how a table should be set, how fresh flowers should be arranged, how to send a thank-you note, or how a proper young lady should dress. That's when our relationship began to grow into a teacher-student friendship. Frau Samson became a mentor, and I valued her advice. While I could not wait to spend my quiet Sundays with Papa, by Monday, I looked forward to my return to Frau Samson. It became clear that my new life was destined to be quite different from my last.

◆

Most routines find their rhythm, and it was not long before she and I settled into a familiar pattern. When the
weather was fine, we would walk for a bit in the Tiergarten and then find a bench near a pond where a flock of
ducks or geese might be viewed. Other times we would
sit and watch the wanderings of people as they happened
by. These were moments when Frau Samson would engage in a continuing commentary as she had many opinions to offer, many that were critical, particularly when
she did not believe people were properly dressed for the
occasion.

From time to time, we would go out for dinner or our
midday meal, but generally she preferred to stay in. Frau
Samson was also a fan of the cinema. Berlin had many
movie theaters, and Thursday afternoons were reserved
for that form of entertainment. She also loved the theater, opera, ballet, and the symphonies at the concert
halls, so I found myself treated to a world I had never
experienced. The little I had seen had been from the outside, always looking in.

As for her habits, they were simple, repeated daily,
somewhat rigid, and extremely punctual. Her clock was
set by the sun. She rose by daylight and ate a light breakfast: coffee, toast, and a soft-boiled egg, cooked for precisely two and one-half minutes. She devoted most of
her morning hours to the newspapers, which were read,
again with much opinion and always very thoroughly.
Then we would make a brief visit to the markets, typically the vegetable, then the butcher, occasionally the

fishmonger, usually the baker, and always on Fridays to shop for fresh flowers.

Lunch would consist of three very thin slices: dark bread, cheese, and sausage. Mid-afternoon she had a cup of coffee accompanied by a small piece of dark chocolate or slice of torte. She had a preference for Sacher: chocolate covered with apricot jam and chocolate icing. She had a small glass of wine with dinner, always red and decanted, and tended to be asleep in bed well before nightfall.

Herr Doktor Samson came to visit at a quarter past four each Wednesday afternoon, spent much of the day with her on Sundays, and telephoned her at precisely the same time each morning, when she would answer on the first ring. Since I would be sitting nearby, I often thought that there was little need for the telephone to ring at all. Frau Samson appeared to know the exact moment to lift the receiver and would carry on their conversation as if the previous day's had never been completed.

As for our conversations, they were wide-ranging as her interests were many. I was challenged to prepare and never knew what she might ask. She was entertained by the newspapers, so I developed the habit of devouring them from front to back each morning. Through conversation, I adopted many of her interests, particularly two of her favorites: fashion, which she observed very carefully with a great deal of criticism and often unflattering comment, and literature. I was expected to read whatever book she was currently reading and be prepared to discuss it whenever this struck her fancy.

As far as I can recall, there was only one topic that was considered off limits. This was anything to do with the life or activities of her son, a topic that was never spoken of and never shared. Herr Doktor Samson's affairs were always kept private. On these matters, she was possessive and protective. It quickly became very clear that Frau Samson considered the life of her son a privilege she reserved only for herself.

As for her opinions and questions about everything else, they were overwhelming and often exhausting. I found myself totally drawn to this world I had never known and hardly imagined had ever existed.

Forty-Four

It's odd how suddenly things can change, often in only the briefest instant. I suppose what made this particular incident so remarkable is how it altered the course of events that were to follow. Late one Wednesday afternoon, several weeks after I began my duties, Frau Samson came to my door and invited me to join her and Herr Doktor Samson in the sitting room, the first time such a gesture was proffered.

There was a question that had been troubling him since the first time we had met, and with my permission, he wished to inquire. After learning my name, he later recalled that he had once treated a young man with the surname of Kasmund when he had worked at the Am Urban Hospital in Kreuzberg. His recollection was that this took place not long after the war began and that the otherwise quite healthy teenaged boy was quite ill.

As he recounted this, Herr Doktor Samson became quite apologetic. He had no intention to intrude upon my personal life but was concerned about my feelings.

He realized that I must have been a very young child at the time, and his patient had had such a sad outcome. Was there any possibility that I was related?

It was that connection, that one simple question, his inquiry about my brother Fritz and my welfare, and the gentle and polite way it was asked, that made me reconsider this much older man. That afternoon, Josef and I found we shared someone in common. I had no idea that a physician of his stature could be so interested and willing to divulge his own emotions in such a simple and forthright way. That was when I concluded that my first impression might have been mistaken.

Josef was not as stiff and stuffy as I had initially thought. I had been confused by the nature of his work and the habits of his training. Instead, I discovered that he was kind, thoughtful, and very devoted to the care and well-being of his patients and their families. Most of all, I learned that he was a serious man who was willing to give me his undivided attention. He instinctively knew how to look deep into my eyes and patiently listen. I must confess that I was immediately confused. Except for Papa, these were things I had never known any man to do before.

◆

Having never experienced the twists and turns that begin intimate relationships and cause them to grow, I now find myself somewhat self-conscious and at a complete loss for words as I attempt to explain the events that followed, only that they happened slowly and were surprising and that each lingering moment was satisfying and delightful. I found myself overwhelmed and entertained. Nothing was rushed. Everything was gentle. There was no hurry.

From the little I know, I can only imagine that my experience was quite unlike anything that might be described as the chaotic fumbling of a youthful romance. What I do know is that at some point, I no longer noticed that Josef was as old as my father, and he chose to forget that I was young enough to be his daughter. Both of us were entertained by the notion that somewhere near the middle, we fit perfectly together.

◆

Of course, a relationship such as this can never be simple. It was filled with many deeply hidden passageways, and there were quite a few bridges that needed to be crossed. Sometimes there was waiting and hoping, and at other times, disappointment and annoyances, often frustratingly so. We found little time to be together, and out of necessity, we needed to remain silent and secretive, certainly far removed from the curious and watchful eyes of Frau Samson.

We both understood that Josef's mother might become quite disturbed were she to learn that we were both recipients of Herr Doktor Samson's private affections and attentions, no matter how different. Nevertheless, we managed to find our moments, and it helped that

Frau Samson chose to follow the moon and the sun when it came to her daily habits.

I suppose Berlin was a big help, too. These were the golden years in Berlin, when we believed that nearly all things were possible and what remained was permissible. After months of agonizing, I chose to confide my secret with one other person, and that was Papa. And just as he was with everything else, he stood by my side and gave me his unbridled support. That's when, with a few adjustments to everyone's Sunday schedules, adjustments that remained undetected, Josef was able to join Papa and me at sunrise for early morning walks. Then, before he left to spend the remainder of the day with his mother, I would take my steps between the two and had both arms to cling to.

Forty-Five

We continued in this manner for many, many months. For me, "languishing" would be the word that best describes this golden era, the end of the 1920s. We languished comfortably, with seemingly few cares in the world. And it wasn't just us. It was Josephine Baker, the Bauhaus artists, the Threepenny Opera performers, and the short-skirted girls walking the streets with their umbrellas. I suppose "languishing" describes all of Berlin: a collective of cafes, coffee houses, clubs, and theatres, where we were all free to be entertained by these prosperous times.

I think I was clear-eyed, but I am not entirely certain because I believe, for most, it is the nature of a love affair to be afflicted with widely conflicting emotions. Even today I sometimes imagine Mutti's voice in my head. Had she been there to stop us, I am certain she would have done so. She would have been troubled by the more than thirty-year difference in age and would have advised me to reconsider. "You have your life to look forward to, and he is an old man." She would have wondered about the prospect of marriage and children. Perhaps she would have been concerned that Josef was of a different faith. Having no way to know for certain, I cannot say. Unlike Papa, who only wanted what made me happy, Mutti had her own set of expectations and might have arrived at entirely different conclusions.

I suppose, in some ways, the wonders and mysteriousness of secretive liaisons are like sampling a fine chocolate with the slightest touch of a sweet liqueur inside. Why should one stop when there are few reasons to do so? Two years quickly passed. Rather than feeling unsettled, I found our involvement calm and reassuring. I was content, and Josef was worldly.

Of course, one can be mistaken, and many are misled, but my expectations were simple. I enjoyed it just as it was. I was young and hoped we could go on like this forever, that there would never be a reason to change. But like so many things beyond one's control, there came a time when we learned that this was not to be. Things began to change when the world began to unravel. Then Josef and I watched in fear as events began to collide and the unthinkable result became the unstoppable outcome.

The tidal wave created by America's Great Depression rolled mercilessly across the Atlantic, crashing against Europe's shores and wreaking havoc with everything in its path. That's when Germany's prosperity came to a sudden stop. Right before our eyes, the good and fun-loving times of Berlin's roaring twenties were no longer.

When the bubble burst and America's markets crashed, Germany's lenders recalled the huge loans used to stabilize the economy and finance the debts imposed by France and Great Britain after the Great War. Once again, Germany was plunged into economic chaos. Unemployment soared. Paychecks shrank. Banks ran out of money. Millions lost their jobs, and businesses were shuttered. Angry mobs took to the streets, demanding action. In Berlin alone, a city of four million, the streets were filled with 750,000 unemployed workers.

Most of Germany's restless wanted to be freed from the obligations imposed by the Treaty of Versailles. Many felt that we had been wrongly mistreated and humiliated, and they wanted to avenge what had been lost in the Great War. They wanted Germany to be given its rightful place in the world, to return to the way things had once been destined to be.

Germans began by searching for a strong leader, someone to offer a clear vision and a voice for the working man. And when a new leader was chosen, it didn't seem to matter what path he chose to follow or whom he chose to blame. Germany became a nation of obedient disciples, or as Josef called them, "a flock of sheep." Hunger, anger, and desperation created the perfect storm. Adding a strong dose of nationalism to patriotism was like pouring gasoline onto a smoldering fire. Anyone could have foreseen the result before it even occurred, but few chose to. That's when the flames began to burn.

And when there was no one strong enough to extinguish the flames, the fires began their deathly march. Then they began to rage.

◆

During these same months, the latter half of 1932, Frau Samson's health began to decline. It wasn't one single affliction, more the frailties of old age, the loss of first one function and then another. We both stood and watched helplessly. Other than providing our own manner of comfort and support, there was little else that either of us could do. I continued to be her companion and sat attentively by her side. Josef continued his Wednesday and Sunday visits and telephoned her every morning. She was always the proud mother, and he remained her dutiful and attentive grown son.

Frau Samson died peacefully one afternoon in the natural order: never expected but not unanticipated, not unimagined, sudden and sad, but not surprising. I don't believe that she ever had any inkling of Josef and my relationship, and if she had, she never said. As opinionated and protective as she was, I am quite certain we both would have known and been given some very strong advice. I really have no idea what she would have thought, but I like to believe that instead of sending me on my way, after some quiet moments of reflection, she might have understood our attraction and, perhaps, been a little entertained by the notion of me, the fair young maiden, and her son, the worldly king.

On one matter, I have no question. She would have never invited me to share their private times together. No intruders were allowed, and that would have been a point of unimagined resentment. She was ferociously jealous and controlling of that personal space. Nevertheless, despite Josef and my differences and the necessity of having to share her one son, she might have considered us to be a reasonable match. Frau Samson died knowing that Josef was a very good and devoted son, and she did want him to be happy.

As for me? Somehow I think she found me a respectable companion, and that, in some odd way, I was now prepared to look after Josef in much the same manner I had looked after her.

◆

The day after Frau Samson died, Josef suggested that I continue to live in her apartment. He thought it best that her home remained occupied, particularly since there was little opportunity to sell it for a fair price in Berlin's troubled economic times. Having never considered whether there could possibly be any other reason, I found his invitation to be a perfectly splendid idea, one that I embraced with enthusiasm. Why not? I would no longer need to share. Now I would have Josef all to myself.

Forty-Six

I think most would agree. As terrifying and improbable as it was, Adolph Hitler's rise to power was astounding and a frightening indication of his genius. The world should have paid closer attention. I can only repeat what I wrote down when Josef told me. He was studious when it came to these sorts of things. From a mere 17,000 members in 1926, the Nazi Party grew to 120,000 by the summer of 1929 and then to 210,000 by the following March.

By that fall, the party claimed one million members among its ranks. And as the elections demonstrated, millions began to believe in a man imprisoned seven years earlier when he had attempted to seize power in a failed coup in Munich, a man who had failed at nearly everything else he had ever pursued, a man who somehow convinced his fellow countrymen, largely by the tactics of his followers and the power of his oratory, that he alone possessed the skill and intelligence to solve the nation's problems.

Germany's economic uncertainties provided Hitler and the Nazis the ideal political climate for the 1930 election. Every week thousands more men lost their jobs and their incomes. They lost their ability to support their families. Their Fatherland had failed them. We watched men stand in line, waiting for their unemployment payments and at the breadlines and soup kitchens. They wandered through the streets of Berlin. They donned brown shirts, wore black boots, and organized themselves as stormtroopers, the paramilitary wing of the Nazi Party.

That fall, the Nazis, who had held only a dozen seats in the Reichstag, received six and a half million votes and won 107 seats. Suddenly they had become the second-largest political party in Germany, and Hitler gained an army of new supporters. His followers were not only the unemployed. They were the industrialists who feared the wrath of the communists, the women who supported the conservative right, and, most importantly, the younger generation, who wanted things to change.

The Nazi Party became the party of youth and revolt. Many of the children of the war, like my brother Karl, who had seen his opportunities denied in the war's aftermath, were now disillusioned once again, out of work, and raging with anger. The Nazis were their answer. They would not back down. They were defiant. They raised their fists to the world. They would restore order. Adolf Hitler convinced his followers that Germany would rise again and he would solve Germany's problems – once and for all.

When the Reichstag convened their session, the Nazis immediately demonstrated how they planned to use their victory. Although demonstrations were forbidden in the neutral area surrounding the Reichstag building, thousands of party members gathered, shouting their slogans. Their delegates to the Reichstag were determined to be disruptive. To show their solidarity, they wore the brown uniforms that they had smuggled inside. That day, after the police dispersed the crowd, the Nazi leaders led an angry crowd of protesters to Leipziger Straße, where they smashed store windows and attacked those they could blame.

◆

Two years later, in July of 1932, only months before Frau Samson died, there was another election. This time, the Nazi Party won more than one-third of the vote and became the largest political party in Germany. When a parliamentary majority couldn't be formed, another election was held in November. This time, the Nazis lost slightly, and the Communist Party gained. But by the end of the year, the small circle around President Hindenburg concluded that the Nazi Party was Germany's best hope to stop the political chaos that would result from a communist takeover. At the end of January 1933, Adolf Hitler was named chancellor of Germany, and the stormtroopers celebrated his appointment by staging a massive torchlight parade along the streets of Berlin.

I remember how glad Josef was that his mother had not lived to see this. She hated that dangerous little man, whom she referred to as an incompetent illiterate.

◆

We sat on the sidelines and watched as these events occurred. Most Germans did. I must say that, before becoming Frau Samson's companion and Josef's lover, I had paid little attention to the politics of Germany. I tended to agree with Papa's approach of "Why should I worry about these sorts of things when there are so many better things to do?" I'm not certain that I had formed my own opinion. But after reading the newspapers each morning, listening to the opinions of Frau Samson, being forced to answer her questions, and spending time discussing the issues with Josef, I, too, began to understand.

I agreed with Josef's assessment and what many others were saying. Things did need to change in Germany. More decisive action did need to be taken. The Treaty of Versailles had put too much strain on Germany. We were being forced to pay the costs of a war others had chosen to fight. The German government had failed us. I think most Germans agreed. We wanted something better but should never have settled for this.

I must tell you. History has taught us. We must always remain vigilant and always remember. In 1932, it was a minority of Germans, one-third of the nation, who believed that Adolf Hitler and the Nazi Party were the ones to lead Germany. Once they gained power, though, many others gave their consent.

Time after time, Hitler's enemies underestimated the strength of his followers. To be sure, there was nothing inevitable about Hitler's triumph. I think Josef said it best: "While Hitler and the Nazi Party may have led, they only did so because a nation of sixty million Germans agreed to follow." The signs were always clear, and the result was preventable. No one should ever cast doubt as to who was responsible. The citizens of Germany can be blamed for what was to follow. We allowed this to happen.

◆

From Josef and his mother, I also learned something else I knew little about, a lens that will define much of my story. Although Josef was a proud and patriotic German, a descendant of Germans who had served their country, he had additional reasons to fear. He was Jewish by birth. This was new to me.

I had never met any Jews before. Few Germans had. Jews were only a small part of Germany's population. I only knew what others had told me, the words and descriptions others had repeated. I had little knowledge and had never formed my own opinion. Mostly I didn't understand why any of this should matter.

Forty-Seven

I n the blink of an eye." Those were the words Josef used when he explained the events that occurred during those weeks. In the blink of an eye, Adolf Hitler had become dictator of Germany, and now there was little one could do.

We had this conversation on the evening of Monday, March 27, 1933. That day the Enabling Act had gone into effect, and Hitler was granted his authority. I remember the date for an entirely different reason. It was the very next day when, without any forewarning, Josef suddenly announced that he would be leaving Berlin. He was fleeing to Paris and would never return.

He begged me to join him. First, I should wait until he was settled. Then he hoped I would follow. I had no idea, not any clue that he was about to say this, and not a moment's notice to collect my thoughts. I felt my head start to spin and tensed my body to stop shaking. As I struggled with my emotions, slowly drawing in steady breaths, I was too stunned for tears. I could only softly ask, "When?"

He stared at me, paused for a moment to gather himself, put his hands on my shoulders, swallowed hard, and carefully whispered one word: "Tomorrow."

◆

Four weeks earlier, on the last day of February, the newspapers awakened Berlin with large and bold headlines. There had been a fire in the Reichstag, Germany's Parliament building. When the police and firefighters arrived, the main Chamber of Deputies was already engulfed in flames. And nearly three hours later, after the fire was put out, most of the building had been gutted by the blaze. When the ruins were searched, convincing evidence of arson was found. There was little question. The fire had been intentionally set, and the question was: "By who?"

By day's end, the Reichstag Fire Decree had been signed into law, and most civil liberties in Germany suspended: habeas corpus, freedom of expression, freedom of the press, the right of free association and public assembly, and the secrecy of the post and telephone. After obtaining these emergency powers, Chancellor Hitler angrily declared that the fire was the work of communist agitators, the start of a communist plot, a conspiracy to take down the new government.

That March thousands of members of the Communist Party and others were imprisoned. Then the government was emboldened to form a new majority co-alition. Legislation was passed enabling Adolf Hitler to rule Germany by decree. He was now Germany's dictator and had been granted the powers to do as he pleased with little or no restraint.

◆

Before that evening, we had never discussed the possibility. There had been no mention. Josef had given me no hint of his plan; not a single word had been said. Of course, I knew of his grave concerns about the events that had taken place in Germany. We had listened to Hitler's speeches and were both fearful of what might come next – what this might mean for the world and the Jews of Germany. Together we had watched as these unimagined events had unfolded.

But to suddenly decide to flee Germany and move to Paris? No, I had no idea. He had given me no notice, not taken me into his confidence. He was fifty-four years old and had lived in Berlin his entire life. What had suddenly happened? How was he involved? Nothing made sense. Why was he running? What about me? And why tomorrow?

Neither of us slept that night. Over and over, I asked why. I pleaded with him to tell me. His answers were incomplete and, to me, made little sense. All he would say was that he could no longer live this way, that he had a friend who had now become his enemy. And when I asked, "What have you done?" he shook his head, col-lapsed to his knees, and replied, "I can never tell you."

◆

By morning, there was little left for us to say to one an-other. The words had all been spoken. Before leaving for the train station, Josef encouraged me to stay in the apartment for as long as I wished. If I decided to move out, I should notify the doorman. He had been given in-structions and knew what should be done with Frau Samson's furnishings and possessions.

As for his apartment and his medical practice, all ar-rangements had been made. There was nothing I should do. His things had been packed and would be shipped to Paris. Others at the hospital would take care of his pa-tients. He would write after he arrived and was settled. I could give him an answer when I decided. He would wait. I should not rush. He understood that I needed time to think this through.

My heart pounded, and my pulse raced. I was angry. I was hurt. I was upset, and I was lost. "How could he do this without my knowing? What else has he hidden? What has he not said?" Mostly I was frightened – both for Josef and for myself. There was little else I could do or say. All that was left for me was to go home. I needed to be with Papa. I needed his arms around me. Josef had been right: "In the blink of an eye."

Forty-Eight

I never asked again, and Josef never chose to tell me. I have always thought that when he said he would never return to Berlin, he must have had very good reasons. When he left for Paris, Josef gave up so much, all that he had worked for: his home, his medical practice, his friends, and his life in Berlin. And when he chose to leave, he chose to risk losing me.

His decision was enormous, particularly at his age and station in life, one few of us would ever be able to make no matter the circumstance. When he told me, I am sure he understood what he might lose with this decision.

That was what hurt me the most. He never asked for my opinion, and when he left, he had no idea whether I would follow. Josef was not a man to make rash decisions. He was careful and deliberate. I knew his reasons for leaving must have outweighed his reasons for staying. So, when I finally made my decision, I chose to respect his explanation and was reluctant to pry any

229

further. We each decided to bury this memory. That was what life required. It was better that way.

◆

I must tell you, when I went home to Papa, as upset as I was, I felt much better when I learned that he had already been told of Josef's plans. That day, before Josef told me that he was leaving, he had been to see Papa. He wanted Papa's blessing before asking me to follow. Josef understood how I would be torn by the difficult choice he was asking me to make.

When I begged Papa to tell me what to do, to give me his advice, he refused and said that only I could make that decision. He would support whatever I decided. He only asked that I be patient and choose what I wanted, not what I thought anyone else expected.

My decision took time. It was difficult. I had to decide between the known and unknown. My biggest concern was Papa's welfare, and despite my disappointment and longing to continue with Josef, at first, I decided that I would not go. Berlin had always been my home, and I was accustomed to and familiar with its ways. Berlin was all I knew. I was German. This was my culture. German was my language. It was easier to stay. I didn't have the self-confidence or courage to leave.

On one question, I had no doubt. I knew that I was in love with Josef. Even with his sudden departure, even though he had not shared his reasons, on that matter, I remained certain. And because he begged me to join him, I was convinced he felt the same. Being with Josef was really all that I wanted. It didn't matter where. My heart ached for the warmth of his arms around me. I knew that if I chose not to go, I would never feel that warmth again.

He had not proposed or made any commitment to marriage, and I had never asked. We had never discussed having children or raising a family. All he asked of me was that I follow. I wasn't a starry-eyed Pollyanna. I was old enough to know that I had to be realistic. I would be following a much older man, a man closer in age to Papa. He would grow old while I was still young. And certainly, as is true with any adventure, there was also a risk. The rewards could not be guaranteed. What would I do if we were not happy? What would I do if he chose to leave again? How could I know? How could I trust him to stay?

I presumed we would share the same apartment and live as man and wife, but I was not certain, as there had been no time to have this conversation. And I assumed that in France, particularly in Paris, this behavior, even for a Jew living with a Gentile, was far more acceptable than in Germany, but I did not know enough to be sure.

Finally, there was Papa. How could I ever leave him? He was the most important reason to stay. I was unsure whether I would ever return to Berlin or if I would ever see him again. Papa offered no help. All he would do was look at me carefully and remark, "I hear the flowers in Paris are wonderful in springtime."

◆

What helped me decide were our letters. We wrote to each other day after day. I think the beauty of a letter is that you can hold it, read it over and over, and reflect on every word. And that's what I did. Josef's letters assured me of how much I was desired, and for any complication I offered, he gave me a perfect answer.

That September in 1933, six months after Josef's sudden and unexpected departure, Papa accompanied me to the train station. There wasn't much to carry, only a suitcase filled with my clothes and the Hofuhrmacher clock that had been by my bedside. I had no other possessions.

As we sat on the wooden bench, waiting for the train to arrive and the departure to be posted, I felt the rush of my emotions and a heaviness in my chest. When I saw the expression on Papa's face and the tears in his eyes, I nearly crumbled and changed my mind. And when he hugged me and said goodbye, I held him tightly. I needed to. I didn't want to let go.

I couldn't tell if my world was still spinning or beginning to slow down. What I did understand was that I might never see him again. That afternoon, as the train departed for Paris, I watched Berlin disappear in the distance and blinked the tears from my eyes. I knew that the memories I have written on these pages would be forever left behind.

Forty-Nine

Josef was there to greet me, running beside the train and waving frantically so I could spot him through the window as we slowed to a stop at Gare du Nord. And when the doors opened and I stepped off the train, he swept me into his arms and held me as if we had never been apart. I pressed my body close and felt the stirring of my heart. I was overwhelmed by the moment and surrounded by the delightful sounds, smells, and sights of Paris, so distinctly different from those of Berlin. They filled the air: the flowers, the food, the voices, the way people dressed, and, most of all, the sense of c'est la vie.

It was such a curious sensation, as if I were still dreaming. One moment I had fallen asleep as a Berliner, a *Fraulein*, and the next, when I awoke and opened my eyes, I had become a Parisian. Now I was a *Mademoiselle*. Paris was radiant that day, and in the warmth of his arms and from the loving smile on his face, Josef made me feel that way, too.

He had found us a perfect place to live, a wonderful, spacious apartment designed for sunlight and fresh air on Avenue Brunetière in the Plaine-de-Monceaux district of the 17th arrondissement. It was beautifully furnished with his favorite possessions, which had been sent from Berlin, things I had never seen before. I was greeted by a brightly polished silver tea set perched on an art deco table in the entrance hallway. Lining the walls of the study were glass-fronted bookcases filled with an interesting collection of old medical textbooks and an assortment of literary classics, some written in German and others in English. In the room's center was a huge desk with an old typewriter sitting on one end and a telephone on the other.

Another room, a sitting room, was nearly overtaken by an opened and polished Ritmüller & Sohn baby grand piano. A wooden chair and a very old settee sat along the wall, and in one corner was a small table that held a gramophone. In another was a cabinet with many small drawers for sheet music and, resting on top, a radiola to listen to broadcasts from around the world.

The walls in nearly every room were covered with an interesting collection of oil paintings, etchings, and watercolors, and oriental rugs lay on the polished parquet floors. In the small kitchen stood a round table with two chairs, and placed on top was a silver vase filled with fresh flowers. In the corner was a large glass-covered cabinet filled with an assortment of crystal and china. And in the bedroom, next to the bed, was a small, rectangular table, the perfect home for my Hofuhrmacher clock. When I opened the shutters to take in the view, I had to blink several times to clear my eyes as I was greeted by much sun, a small park with a bench, and the lavender scent of flowers that filled the air from the garden below. I could not have been more pleased.

Josef had important news to report, too. He had received word that he'd been given a position at the well-known Hôpital Lariboisière, one of Europe's largest hospitals. He could finally resume his profession. I knew how much this meant to him. He had practiced medicine in Berlin for nearly thirty years, was quite respected in his field of pulmonology, and had been encouraged by French colleagues to sit for a set of exams. As he was fluent in French, he never worried about the exams but had been anxiously waiting for the approval. At long last, the papers had arrived, and Josef could begin his work.

◆

So, that's how it happened. That is how I moved from Berlin in September of 1933 and stepped into my new life in Paris. That night we shared a bottle of Champagne and amused ourselves. We had so many reasons to celebrate and the freedom of Paris to do it. One day I gently left the comfort of Papa's arms, and on the next, I found myself delightfully swept into the arms of Josef.

How quickly my world had changed. I had survived the Great War, lost most of my family, and left my home. Now I was twenty-three years old, about to discover the wonders of Paris and share this new life with le Docteur

Samson. And again, despite the difference in our ages, I knew we would find our happiness. It really didn't matter that he was quite settled and I was still quite young. Just as we had done in Berlin, we would be perfectly content to meet somewhere near the middle.

Fifty

When I think of those wonderful years in Paris, I am struck by how happy we were and the simple and carefree life we lived. We didn't have much, but we had one another, and that was all we needed. Glorious. That is how I felt each morning when I threw open the shutters and looked out upon the city. Each day was full and complete, from early morning to past midnight.

In Paris, we found a home that could be shared with painters, sculptors, composers, dancers, poets, and writers. The days and months went by all too quickly. At first, there was so much I had to learn, and not unexpectedly, necessity challenged me to adapt – a new culture, a new language, new friends – but slowly and steadily my feet found their footing, and I overcame my uncertainties. And once again, I was pleased to discover a world I had never imagined.

Before arriving, I had considered many things, but I quickly recognized I had given little thought to the adjustment that would be required by the change in our living arrangement. Having a secretive romance requires one to observe a certain set of rules but also entitles one to be freed from the binds of many others. Living together day after day (and assuming the roles of husband and wife without the vows of marriage) is an entirely different circumstance, one that must be taken seriously, has its obligations, leaves little to the imagination, and requires adjustment to the peculiarities and peccadillos of another, including the necessity for patience and compromise.

In Berlin, during the months after Frau Samson died, we experienced some of this as we spent more time together, yet Josef expressed certain reservations and was cautious. He never invited me to his home, preferring to keep our relationship guarded and private. That seemed quite understandable. Germans take great pride in a culture of formality and discretion.

While no reason was ever given as to why we continued to keep our relationship completely hidden and away from the prying eyes of others, I understood that Josef had other responsibilities and interests, and I recognized that our age difference and circumstance could raise eyebrows among some of his friends and colleagues. In Berlin, I shared his concern and wished for my reputation to stay untarnished.

Now our situation was much different, and there were no restraints on our behavior. There were no judgments to be made by others, and there were no prescribed rules we were expected to follow. In Paris, apart from the demands of Josef's profession, we were unbridled and free to spend our days and nights together. We could do as we pleased.

I believe we adapted and adjusted well to this new arrangement, and I think Josef would agree. As in life, there are times when one has to give what the other might take. And though nervous and perhaps a bit intimidated at times, I found myself fully practiced and prepared to become the lady of the house, a task I accomplished quite well. I relished my wifely role and the responsibility of taking care of Josef, and he made it perfectly clear that he rather enjoyed looking after me. While he worked, I made certain the apartment was kept tidy, the daily shopping was done, and the meals were prepared to his liking.

I soon found out, but was not surprised to learn, as he was much older and also his mother's son, that Josef was quite set and fastidious in many of his ways. That posed little issue for me as mine were quite flexible and still being formed, and I was open to his suggestions.

I can only recall one topic that caused minor discord and required a period of debate. It was the round piano seat, an item Josef was quite fond of. My concern was the size of the seat. On this matter, our differences were satisfactorily resolved after I brought home a two-person piano bench, purchased with my own funds for a small price at a used furniture shop on the Boulevard des Batignolles. Oddly, in all the years that followed, this bench would be the only contribution I would ever make to our household furnishings apart from my clock.

Thereafter, each morning, I joined Josef on the seat in front of the piano. With great dedication, he would practice for one hour before leaving for the hospital. This time together became a beloved daily ritual. Josef would play, and I would share the bench, silently observing until the precise moment for my single responsibility. Then, with the care that no note was missed, I would reach across the keys and turn to the next page of his music.

◆

Our weekends and weeknights were filled with discoveries. Although the Années Folles, the crazy years, were over and the Great Depression had darkened the mood of Paris much in the same way it had brought hardships to Berlin, the city was rich in its culture and history, and its streets remained filled with expressions of art, music, literature, and cinema. I quickly learned that our neighborhood was a favorite of many authors and artists and dotted with small shops and market places, all necessary for our daily existence: butcher, baker, fishmonger, flowers, vegetables, and, of course, the many small cafes, where, in late afternoon, it seemed the entire world gathered.

We soon determined that the museums of the Louvre, neighborhoods of Montparnasse and Montmartre, Arc de Triomphe, Jardin des Tuileries, Grand Boulevards, Petit Palais, Paris Flea market, Eiffel Tower, Notre Dame, and the Latin Quarter all could be reached within an hour on foot, and no matter which direction we chose to follow, there were always curious streets and passageways to explore and wonderful sights to be revealed. So different from Berlin's straight, methodical, and unromantically clean streets, Paris's dark, winding, and crooked alleys filled my imagination with mystery and the visions of past centuries.

Our weekend activities were largely decided by the weather. If it was cold and rainy, we would explore the halls and galleries of one of the Louvre museums or the Luxembourg or visit Sylvia Beach's enormous Shakespeare and Company bookstore on Rue de l'Odeon. And when the weather was fine, which seemed to be often, we chose to wander the streets, sit in the sun and share a picnic on a bench near the Seine, or join the crowds at the Place de la Concorde, where one could spend the afternoon watching the mimes and musicians perform. I can't recall a time when either of us was bored or could find nothing interesting to do.

Josef was thrilled to resume his favorite hobby, actually a passion, one that necessity had forced him to set aside the past few years in Berlin. Less than a ten-minute walk from our apartment, at the junction of Boulevard de Courcelles, Rue de Prony, and Rue Georges Berger, was the Parc Monceau, a delightful and expansive park that had once been a fashionable resort before the French Revolution. On weekends and sometimes in the late afternoon, when the clouds and the light were just right, Josef would carry his easel and paints and join the collection of artists, some renowned and others unknown, but all equally passionate, who pursued their talents and sold their works. Josef loved to set his easel up aside the Pavillon de Chartres, near the entrance, by the monument to Guy de Maupassant.

The park was a lovely labyrinth of curved walkways, full of randomly placed monuments and any number of vistas to be captured on canvas. On those days, I would be quite content to silently sit by his side for hours in quiet contemplation, watching him work. Perhaps others who observed us might have been curious, finding my role as the silent onlooker a trifle confusing. I can only respond by saying that we are each entitled to find our happiness by doing what we choose.

Late in the day, after the park's gates were closed and locked, we would often rendezvous with Josef's fellow artists for bottles of wine at one of the many outdoor cafes that lined Les Batignolles. There we watched dusk turn to darkness in the impassioned company of new friends and acquaintances. Other evenings, when the mood struck, we walked to Montparnasse, where colonies of artists had settled. There we joined the conversations in one of the open-air cafes along Boulevard Montparnasse and Boulevard Raspail: Le Jockey, Le Dome, La Rontonde, and La Coupole.

◆

One thought always troubled me and was difficult to understand. When I first arrived, what I knew of Paris was through the German telescope of the Great War and the filter of my German education, a view that taught the superiority of the Fatherland. From my teachers, I had always been led to believe that there was a competition, that we had been challenged, that the French were condescending, which was why Kaiser Wilhelm II was never invited to Paris. We were told that the French were our enemy and they wanted to take everything good that belonged to Germany.

When I lived in Paris, I began to understand a much different story. I realized the truth of war is that neither victor nor vanquished is spared from pain and loss. All sides suffered horribly in that war. In Paris, I learned that in war, some are villains and others are victims. Years later, when we were forced to leave the city, when we feared for our lives and watched in horror as Germany brought terror to the world, I understood the danger of superiority, of teaching children to believe that they are entitled and better and more deserving than others.

Although Berlin may have been a grand city and Berliners may have had pretensions to greatness, we must always remember this important difference when we try to compare the two countries in those times. The Germany that I knew, where I was born and lived, cared more for itself than it respected the lives of others. The Fatherland was self-centered and proud and rarely considered the rights of anyone other than itself. France was not the aggressor. It was the defender, and it was welcoming. I remember when the Ministry of the Interior declared that those who sought asylum were to be welcomed in accordance with the traditions of French hospitality. The France I came to know and love and the open-armed French people who adopted us cherished life. They cared about more than themselves. They were passionate about the welfare of the world.

Fifty-One

Papa arrived by train for a visit late in the spring of 1934. When he wrote, he told me he wanted to see the flowers in Paris and wish us goodbye, that these were his last wishes, that he had little else to ask for, that doing this would satisfy what was left of his life. I was completely devastated when I read his letter. I cried for hours and could not bear to see these words.

If I had known about his illness, if he had told me before I left, I think my life would have turned out much differently. I am certain that I would not have chosen to follow Josef to Berlin, at least not when I did. However, Papa kept his illness secret and chose not to tell me. More than anything, he wanted me to live my life and not be restrained by his. But now, his health had interfered. He wrote that his body was failing and there was little anyone could do to stop this decline.

When I met the train at the Gare du Nord station, I barely recognized Papa. He was so stooped and hunched over, his hair all white. I felt a head taller. As my eyes filled with tears, I saw only a shell of the Papa I had known: gaunt, pale, thin, and weakened. It had only been eight months since I had left him at the station in Berlin, but now he appeared to carry the burdens of his years.

As he stepped off the train and we slowly walked arm in arm along the platform, I wanted my eyes to deceive me, but they refused and only showed the bitter truth. Somehow Papa had been defeated by his battles. He was an old and tired man. As I watched him, I was heartbroken. I was sad and helpless. Now it was my time to put my arms around him and hold him close. That was all that was left for me to do.

Papa's visit was short, less than a week. This was his decision. I am sure, in his condition and with his pain, any longer would have been too much. In those few days, Papa, the man of very few words, the man who valued his silence, gave me a wonderful gift. He looked into my eyes and spoke honestly. He opened up and said things I had never heard before. He told me how he felt – about Karl, about Mutti, about Germany, and about me.

Papa knew few details about Karl – from a postcard now and then – but more than I did, as I knew nothing at all. And when we spoke of Karl, we did so in our private moments, out of earshot of Josef. There was no need for Josef to be part of this conversation. We both understood how angry and upset he would become because of Karl's strong ties to the Nazi party.

I certainly disapproved, but there was some part of me that needed to know. I wanted to understand. Despite the enormous differences between Karl and me, I am not certain that it is ever possible to fully sever the relationship between brother and sister. There was too much we still had in common. As hard as I have tried to forget and hide these memories, there will always be moments that only Karl and I shared, times when we were close, when we cared, when we needed and supported one another. Those times can never be totally erased.

For years, my contact with Karl had been very limited. After the war, when he raged with anger and left for Munich, he became an entirely different person, someone I had never known. One Sunday, not long after I began sitting with Frau Samson, Karl returned to Berlin for a visit with Papa. When he learned that she was Jewish, he spit out his hate and disgust. "How can you care for a Jew?" I was at a loss to understand. Our words became heated, and Karl shouted vile and cruel things about Jews, words that can never be forgotten. There was no reason to say more. We angrily slammed the doors shut to one another's lives and never spoke again.

From Papa, I learned that Karl had married and I had become the aunt to two young nieces, who were good and sweet, as most young children are regardless of who their parents may be. But Karl's hate never stopped, and his outrage continued to grow. After Hitler came to power, he advanced through the ranks and was awarded a position of authority within the Nazi regime in Munich.

Papa offered little opinion, only that Karl was now a grown man and certainly old enough to make his own decisions. While he chose not to agree with all of Karl's views, he was sympathetic with many and understood the reasons for his anger. He wished that Karl would someday find what he was searching for. To my disappointment, Papa explained that as a parent, no matter what, he could never end his relationship. How could he stop loving his son? I closed my eyes and hid my sadness and disgust. I chose not to respond or react. What could be said? On this matter, I refused to learn any more.

As for Mutti, Papa only offered that life had given her too many disappointments, ones that he had been unable to change, defeats that had left her troubled and despondent. She had been taught to expect more and never understood why life had given her less. Papa wanted me to know that despite what I might have thought, Mutti had always loved me, that she had loved me as much as her heart would allow. Even if there had been times when I failed to meet her expectations, she had still wanted me to be happy. She had just been unable to show her love.

When Liesbeth died, they both were devastated. They had hoped and prayed but had always known that Liesbeth's life was fragile, that how long she might live was in the hands of God. They were told of her heart defect shortly after her birth. But then she survived longer than they had expected. They were fortunate to have her in their lives and blessed that she had lived until past her sixth birthday. After Liesbeth was lost, Mutti gave up her belief in God and lost faith in much of the rest of the world. For her, every day was a struggle, and she never overcame her disappointments.

When the war came, Mutti told Papa that she was unsure if she wanted him to return. There was a time when
she even threatened to take her own life. She only chose
to continue because of Karl, Fritz, and me. We were her
reasons for living. Then, when Fritz was lost, her heart
broke again, and she was only able to do what was required. She held on until Papa returned from the war,
but she could do little more because that was all she
could give.

Papa had tried to make up for this in the years that
followed. He told me he was glad that Mutti hadn't lived
long enough to see the anger in Karl's eyes. She would
never have understood and would have been terribly
hurt. Neither intended their lives to be this way, but
sometimes that is the way life works, and the children
are left to suffer. Papa wished I had known Mutti the way
he had when they had first been married, when she had
been happy. That was his regret.

Before Papa left to return to Berlin, we had many conversations about Germany. I remember how shocked he
was when I told him how disgusted and outraged we
were over what was occurring. How could he not know?
What had Germans been told? When I asked Papa what
he thought, I became angry with his response. I wanted
him to reject the views of the Nazis, but he refused. He
told me he would always be a proud German. He remained faithful to the German cause and could never
bring himself to criticize it. Germany was his home, and
he wished for Germany to find a way to greatness. He
was not as outraged as Karl, nor did he wish any harm to

the Jewish people, but the best solution would be for the Jews in Germany to do what Hitler asked. He felt that Hitler was showing compassion for the Jewish people when he urged them to leave. What harm would there be? Why should people stay where they do not belong? The Jews were not real Germans.

Papa held no grievance against Josef. He bore him no ill will. He told me Josef was the first Jew he had ever met and he considered him a friend. But he also believed that it was best for Josef to have left Germany, and if I wished to be with him, then it was best that I leave as well. We would all be happier if Germany was left for the German people. When I asked who else shared this selfish anti-Semitic view, he told me that this was the opinion of everyone he knew. This was what Germans wanted.

I cried that night. There was no sense in repeating Papa's words. He had told me the honest truth about Germany, not what I had wanted to hear, but about its arrogance and ignorance. Germans were convinced in what they knew and patriotic in their beliefs. They would never go against their leaders. Nothing could be done to change this.

When he left the next morning, we set our differences aside, and Papa asked that I remember to do one thing. Every eight days I should take the brass key and carefully wind the clock. That way, when it chimed, I would be reminded of his love.

◆

Weeks later I received an unsigned postcard sent from Munich informing me that Papa had died. Now more than seventy years have passed since Papa's visit to Paris. That was the last time in my life I had contact with anyone in my family.

Fifty-Two

The summer of 1936 was a good time to escape Paris for a few weeks. When Josef surprised me with a trip to Italy, he told me we needed to get away from the restlessness on the streets and the madness in the world. Although he had traveled extensively, he had never visited Naples and was curious about its history and culture, and he was quite taken with photographs he had seen of Capri, Sorrento, and the Amalfi Coast. As my travels were quite limited, having only experienced Berlin and Paris and the view from the train that connected the two, a trip to Naples sounded like a marvelous idea. I had never taken a summer vacation.

◆

We were both very much aware of the world's events, particularly in Germany, and shared the sentiment that if we didn't do this now, there might never be a chance. Each morning we read the papers from front to back and knew that the situation in Europe was worsening by the day. We listened closely to evening broadcasts on the private and state-run radio stations.

The news reports were concerning. We learned about the failed attempt by the Nazis in Austria to take control of the Austrian government, the vote in the Saar region to rejoin with Germany, the assassination of the king of Yugoslavia when he made a visit to Marseilles, the *Nacht der langen Messer*, when Hitler strengthened his grip on Germany and executed nearly one thousand of his political enemies, the outbreak of the Spanish Civil war, and, most recently, the issuance of Germany's Nuremberg decrees.

Although reports from Germany quieted as Berlin's Summer Olympics approached, Josef remained convinced that this was a ruse, that Germany had disguised its face for the world, and that the Nazis' carefully constructed propaganda campaign was succeeding. The image portrayed concealed the frightening dangers of the situation. He predicted that it would not be long before Germany waged two wars, an external one to expand its empire and the internal one that was already underway: Hitler's war to protect the Aryan race and rid Germany of anyone who did not belong.

Neither of us could understand why more of the world failed to take notice or why others found few reasons to object or refused to voice their alarm. Within the past year, Germany had announced that it was rejecting the military terms imposed by the Treaty of Versailles. It would flaunt these restrictions and begin rebuilding its armed forces. And when the Nuremberg Laws were adopted, extending the 1933 decrees, Jews were excluded from most aspects of public life. Jewish doctors were no longer able to be reimbursed from health insurance funds. Berlin forbade Jewish lawyers and notaries from working on legal matters. And the mayor of Munich forbade Jewish doctors from treating non-Jewish patients.

Jews were no longer defined by religious belief but by ancestral lineage. They were stripped of their rights of German citizenship and now were considered state subjects, excluded from the workforce and universities and banished from most aspects of society. They were betrayed by their country.

Just as Papa wished, Jews were strongly encouraged to leave Germany. Many had lost their livelihoods and were left with no choice. My brother Karl must have been delighted. This was what he wanted. German citizens were being given jobs and positions that had been held by Jews, and Jewish-owned businesses were being forced to be sold for a fraction of their worth.

◆

With good reason, there was not a day that passed that Josef did not express fear for the welfare of his friends and family who remained in Germany. He had a number of cousins who lived near Hamburg, and he maintained his correspondence with a wide network of friends and acquaintances. He explained that most were unwilling or reluctant to leave, particularly those with obligations and family. Others who remained were convinced that the Nazi regime was a passing phenomenon, that things would surely change.

Josef tried to shield me from much of what was happening, and I knew little about the nature of his contacts, but I was not as naive or innocent as I once had been when he told me that he had an enemy who once was his friend. While he refused to speak about the details of his activities, I was convinced that somehow he remained connected and, despite having left Germany, there were important things left behind that he chose never to tell me.

◆

I was so glad to have followed Josef to Paris, where we could be together and he felt safe from harm. I never once doubted this decision. In France, Jew or Gentile, there was no distinction, at least none that was apparent or affected our lives. No one cared if I lived with a Jewish man. The only thing anyone noticed was my German accent. For some Parisians, this aroused suspicions and displeasure, so I was cautious and respectful of this concern. Fortunately, Josef had only a trace of an accent, and we had good friends who understood our situation. They welcomed us and made us feel that Paris was our home.

◆

France had difficulties, too. Though different, their origin, like much of Europe's unrest, could be traced to the struggle to regain the prosperity that had suddenly vanished after the Great Depression crashed on Europe's shores. Factories closed because they produced more goods than consumers could afford to buy, and fewer wealthy tourists came to Paris, reducing the demand for luxury items. And when other countries devalued their currencies, French exports became too expensive. Then factories that had managed to survive were forced to lay off their workers.

For the past two years, there had been riots, protests, and worker-staged strikes. During one large demonstration, eleven Parisians were killed, and three hundred were injured. The political extremes, the communists on the left and the new movements on the right, the Croix de Feu, Jeunesse Patriotes, and Solidarite Francaise, had formed semi-military organizations, and Paris was where they clashed.

At the Bastille Day celebration in 1935, the political parties on the left, the communists, socialists, and workers, linked arms together and marched together as the Popular Front. And in the spring of 1936, they won the national elections in France and the municipal elections in Paris. Then, even before the new government could take office, the labor unions, inspired by the workers' victory, declared a national strike. Over one million workers, from construction, transportation, department stores, insurance companies, cafes, and restaurants, took to the streets.

◆

Josef was right when he told me that we needed to get away from the madness. The streets were crowded, and world events were unfolding. The summer of 1936 was a good time for a vacation. We all needed a break.

Fifty-Three

Our train arrived at Naples Centrale shortly after midday. The journey was lengthy, nearly three days, and more tiring than I had expected, with too many stops and a number of connections. We traveled from Paris to Lyon and then from Lyon to Geneva, Geneva to Milan, Milan to Rome, and Rome to Naples.

Neither of us was able to get much sleep as there were interruptions at the many intervening town and village stations. It was as if the train conductors were playing a game and chose to announce the next stop as soon as they saw that we had closed our eyes and fallen asleep. To me, little of this mattered. I didn't care too much about sleep and had no wish to miss the view. I hadn't seen these sights before. Nearly the entire trip, whenever there was enough daylight to see, I kept my face tightly pressed against the window and eagerly watched all that passed along our way.

Josef had extensively researched the route and made all the arrangements and reservations. Unlike me, he tended to enjoy these intricate details and would frequently stay up late in the night to consult his maps and make notes in his guides. I had little patience or interest for this exercise. And as for geography, I knew little and was content to leave Josef in charge.

At first, he proposed to travel from Paris to the southeast of France, to Menton, the hilly, medieval old town that is home to Basilique Saint-Michel, with its eighteenth-century bell tower. He excitedly informed me that we would take the Calais-Méditerranée Express, *Le Train Bleu*, a train composed exclusively of first-class carriages and a dining car renowned for its haute cuisine and five-course dinners.

I had observed that there were times when Josef was impulsive in this manner and yearned for this kind of life, perhaps trying to relive something from his past. However, my taste in food was rather simple, so I thought the idea unnecessary and a bit silly, given its exorbitant cost. But then, as it turned out, none of this mattered. The plan was quickly abandoned. Josef explained that he had encountered a difficulty in finding a way to get from Menton to Ventimiglia across the Italian border, where we would need to catch the next train.

I only take time to share these unnecessary details now as they were hurriedly imparted as an excuse when Josef woke up with a start. That was when he suddenly remembered that he had neglected to write and reserve a room for our stay in Naples, an oversight I learned of as we passed through the Mont'Orso Tunnel and were fewer than two hours away from Naples Centrale.

He proposed a solution. Once we arrived in Naples, we would taxi to the Villa Comunale, the long, leafy seaside park that borders Via Caracciolo, the home of many pensiones, a location he had previously identified as an ideal spot for his paintbrushes and easel. There I would be deposited in the gardens near the fountain and could sit with our belongings while he went off in search of available lodging. And that was how I found myself abruptly abandoned in the middle of Naples on a hot summer day.

I remember how hurried, distressed, and ridiculous Josef looked as he ran down the street wearing his painter's beret. He was so anxious to find a room that he had forgotten to leave me his frock, the one with the hideous bluish-green paint smudge on the lapel, the one I disliked and he always insisted on wearing. Not having the faintest clue when Josef would return or where I was, I sat patiently on a wooden bench and spent much of the afternoon guarding our suitcases and his easel and painting supplies in the company of hundreds of pigeons, who seemed as entertained by me as I was disinterested in them.

I know that throughout these pages, I have given the impression that Josef was older and wiser, that, as a couple, he was the mentor and I was the student. I choose to include this particular episode as an illustration of Josef the younger, when he would revert from a rather self-confident and cocky personality to an extremely quiet, apologetic, and exceptionally nervous person. In these situations, I could only laugh. Truthfully, I found these latter traits to be some of his more endearing qualities.

Josef returned quite some time later and proudly announced his success. He had secured a room at the nearby Pensione Alexandra, which, oddly, given the time he had taken to find it, was less than four blocks away. Apparently, at first, for reasons he claimed were the result of his nervousness, he had begun his search in the wrong direction. Fortunately, this had been corrected when he had had a rather odd encounter. An older man sitting on a doorstep, drinking from a bottle of wine, had inquired about his destination. Then he had been turned around and pointed the right way.

When we arrived at the third-floor reception area, the proprietress, a quite pleasant and friendly woman, Signora Oulman, was there to greet us and introduce herself. Josef was momentarily confused, concerned that he had taken us to the wrong establishment, as he later claimed that the reception areas of many look much the same.

Earlier he had spoken to a young German woman, a girl named Lotte, who had taken his reservation. To his relief, Signora Oulman quickly explained that Lotte had left to teach a German lesson. She held a second position and was the tutor for two children who lived down the street. She assured us that Lotte had briefed her on the details of our unfortunate situation. Then she turned to me, smiled warmly, and remarked that Lotte must have been confused because it was clear she had misunderstood our requirements. "Herr Doktor, Lotte explained that you were on your honeymoon and in need of one room. I am pleased that you will join us and look forward to meeting Frau Samson. How nice that your daughter is with you for such an important occasion. Obviously, you will require two rooms."

I hope we all have cherished memories like these, moments that make us smile and laugh, moments that we always remember. I will never forget that special day in Naples, when Josef left me at the Villa Comunale amidst the pigeons and rushed off to find a room for us at the Pensione Alexandra with the excuse that we were on our honeymoon.

◆

Josef and I fell in love with Naples and Southern Italy during our visit that week. In the years that followed, we chose to return often for our annual ten-day holiday from Paris, always staying at the Pensione Alexandra, the interesting sixteen-room guesthouse overlooking the Bay of Naples, operated by the Oulman family. And when we arrived, I would always receive a big hug from Consolato, the dishwasher, who remembered us. He was the old man sitting on the steps who had given Josef directions that first time we visited.

During each stay, we followed a simple and familiar daily routine, a pattern that was seldom varied and reminiscent of the rather precise habits of Josef's mother. Without fail, we began each morning with a light breakfast and coffee in the breakfast room and a visit with

Signora Oulman, who would review Josef's detailed sightseeing plans, gleaned from his dog-eared copy of the Baedekers guide, and offer her own wonderful suggestions and ideas for the day. Then Josef and I would set off on our way and explore the streets and sights of Naples, always returning by early afternoon to avoid the midday heat. This was the ideal time for a light lunch, followed by a brief and restful nap.

Later in the day we would carry Josef's paintbrushes and easel to the Villa Comunale, where I could sit quietly on a bench and patiently watch him work. Finally, after a dinner prepared to our liking by Signora Oulman, we would take a long walk along the Bay of Naples waterfront on Via Caracciolo to the public aquarium and back before joining the Oulmans on their balcony for a relaxing late-night aperitif and interesting conversation. It was the perfect place to watch the moon rise over the Bay of Naples.

The Oulman family became dear friends. They were wonderful and engaging hosts. Signora and Signor Oulman were both close in age to Josef – he two years older, and she two years younger – and we quickly learned they shared much in common. They were both originally from Germany, having moved to Naples as young adults decades earlier, Signor Oulman in the early 1890s and Signora Oulman shortly after the turn of the century. Owning and operating the pensione was a more recent enterprise. The guesthouse was clearly the pride and joy of Signora Oulman, who had acquired it that year from the previous owner, an Englishwoman, who had operated it for forty years.

Signor Oulman tended to be on the quiet side, usually with a cigar in hand and always pleasant, but reluctant to interrupt the conversation and rarely offering his own opinion on any matter other than the weather. By contrast, I found Signora Oulman to be a natural conversationalist, animated, opinionated, and curious about everything, always asking questions. She was interested in a wide range of topics and very much enjoyed speaking with us in her native German tongue.

Their daughter, Emilia, and German employee, Lotte, were both very close in age to me, within a few years of one another, perhaps two or three. Signora Oulman tended to treat herself, Josef, and Signor Oulman as contemporaries of one generation, with the view that Emilia, Lotte, and I were of another. At times, I thought Signora Oulman acted as if we all were her daughters, myself included, and, therefore, could benefit from her advice. I must say that at first, I was resentful and became quite annoyed.

I took great offense at the idea that we could be divided in lots by age, as I expected mine to be rightfully cast with Josef, which was where I belonged. In that regard, I distinctly remember reminding Josef of this point when we returned to the privacy of our room one evening. I told him that this was an issue with consequences, one that he sheepishly claimed not to have noticed. Before nightfall, at his urging, Signora Oulman quickly adjusted her behavior.

In any case, I did soon learn that my feet were in both camps, with Josef and Signor and Signora Oulman and also with Lotte and Emilia, whom I began to accept as my contemporaries. In Berlin, I had never had the opportunity to develop close friendships with young women close in age and had never been particularly interested. I was always too busy, at first during my years with Papa and later with Frau Samson and Josef. Even in Paris, my attention was occupied with friends and acquaintances who were generally older, closer in age to Josef.

I learned that Lotte had recently moved to Naples from Germany with the encouragement of her mother, who was a childhood friend of Signora Oulman and upset by the turn of events in Germany. She thought that life in Italy would be safer and present more opportunities.

With Lotte, I found an immediate sisterlike kinship, perhaps because we were both from Germany, but I think mostly because I found her to be of similar personality, very much of the German way, a bit formal and reserved, always respectful, and not too inquiring. From the moment I met her, it was clear we agreed. Lotte valued a certain amount of personal privacy.

Emilia, on the other hand, was quite different than anyone I had ever met, rather remarkable, earnest, and unusual in her own special way. I really did not know what to think of her, only that perhaps she was more of the Italian influence, although I really can't say that with confidence, as she clearly had traits quite similar to her mother. I knew she meant well and was genuinely kind, but she was also exceptionally curious; some would say nosy. She tended to ask many questions that I found inappropriate and intrusive, often too personal or inquiring to warrant an answer. It was clear that she found Josef and me a mystery.

Upon our arrival, the Oulmans and Lotte considered Josef and me an odd couple – because of our age difference and the way we suddenly appeared on their doorstep. The age difference, I understood as I had been confronted with questions about it before. But I had no desire to give up my privacy. Why or how we arrived seemed none of Emilia's business. So, with that in mind, I chose not to engage too much with Emilia, and she continued to find us a question in need of an answer.

I am afraid she and I did not get off to a good start, as I soon learned that she was quick to tears and sensitive to criticism. I also had the distinct impression, largely from the nature of her questions, that she had it in her mind that Josef and I might be foreign agents, spies of some sort, and that we had come to Italy on a secretive expedition. Evidently, she got that idea because we were Germans living in Paris, although Signora Oulman mentioned one day that Emilia spent much of her time dreaming, so I suppose that could be another reason.

In any event, our visit was delightful, and by its end, Josef and I agreed with the assessment written in the 1930 *Baedeker's Guide to Naples and Southern Italy*. Of the many pensiones on Via Caracciolo, the Pensione Alexandra deserved the highest marks. The only thing I would revise was the guidebook's description, which read: "English and good." This needed to be changed since the new owners were German.

That morning, as we were saying farewell, before we left for the train station, we mutually agreed to drop some of our initial formalities. We became Josef and Kaethe, and they became Paul and Elsa. However, I had one additional, more personal request, having developed a certain closeness with Signora Oulman by the week's end, a sense of family. From that day forward, I preferred to refer to her as Emilia did. Signora Oulman became Mamarella to me, the lovely name her children had bestowed.

And on our way out, I could not help but hear Mamarella give one more piece of advice, as she was wont to do. She pulled Josef aside and reminded him that he was not getting younger. Before it was too late, he should ask for my hand and marry me. Then Consolato helped load our belongings into the waiting taxi, and we opened the windows, reached out our arms, and waved our handkerchiefs goodbye.

◆

Throughout these visits, our friendship with the Oulmans continued to grow, and their balcony, with its wonderful view of the moon rising over the Bay of Naples, became a welcome place to enjoy our evening conversations. When we visited the next year, in 1937, we were delighted to learn that Lotte had married

Mamarella's son, Alex, a charming and entertaining young man the same age as me, who had returned home after two years in the Italian army.

Our 1938 visit took place at a very difficult and confusing time, only weeks after Adolph Hitler, with his entourage of three bulletproof trains and five hundred party officials, conducted a six-day state visit to Italy to thank Mussolini for not interfering with Germany's invasion and annexation of Austria.

The Oulmans told us of his visit to Naples, how black-shirted security guards had been posted on their balcony and a half-million people lined the street to watch Hitler and Mussolini pass by. Hitler stood in an open car and saluted and waved to the cheering crowd as they drove down Via Caracciolo. That day they had a bird's-eye view of the two dictators as the motorcade slowed and turned around directly in front of the Pensione Alexandra.

These were difficult years. Months later, not long after we returned to Paris, we heard that Mussolini had issued the *leggi razziali*, the set of Italian racial laws patterned after Germany's Nuremberg Laws. And then, in November, we learned of Kristallnacht and the devastating horrors inflicted on Jewish families in Germany.

◆

We became close friends with Paul and Mamarella at the beginning of such a dreadful time. In many ways, I think we were drawn together by our mutual confusion.

Throughout our visits, as we spent our evenings together, we slowly became familiar with each other's histories. Some things took us years to learn, and many other things were left unsaid, but I think that is how good friendships grow, slowly and steadily, trusting and more trusting. At first, we were all a bit reluctant and uncertain about saying too much. I remember when Josef asked about Mussolini. Mamarella warned us that in Italy, one needed to be careful and said, "You never know who may be listening."

Another evening Mamarella remarked that she had never known she had an accent until she moved to Italy. Although she had lived in Naples for more than thirty years at the time, she was still surprised when people asked about her accent, as she never heard it.

I understood. I felt the same way in France and wondered whether I would ever fit in. And much like Josef, the Oulmans had Jewish ancestry and relatives still living in Germany. I was never given the impression that their Jewishness was a function of their religious beliefs. Mamarella said they observed few traditions and had never visited the synagogue. They seemed to act the same as Josef. Their Jewishness was in their blood, and they were proud of their heritage. It defined who they considered themselves to be.

I suppose that we recognized, each for our own reasons, that we were adrift in the world, with little idea as to which part we now belonged. Papa and Mamarella told us about an encounter they had had at their German club in Naples when another couple had ended their forty-year friendship because the Oulmans were Jewish. As she spoke of this, Mamarella said she didn't understand their behavior because her family had always been German. "Who had the right to act this way?" she asked. "Could one be German if one was a Jew? Could one be Jewish if one were German?" These were the same questions I know Josef struggled with, and these were the same questions that left me confused when I tried to understand why my brother Karl and the Nazis felt so entitled.

◆

Our last visit to Naples took place in the spring of 1939. We arrived unannounced at the Pensione Alexandra. I had no idea how Josef had secured our train arrangements, as this was a very difficult and confusing time, but Josef was insistent, only telling me that it was important that we go to Naples. All he would say was that there were things he needed to see and information he needed to gather. And once again, I was at a loss to understand. It was clear there was little about this that Josef would share with me.

I am always amazed at those times when things can be so different yet still appear to be exactly the same. That is how I felt about this visit. Despite the behavior of Hitler and Mussolini, most of Naples seemed unchanged. People went about their business as if little had occurred. And with only minor adjustments, like setting up his easel near the port (for different scenery, Josef said) and seeking out different destinations for our walks in the early evening, Josef and I continued to follow our established daily routines. We did notice that the number of tourists roaming Naples's streets seemed to have decreased, but this was to our benefit as we did not have to stand and wait our turn in lines at popular tourist sites.

It was only when we looked below the surface, at those things that might not have been as obvious to the casual visitor, that we were able to recognize how much life had changed. And nowhere was this more evident than at the Pensione Alexandra. When we arrived, we learned that the Oulmans were no longer the owners. They were planning to leave Italy and move to the United States.

Fifty-Four

Mamarella told me how surprised they were when Mussolini suddenly changed his behavior and issued the *leggi razziali*. Throughout his years of rule, Mussolini had consistently voiced the view that Jews living in Italy were not a threat and should be left alone to live peacefully and in harmony. Mamarella never particularly cared for Mussolini and distrusted the fascists, but unlike Germany, Italy did not discriminate against its Jewish population. Italians did not care or ask about race.

In Italy, one couldn't tell who had Jewish, Catholic, Muslim, or Protestant blood in their veins or who had descended from Teutons, Langobards, Goths, Visigoths, Normans, or Spaniards. Some claimed it was as if nearly everyone had a friend or someone in their family tree who was Jewish. Italy was a melting pot of tribes and races. This attitude was part of the Italian culture. For years, Mussolini had claimed that anti-Semitism did not exist in Italy, and Italians embraced that belief. Italian Jews were assimilated. Mixed marriages were accepted.

Jews were few in number – in Naples, perhaps a few thousand out of a population close to one million. Even if you took all the Jews in Italy and stood them in the same field together, there were less than fifty thousand, hardly more than one-tenth of one percent of Italy's population, one Jew in a crowd of one thousand. Why would a country of forty-four million people concern itself with such a small group of people who had contributed so much to all aspects of Italian society? Mamarella claimed that in Naples, the anti-fascists were more of a threat to Mussolini than the Jews.

While the Jews might not have been Mussolini's biggest supporters, many were his advisors and allies. Most Italian Jews believed that Mussolini would shield them against the hatred of Hitler, that he would shoulder this burden and be their protector. After all, it was widely known that his mistress was a Jew.

All Mamarella would say was, "Il Duce sacrificed the Italian Jews. He chose to protect his empire. He needed Hitler to remain his friend and not become his enemy. That's why he turned against the Jews. He was afraid that Hitler would do to Italy what he had done to Austria, so instead, he did what Hitler told him to do. We were his gift to Hitler."

After Mussolini issued the *leggi razziali*, Mamarella's son, Emilia's twin brother, Arthur, who was living in Milan, announced that he would move to the United States. Then the others, Emilia, Alex, and Lotte quickly decided they would do the same. Mamarella told me that it would not be fair to ask the children to stay. "What is there for them to do in Italy? Alex has served his country in the army. Yet, they have no opportunity. They have no future here."

That was when Mamarella and Paul gave up their dreams and decided they would leave as well. As soon as they could get their visas approved and find passage, they would all leave Italy and move to the United States. Mamarella could not bear the thought of staying in Italy with their children so far away. And since the new rules in Italy prevented them from owning the pensione any longer, they had transferred the ownership papers to their landlord, Signor Spinelli. They would leave when they could and, in the meantime, continue to operate the pensione, and Signor Spinelli would make sure that they received an income.

◆

That week we continued our conversations each evening on the balcony. We all knew that our lives would never be the same as we tried to understand the events that were shaping our world. War appeared inevitable. Each day it seemed that the world was spinning out of control. The Nazis kept pursuing their ambitious plans, and Hitler continued his strong-arm tactics, taking every opportunity to test how far he could push the European powers. And at each turn, it seemed that his opponents chose to back down and appease him. Josef kept asking,

"Why did the politicians think that if they gave Hitler a little, he would not ask for more? How many times does that lesson need to be repeated before the world understands?"

◆

Our visit seemed to end as quickly as it had started. Mamarella and Paul accompanied us to the Centrale station when we left. We knew that it was doubtful we would ever see each other again. How would that be possible? When we said farewell, the world was changing before our eyes, and there was little anyone could do to stop it.

◆

While our trip from Paris to Naples that year was largely uneventful, the same cannot be said for the return. Security was heightened. After we changed trains in Geneva, we were stopped on our way to Lyon and detained and questioned by French patrols at the border crossing near Annemasse. It was easy to see that these young men were nervous. They did not know who they could trust.

My German passport seemed to be an issue. Why was I traveling from Italy to France? What had I been doing in Italy? One guard couldn't understand why I was traveling with a Jewish man as old as Josef. Neither of us were French citizens. I had never renounced my German citizenship, and the Nazis had stripped Josef of his citizenship, so now he was stateless.

At first, we thought these might be minor distractions. But then somehow they connected me to my brother in Germany, and we were required to wait two days for the police authorities in Paris to confirm that we were no danger, that we were registered aliens and legal residents. Needless to say, by the time we returned to Paris, we were both quite shaken.

Fifty-Five

Although we had been away from Paris for less than three weeks, we were surprised to see the war preparations underway upon our return. As Paris braced for war, city workers were digging trenches to be used for bomb shelters in city squares and parks. Sandbags were being placed near public buildings. Strips of paper could be seen covering the glass windows of many shops to prevent glass from shattering should an aerial attack occur. And days later, Paris civil defense officials began distributing gas masks to citizens and posting signs with directions to shelters.

Josef wondered whether diplomatic negotiations would prevent war from occurring, that perhaps the non-aggression pact being discussed with the Soviet Union would temper the moment. And like most Parisians, we found it difficult to get a clear sense of events, to distinguish rumors from fact. Speculation was rampant. So much was being said, and everyone had an opinion.

The evening news broadcasts offered only sketchy details, mostly unconfirmed suspicions, and many of the newspaper reports were censored, particularly those newspapers with communist leanings, like *L'Humanité* and *Le Soir*, whose copies were seized after they praised the Hitler-Stalin alliance. There was talk that the British were still pursuing a policy of appeasement, which infuriated Josef as he remained convinced that appeasement was political folly and did little to deter Germany's aggressions. One day we heard that the Vatican had become involved and was trying to seek a last-minute solution.

Throughout Paris, there were ominous signs that war was imminent. Everyone understood that if Germany attacked Poland, France and Britain were pledged to come to Poland's defense.

Someone told Josef that workmen were removing the stained-glass windows from Sainte-Chapelle, the royal chapel within the medieval Palais de la Cité. Others said that curators at the Louvre were returning from their vacations to pack up and catalog major works of art. With the help of nearby department store workers, valuable pieces were stored in crates labeled with codes disguising their contents. The *Winged Victory of Samothrace* statue, the celebrated Hellenistic marble sculpture prominently displayed at the Louvre, was removed, carefully loaded onto a truck, and taken to the Château de Valençay in the Loire Valley. There were reports that continuous convoys of vehicles, without headlights and under the cover of darkness, were carrying very important collections of paintings and other priceless works of art to be hidden in safe destinations.

In late August, we learned that the French authorities were beginning to evacuate children out of the city to safe areas surrounding Paris. Streetlights were extinguished as a measure against German air raids. Normally busy, the streets of Paris suddenly became dark and deserted. Those who could afford to flee Paris were leaving.

Then one evening we listened to the frightening news reports. Negotiations had stalled, and Germany had invaded Poland. We were told that France would soon be at war. Hitler, without fear of Soviet intervention or reprisal, had done what he had always threatened to do, what he had already done to Austria and Czechoslovakia.

This time he claimed he was provoked, declaring that Poland had been the instigator. But we all knew better. The German view was that war was a necessity, survival of the fittest. Just as in the past, they were invading. They were the aggressors. Hitler was rebuilding the German empire, conquering territory for his fellow Germans, vowing that Germany would never be defeated again due to a lack of the resources necessary for the fight.

France and Britain had given their word. They would not step aside and allow this to happen. The two countries stood by the people of Poland. Two days later, they declared war against Germany. Our worst fears had become true, and for the second time in the twenty-nine years of my life, I found myself in the middle of the darkness and confusion that surrounds every war.

Fifty-Six

When I opened the apartment shutters to abundant rays of sunshine the next morning, the small park across the street looked exactly the same as it had in the weeks and months before. I could still smell the fragrance of the flowers from the garden below and look out across the Paris rooftops. The buildings still stood. But anyone who looked out their windows that day, the day after France and Britain declared war on Germany, understood that Paris had changed. The people were missing. The streets were quiet, eerily quiet, in a way we had never seen before. We were all on edge, not knowing what to expect next. There was a collective sense that something bad was about to happen, but no one knew where or when.

As for the fighting, that day it took place elsewhere, on the seas and in the Battle of the Atlantic. It did not take place on the streets of Paris. That day we had no idea. Everything was unknown. No one was able to predict that it would be eight months before Germany

282 | RALPH WEBSTER

would begin its major ground offensive in France and Belgium and its assault on Paris.

Paris, like most of the world's great cities, seldom sits still and rarely sleeps. The quiet did not last long. Although the uneasiness continued, Parisians were accustomed to living their lives on the streets and boulevards, in shops, at the markets, in the small squares and parks, and in the brasseries and cafes, and within weeks, they would continue to do so.

As the days passed, even as the men went off to war and France's armies prepared for the battles, the city returned to the way it had always been. Children who had been evacuated returned to their parents. Families who had left returned to the city. Restaurants were filled once again with their patrons. Shops reopened. Fishermen, booksellers, and street performers returned to their favored spots along the banks of the Seine. Theaters and cinemas scheduled their matinee and early evening performances. Some understood what war meant, but when one gazed across the city's rooftops, it was as if little had changed.

◆

There is a sad and terrible truth about every war. Early impressions can be too simple. Usually, hindsight is required. War is filled with complexity, contradictions, and appearances that can be misleading. Much might remain undercover and out of sight, but one should never confuse the cloak of camouflage with war's reality. Once wars begin, the effects can never be truly hidden. Wars do change things, particularly for those caught in the middle, where, no matter how hard one tries, life can never be normal.

Events occur that are beyond one's control. Most cannot escape, and nearly everyone lives in fear. There is a depressing inevitability, a downward spiral, a feeling there is little one can do to change the world's trajectory. Families do not remain the same. Children grow up without their fathers. Husbands, brothers, fathers, and sons depart for war, and all lives are disrupted.

As I hold my pen and write these words, I am haunted by the thought that all too often, we fail to remember. We repeat history's most important lessons. Once war begins, hunger, misery, confusion, devastation, and loss of life are sure to follow. I know this to be true because I have lived through wars. No one ever really wins.

◆

Two days after France declared war against Germany, on September 5, 1939, an announcement appeared in the newspapers ordering all German males residing in France under the age of sixty-five to report to *camps de rassemblement*, assembly centers, for interrogation and transport to internment camps, where they would be detained for an undetermined length of time. Detainees were advised to bring a small suitcase for their clothes and personal effects, a two-day supply of food, a warm blanket, and cutlery. Failure to comply would result in arrest and prosecution. Within days, similar notices appeared on posters and billboards throughout Paris.

I know that I should not have been surprised. Josef had always said we should prepare ourselves for this moment, that something like this was bound to occur. Detaining enemy aliens, removing them from the general population to prevent possible dangers to national security, was not a new concept. Taking this action was not unique to France and certainly not unjustified. Anxiety was heightened.

In times of war, every nation has the right and responsibility to be concerned about the security within its borders. And in the rush to judgment, it should not be surprising that those in authority may take a broad brush and identify and detain everyone who arouses suspicion or may be considered a potential threat. No further justification is necessary.

There were no exclusions and no appeal. Reason did not matter. Most understood, and few complained. The authorities chose not to exempt refugees. Why would they do so? The answer was obvious. There might be suspicious persons among them.

The order included Germans Jews, like Josef, who had had their citizenship revoked and been declared stateless by the Nazi regime. The Nazis had been clear. Josef and other German Jews who had left were no longer welcome to return to their native Germany. In France, Josef had been welcomed and allowed to live freely without fear of persecution. The fog of war changed all of this. Because Germany was the country of our birth, now France considered us to be loyal to the enemy, at least until they could be convinced otherwise. We were classified as enemy aliens and considered a threat.

◆

When we had arrived in France, we had been given hope and expectation. We had been welcomed with open arms. Now suddenly the ground had shifted. Now we were faced with disappointment and despair.

Fifty-Seven

Devastated and frightened, I wanted to shut the world out. I had nowhere to turn. How could this be? Josef was a sixty-year-old man. He had fled Germany. He was no threat to anyone. I knew this man well. He was a physician, a healer, a person who had spent his life caring for others. What reason could he possibly have to be an enemy of France? Yet there really was nothing he could do but comply. What choice did he have? He was calm and reassuring and told me there was no reason to fear. While I worried about him, he was far more concerned about me and how I would fare during his absence.

Later that evening I helped him pack his suitcase with a few clothes and his supplies. And the next morning, before he left, we rose early for our everyday ritual, just as we had nearly every morning for the past six years. We sat side by side on the piano bench, and I turned the pages of his music, content to watch his fingers dance across the keys. I think we both knew that this morning was different, more intense and more serious. We were anxious. What would come next? I watched Josef carefully, wanting to remember the sound of every note and every expression on his face. I had no way of knowing whether he would return to do this again.

As we stood by the door and he was preparing to leave, he handed me a small leather-bound notebook, a book he had never shown me before. As I slowly leafed through the gilded-edge pages, I saw that many were filled with his handwriting. Some contained small drawings, while others were empty, and I noticed that several pages had been torn out and appeared to be missing.

When I asked, Josef explained that when he was a child, the notebook had been a gift from his grandmother. He had received it on his ninth birthday, and he pointed to the inscription on the first page. She had hoped he would use it to write about special moments in his life. Josef told me that at times, he had done so, not always well or faithfully and sometimes with misgivings, but he had attempted to do as she had asked.

Now he urged me to do the same. "While I am away, use these pages to write about the special moments in your life, not a daily diary, but the things I do not know. Tell me your secrets. I will have this to look forward to reading when I return. I want to know all there is to know about you, all the things you have chosen not to tell me." Then his eyes twinkled as he gave me a kiss and went out the door.

From the apartment window, I silently watched Josef cross Avenue Brunetière. As he slowly disappeared from my sight, I could only smile when I noticed that he was wearing his painter's beret and the awful frock with the bluish-green paint smudge on the lapel. Josef was true to his passions. As I lingered by the window's edge and the tears began to well up in my eyes, I thought about how fortunate my life had been to have this very special man by my side. Then I closed my eyes and prayed for his safe return.

◆

It would be more than three months, more than a dozen weeks, nearly one hundred days and nights before Josef would return, and when he did, I was given no notice. His arrival was as sudden as his departure. I only learned of his release when I heard the familiar sound of his footsteps on the stairs and he opened the door. Apart from some loss of weight, he appeared to be in reasonably good health, tired and sore, his face a bit more drawn, but he was in good spirits and glad to be home. As for me? I was overjoyed and unable to speak. Tears were streaming down my face. A weight had been lifted. I could finally breathe again.

Josef had been detained at Les Milles, an abandoned brick and tile factory located between Aix-en-Provence and Marseilles, one of many sites scattered across the French countryside that had been converted into internment camps to house enemy aliens. He and a number of men were taken there by train. While he was detained, I received a few brief letters. He could only write sparingly to tell me that he was safe and not mistreated. The censors would allow him to write little more, and I am not sure that there was much more that he wished to tell me. I was given no idea where he was held or how long he would be kept there.

After he returned home, he told me his release had been totally unexpected, the result of special Ministere de la Justice intervention. His medical colleagues had submitted affidavits attesting to his behavior and a request for release. They hoped he could return to his work at the hospital.

What I write here is what I slowly learned over the weeks following his return. Josef told me little. He chose to share few details, mostly that he was never in danger, that the living conditions were primitive and cramped, and the sanitation poor. There was not enough food, and what little there was was less than satisfactory. The guards showed little interest or concern for the health and welfare of the detainees, who slept on straw bedding that had been placed on stone floors.

He had little idea why he had been sent to Les Milles, as nearly all the detainees held there appeared to be from the area surrounding Marseilles, not Paris. All he could conclude, and he smiled when he told me this, was that when he was screened, his clothing, the painter's beret and frock, might have led the interviewer to believe that in addition to being a physician, he was an artist of some repute. Apparently, there were a number of well-known artists and intellectuals who were detained at Les Milles. Many were like Josef, Jewish refugees who had fled to France from Germany and occupied areas. He was never asked for his reasons.

Discipline was relatively relaxed. There were four roll calls at scheduled times each day and one hour of assigned tasks every morning. Otherwise, the detainees were free to do as they wished as long as they stayed within the barbed-wire fence that encircled the camp. He had been assigned to a group of twenty-four men, mostly artists who chose to spend their free time in a room in the catacombs, where they were able to work on their paintings.

As a whole, he found all the men he had met there to be very organized, educated, and resigned to their fate. Some held literary discussions. Others spent their days discussing philosophy. Another group staged performances.

His biggest surprise was when he encountered an old acquaintance, a fellow artist, a Russian, whom he had met and befriended in Berlin twenty-five years earlier when his works had been displayed at the Der Sturm gallery. Josef explained that he had seen Moïche on one other occasion. They had had dinner one evening in the early 1920s when Moïche had returned to Berlin on a failed mission to retrieve his paintings that had been left at the gallery. Josef recalled that Moïche had been very upset when he was told that these paintings had disappeared. Josef learned that Moïche and his wife, Bella, now lived near Paris. Moïche had given him an address near Loire. Evidently, his works had gained considerable international notoriety, particularly after he changed his name to Marc in an attempt to give them more appeal. When Josef told me this, I was unaware that one of Moïche's paintings hung on our walls.

◆

Having never lived alone before, I was uncertain about how I would react without having Josef close by my side during those months. And having no idea when he would return, I worried about his health, prayed for his safety, and missed him terribly. Being without him left me with such an empty, hollow, and incomplete feeling. He was my other half. His habits had become my habits. His life had become my life. I needed to be held in his arms so I could feel whole.

Yet, in some strange way, sometimes a little good comes from even the most difficult situations. I also knew that there was little to be gained by being helpless. I was not afraid of the dark. I am not fragile and have always been capable and quite able to take care of myself. I can shrug and go on if that is what is required. So, that is what I did. While Josef was away, I seldom was bored. There were books to read, and there were things to be done: shopping, cooking, cleaning, sewing, comforting habits that have always filled my life.

I found no desire to search for company, and by nature, I have little need to be entertained by others. As has always been true, I am content when silence is my quiet companion. I know that others may not understand, but being alone has never made me lonely.

What I did learn was that Josef had left me with the perfect project, an inviting task that required hours of contemplation before even writing one word on paper. And that is how I spent much of my free time, penning many of the stories that fill these pages, all written for an audience of one.

There were days when, in the late afternoon, I found an out-of-the-way seat in the rear of the small cafe around the corner from the apartment, a place where the owner knew us well and was happy to let me be. There I could sit quietly for as long as I wished with a single glass of wine.

Left alone with my pen, notebook, and memories, I suppose one might say (and it does make me smile to say this) that during that time in Paris, I found my way, in the Parisian manner, to becoming a writer. And I found a great amount of pleasure in knowing that someone had already said they would read my book.

Fifty-Eight

The Phoney War, or the Sitzkrieg, as some called it, those first eight months at the start of the war, were a time for France to build up the necessary forces and position its armies in a line of concrete fortifications, obstacles, and weapon installations – the Maginot Line – covering the French side of its borders with Italy, Switzerland, Germany, and Luxembourg. Apart from the French-led small Saar offensive, which was withdrawn by mid-October, there were no major military land operations on the Western Front during this time. Instead, France's armies waited for the Germans to attack, and when they did, France hoped to keep the enemy at bay and minimize the loss of life.

France's leaders were tired, politically divided, and still haunted by the memories of the Great War, when a generation of young men had been lost and more than four percent of France's population killed. The French public was not in a rush to get into another war with Germany, particularly one that would be fought again on

French soil. The French weren't pacifists, but they were wary and cautious. If machine guns, artillery, and barbed wire had soaked their land with the blood of millions during the Great War, surely another war with more advanced technology and air power would be far more destructive. This time the government vowed to be prepared, but their military plan would be passive. They would be patient and wait. Their armies would defend France from invasion, but they would not be the first to strike.

These months were quite difficult, and we had cause for our concerns. After Josef was released from the internment camp, conditions were imposed. He had to report to the police several times each week. The entire time was uncertain; a nerve-wracking freedom would be the best way to describe it. While Josef was able to continue his work at the hospital, we kept to ourselves and were not comfortable straying far from our apartment. Our German accents aroused suspicion. One never knew what might come next.

It would not be until May of 1940, the following year, that Germany launched its attacks on Belgium, the Netherlands, and Luxembourg. Then France's fears were realized. The invasion of the Low Countries marked the beginning of the Nazi incursion onto French soil. Within days of the German offensive, French internal security authorities launched another round of internments to detain enemy aliens. Again they were concerned that there might be spies in their midst, a dangerous fifth column that might be providing intelligence to the enemy.

French surveillance was even more heightened, and their efforts intensified.

Immediately large red posters appeared on the lampposts of Paris, announcing that all *ressortissants allemands*, all those from Germany, were to report at once to the Vélodrome d'Hiver, the winter sports stadium, for interviews and investigation. Again we were told to bring one piece of luggage, two days of food, a blanket, and utensils.

Arrests and detentions were carried out without regard to who might have been previously considered and released. All enemy aliens were under suspicion. This time the order was expanded. For the first time since the war had begun, women and children were included. Now both Josef and I were under orders to be detained.

We complied the following morning. When we arrived at the stadium, in the crowded confusion, we lost track of one another. There were so many anxious people, and we were sent to different lines for processing. I remember how nervous I was, fearful that they would make inquiries about my brother in Germany. I had no idea what kinds of problems that could cause. After my interrogation, I was detained in a room beneath the stadium for two days before being loaded onto a train with several hundred other women and some children. We were taken to the Gurs internment camp in the foothills of the Pyrenees, in Southwestern France, about eighty kilometers from the Spanish border.

When Josef disappeared from my sight, I became frantic and desperate. I knew nothing of his fate, and the authorities were unwilling to assist. Perhaps if we had been married, our situation might have been different, but we did not share the same surname, and despite my anguished pleas, no one cared to take the time to search. I had no way to know.

That week, for the first time in my thirty-year life, the pendulum in the mahogany clock by my bedside stopped its swing. No one would hear the steady ticking or the sound of its chime. The brass key remained untouched. There was no one left to wind the clock every eighth day. Our apartment was empty.

Fifty-Nine

I knew nothing of Gurs. It was a name I had never heard mentioned before the day I was sent there. I soon learned that it was one of the first and largest pre-war internment camps established in France. It was constructed to detain the Spanish refugees who had fled across the border when Franco's armies had advanced into Catalonia during the Spanish Civil War.

After giving this a great deal of thought, I have decided to write only a few words about my experience in Gurs, only enough to record this history. There is little I wish to share and even less that I wish to remember.

My lasting memory of Gurs is the overpowering smell, so strong that it was difficult not to become sick. I had to clench my hands, hold my breath, and close my eyes. I will never forget the horrid odor, how it seeped deep into the pores of my skin. I thought I would never be able to remove it from my body or my clothes or wash it from my hair. I remember worrying whether Josef would ever love me again. Oh, how I cried at that thought. The smell was damp and disgusting, fetid and foul. It filled the air and burned my eyes. There was no way to escape. We could not see it, but it held us tightly within its grasp.

The Gurs camp conditions were horrible, and I was unprepared. There were shortages of food and water. All we were fed was a cup of watery turnip soup with a little bread twice each day. I have no idea how many of us were held there, but it seemed as if there were thousands. The camp was enormous. There were hundreds of barracks, some holding as many as sixty women. A seven-foot-tall barbed-wire fence surrounded the entire camp.

Gurs was built on swampy ground with no drainage. We were not far from the Atlantic Ocean, which others claimed contributed to the frequent torrential rainstorms. The grounds were always muddy, covered with a grayish, slippery clay that never seemed to dry. Small stones had been used to create pathways throughout the camp, but it seemed that the mud would always be ankle-deep whenever one needed to use the toilet.

People would slip and fall. Someone removed the barbs from a piece of wire fencing to create rails to hold onto, but the mud was so slippery and deep that the wire hardly made a difference. If you tried to hold the wire and fell, you would cut your hand or slice your finger. Then you would be in far worse trouble because, while the camp had doctors, they had no medicine.

The barracks were hastily built out of flimsy wood and covered with fabric. There were no windows and no protection from the weather as most of the fabric was severely worn and deteriorated. When it rained, there were leaks everywhere, and it was impossible to keep the inside of the barracks dry. There was no lighting. We were crowded together and slept on crude mattresses stuffed with bags of mildewed straw. The barracks were infested with rodents, and everyone complained about the fleas and the lice.

The toilets were primitive: a board with a hole and a tank that overflowed below. There was no paper or supplies to clean oneself, and there was no privacy. What made this worse was that there were very few showers and not nearly enough washbasins. Most of us had only one change of clothes. None of us were clean, and most of us were filthy. I know some did not wash the entire time we were there. Fortunately, the time I spent in Gurs was relatively short. You can imagine how many suffered from typhoid and dysentery.

One thing I have to say is that the detainees who were sent there were organized. We had to be. It was the only way to keep our situation from becoming worse and to keep ourselves sane. Apart from roll calls, there was little to do, so people arranged themselves into various groups, such as handiwork classes, discussions on different subjects, anything to keep busy and one's spirits up, something that was very difficult to do in a place like Gurs. In the evenings, there were often musical performances of one sort or another. I suppose what made this passable is that we shared this horrible situation together and everyone looked out for one another.

There was little news but many rumors. We knew nothing of the war. Letters were allowed, but I quickly learned that many detainees were in the same situation as me. We were separated from our loved ones and had no idea where to find them or when these days would end. All we could do was lean upon one another and hope and pray that we would survive.

Sixty

Events happened quickly, much faster than most expected. Unlike the Great War, the Battle of France was decided within six weeks. France, Belgium, Luxembourg, and the Netherlands all quickly fell to the Germans. Once the French front was breached, France's defeat was all but certain.

Early on a Friday in mid-June, a little over a month after I arrived at Gurs, German troops marched victoriously into Paris. A line of Panzer tanks rumbled from the Arc de Triomphe down the Champs Elysees to the Place de la Concorde. They were met with no resistance. French and Allied forces had already retreated.

To avoid loss of life and the total destruction of Paris, the French military governor declared Paris an open city, and the government left to reestablish itself in Bordeaux. By early afternoon, a gigantic swastika was flying beneath the Arc de Triomphe, and loudspeaker announcements were heard throughout the city. An 8:00

pm curfew was put in place. Paris had fallen, and the German army was now in control.

◆

The following Monday, six hundred kilometers from Paris, at the camp in Bassens, Josef joined a delegation of detainees who appeared before their camp commander. There had been frightening air raid attacks in the area the night before. The German Luftwaffe had begun their bombing of nearby Bordeaux. The detainees pleaded for their release. They claimed their lives were at risk.

That night the bombing continued, and by the next morning, the panicked camp authorities ordered the gates to be opened. It was a humanitarian gesture. All detainees with families in France or who were persecuted by Germany were released with instructions to proceed southward to be out of harm's way. Suddenly and miraculously, Josef was granted his freedom.

◆

Less than a week later, the following Saturday, an armistice was signed in Northern France, at Compiègne, by officials of Nazi Germany and the French government. France had conceded. The ceasefire agreement divided France into two parts – a German-occupied territory with its capital in Paris and an unoccupied region centered in Southern France, in the resort town of Vichy, where a new authoritarian government would be responsible for the civil administration of France and its colonies. Germany was given marine access to all French Channel and Atlantic ports.

◆

Article Nineteen of the armistice was significant, but in the confusion that followed, its implementation was not immediate. France was required to turn over to German authorities any German national on French territory. This was primarily directed at German Jews, like Josef, who, until the war began, had enjoyed their freedom in France.

Several months later, many of the German Jews detained as a result of this clause would be deported to concentration camps. Josef managed to escape this sentence by the thinnest of margins. Had he not been released from the Bassens camp four days earlier, he might have been one of those imprisoned by the Germans and sent to their deaths by the Nazis.

◆

I, too, was given my release. The evening the armistice was signed, my release order was issued. The following day I was told I was free to leave the Gurs camp. Since the German military campaign against France had been successful, all non-Jewish Germans, pro-Nazis, and communists held in Gurs were immediately released.

◆

304 | RALPH WEBSTER

I don't know how any of this can make sense. Josef and I were both German. Germany had been our home. It was the home of our parents and grandparents. Now we were released from internment camps but for entirely opposite reasons.

He was Jewish. I was not. It was as if we were enemies of one another. Josef was released from the Bassens camp by the French to save his life. Now there was little question. He was considered a threat to the Germans because he was a German Jew. I was given my release from Gurs because I was not a threat to the Germans. I was a non-Jewish German. When I was freed from Gurs, my Jewish roommates were still detained.

Mamarella had been right when she had asked, "Could one be German if one was a Jew? Could one be Jewish if one were German?"

Sixty-One

Our plan was always to return to Paris. That was our agreement, one of the last things we had spoken about before we each were interrogated by the authorities at the Vélodrome d'Hiver. If we became separated, we would reunite at the Paris apartment. Whoever was there first would wait for the other.

There was no other plan we could possibly make, and we knew of no other place to go. That day, we had had no idea how long we would be detained or where we would be held. And while neither of us believed that the German army would succeed in its ambitions, neither were we confident that France could withstand the attack.

When I was told of my release from the Gurs camp, it was sudden and unexpected. I was given no advance notice and knew few details about the progress of the war. Even when the guards told us that Paris had fallen, we did not know what or who to believe or whether this had actually occurred. So much was uncertain, including my status. While my papers were in order, they said little, only that I was an unmarried, unemployed German national living in Paris. There was no mention of my relationship with Josef or that my religion was evangelical. The one thing I knew when I was released was where to go. I would use the little money I had to find my way to the Oloron-Sainte-Marie train station and search for connections to take me to Paris. Then I would wait in the apartment to hear from Josef.

As I silently walked down the muddy, rutted road, through the imposing Gurs camp gates, and took my first breaths of fresh air, I strained to believe my eyes. At first, I thought it was a mirage. This couldn't be possible. How could this be? Josef was standing across the road, smiling and waiting to greet me.

All I remember of that moment was running to him, reaching for his arms, and touching his face. There was no hesitation. I never stopped to consider how I must have smelled. When Josef put his arms around me, I knew he didn't care. Whatever worries I might have had suddenly disappeared. All we could do was hold on to one another and cry. I never wanted to let go. We held each other for a very long time.

◆

It was only through a stroke of luck that Josef was able to be there, waiting, when I was released. What I did not know was that he had been told that I would be detained at the Gurs camp. In Paris, at the Vélodrome d'Hiver, before being sent to Bassens, he had learned this information. When Josef was set free from Bassens, he followed the exodus southward, trying to stay safe. The roads were filled with those fleeing areas controlled by the Germans, and he was able to find a ride that took him to the town of Pau.

Once a flourishing turn-of-the-century winter resort for Europe's nobility, Pau was located at one end of the Canfranc railway, now a crossroads for refugees. The Gurs camp was not far, no more than forty kilometers. In Pau, he found lodging in the Continental Hotel, already becoming known as a friendly refuge for those trying to escape.

That evening, in the crowded bar, he learned that a number of German prisoners were expected to be released from Gurs within days, as soon as the armistice was signed. Hearing this news, he made his way to the Gurs gates, where he joined others who were camped out across the road, waiting for their loved ones.

◆

When we were reunited, Josef promised we would never be separated again because we did not share the same last name. The very next day, Monday, June 24, 1940, I walked a short distance along a dirt road to my wedding and became Kaethe Samson. Josef and I were married by the clerk at the town hall in Préchacq-Josbaig, a tiny village only a few kilometers south of Gurs.

◆

Josef chose to share few details about his time at Bassens. All I learned was that the camp was in an abandoned old powder mill on the bank of the Garonne River that had been quickly converted to hold undesirable prisoners. Eleven hundred men were confined there. Nearly one-third were German soldiers who had been captured by the French at the beginning of the war, a situation that made this confinement very difficult. I chose to refrain from asking Josef any other questions. Too much had happened. I think we both felt better that way.

Sixty-Two

O nce we were together, the question that still remained was where to go next. Returning to Paris was ruled out, at least not until we had more reliable information. The reports were inconsistent: rumors and opinions, with few facts, at least none that we could depend upon. Traveling to Paris could be dangerous, and once there, we were unsure whether Josef's safety would be in jeopardy. It was clear that he would not be permitted to resume his work at the hospital.

My situation was different. With my German papers, it seemed that I might be able to travel freely throughout France, but we couldn't be entirely confident. The best solution was to stay out of harm's way and find a safe place to live until the situation settled. Then we would have a better idea of what the next step should be.

Josef proposed Soumoulou, a very small village less than twenty kilometers from Pau. A gentleman he met at the bar in the Continental Hotel, as I recall a sympathetic Gurs prison guard, had recommended Soumoulou

310 | RALPH WEBSTER

to Josef and given him a card for his friend Baptiste Rey, the owner of the Restaurant du Commerce. When we arrived, Monsieur Rey introduced us to the supervisor of the local train station, a person who had assisted many fleeing refugees. With her help, we were able to make contact with an area farmer who rented us a few furnished rooms in the rear of his house on the edge of the village. Our new landlord's biggest concern was that we had the funds to pay the rent, not whether we were German or that one of us was Jewish.

What an unexpected change this was for me. I instantly fell in love with the tiny village of Soumoulou. Perhaps it was because of all we had been through. I felt safe there, but I think it was something more. This was an entirely different way of living. I was a city girl, accustomed to the commotion and sounds of city streets, and this was the country. I had never lived in a place so quiet and peaceful.

The fresh air was wonderful. It was the perfect setting to forget the foul smell of Gurs. And in Soumoulou, we were finally able to live as husband and wife. This was our honeymoon. No one bothered us. We kept to ourselves and used bikes to ride along the country road to the small shop in the village, though only when supplies were needed. Everywhere Josef looked, he could find wonderful landscapes to paint, and for the first time in my life, I was able to plant a flower garden.

◆

In those days, after the armistice was signed and the fighting in France quieted, Germany's war machinery began to shift elsewhere, and nearly all the French people we encountered were sympathetic to our plight. The local police were more indifferent, certainly more official, and perhaps not quite as friendly. But while they claimed to know little, at least they left us alone. The Gestapo? They remained a continuing threat. But as threatening as they were, even they were confused. That summer it seemed that everyone in France was waiting for orders.

Among the French, at least those in the countryside, on one topic, there was little confusion. The Germans were viewed as unwelcome intruders. Despite the armistice, France did not give up entirely or easily. There continued to be small roving bands of armed militias and pockets of resistance. And although we often heard that the German response would be to take control of unoccupied France, this was an oft-repeated threat that never was acted upon.

As for the Jewish population in France, it would be several months before the Gestapo would begin any concerted action. Everything appeared to be at a standstill as the Vichy government grappled with how to manage the unoccupied areas. And while the Germans turned their attention to Paris and the areas within their control, we were told they needed to undertake a census of the Jewish population. Without this information, no systematic roundup of the Jews in occupied France was possible. The records were incomplete. It had been well over half a century since a census listing religion had been conducted.

Although there were isolated reports of Jewish-owned shops on the Champs-Élysées being stoned by French Nazis, by mid-September, we felt we had learned enough to believe that it would be safe to make a brief return to Paris. Our departure had been sudden and abrupt. Now we needed a few days to close our apartment and arrange our affairs. And while we had heard that the German ambassador had organized an effort to expropriate property from some of Paris's well known and wealthier Jewish families, we knew that this would have little to do with us. If we minded our own business and were careful and cautious, there was no reason to be overly concerned.

By train, the trip from Pau took six hours. We encountered no problems. No questions were asked, even when we crossed the border from Vichy France to the area directly controlled by the Germans. In Paris, we were able to make arrangements for everything in the apartment to be sent to Pau and placed into storage. As it turned out, our timing could not have been better. Only days after we returned to Soumoulou, the Gestapo ordered all Jews in Paris to register with authorities.

There was one surprise, fortunate for us, but for Josef, perhaps bittersweet and a lingering reminder of his past. In Paris, a letter from the United States was waiting. An attorney from San Francisco had written that Camilla, the mother of his first wife, Hilda, had died. Josef was named as a beneficiary in her will and had been left an inheritance of seven thousand dollars, an enormous sum of money to us.

Josef had never mentioned any correspondence with Mrs. Samson, so I have no idea whether Hilda's mother was aware of our difficult situation. All Josef told me was that he had written to her with his address years earlier, shortly after he had moved to Paris. In any event, receiving these funds was truly a gift from heaven.

◆

Josef seldom spoke about Hilda. I never had the impression that he was trying to conceal anything, only that her death was a matter he chose not to share, something that had occurred when I was still a young child.

When he did speak of Hilda, he spoke sparingly, never more than a few words, but always kindly and with gentle affection. He would only say that this was something that had taken place in the past. It had happened long ago, in another life, and had little to do with me. Nevertheless, while I knew little of her, I have always felt a certain kinship, the sense that she and I shared a close connection.

After I moved in with Josef, Hilda's possessions became my possessions. Now her husband had become my husband, and I suppose, in some strange and curious way, I sometimes felt that I was finishing the life that she had once started. We drank from the wine glasses and ate from the plates that she and Josef had received when they were married. I put flowers in vases her mother had given her. I read books that had been inscribed by her uncle. I wore her watches and hatpins, and Josef insisted that I wear her rings, necklaces, and other jewelry. And somehow I have managed to convince myself that our eyes might have met once, that day Mutti and I took my brother Fritz to see the doctor at the hospital in Kreuzberg, the day I remember because Fritz vanished from my life.

◆

Neither of us slept much that final evening. It was one of those times when sleep did not easily come no matter how tired we were. We had spent our days packing the things to be shipped to Pau, and we both knew it would be our last night in Paris.

The apartment seemed lifeless and empty, as if it knew that this was not our home anymore. The dark edges of faded shadows filled the walls where pictures had once hung, and the floors echoed with our footsteps when we walked through the rooms. All that remained untouched was the furniture, left for the movers. They would pack what was left into large crates to be placed into storage.

It was well past midnight when I wrapped my arms around Josef and pulled him close. That night, for the first time, he tearfully told me the story of Hilda's death, the story I had not known, how he had rushed home to find her lying on the floor, how he had lost all that was good, how she and their unborn child had died, how he had spent years trying to forget the events of that day, a history too sad to be remembered.

By morning, we decided to leave all these unpleasant memories behind. Josef's inheritance would allow us to begin a new life in America. Now all that was left was to find our way there.

◆

Before returning to Soumoulou, Josef had one last stop to make. We borrowed a colleague's car and drove to Loire to see his old friend Moïche. We found him with hammer and nails, busily packing his paintings into large wooden boxes. He and his wife, Bella, were preparing to move to Gordes, a half-abandoned medieval village on the foothills of the Monts de Vaucluse, near Avignon and not far from Marseilles. There they had rented an ancient stone house and planned to wait out the war. Neither had an interest in leaving France.

Josef was convinced that Moïche could help with our arrangements. He had a connection, someone who was urging Moïche and Bella to leave France and was able to obtain the necessary papers and find berths on a ship to the United States. Before we left to return to Paris that day, Moïche gave us the name and address of a man in Marseille, and he handed Josef an envelope containing a penned note of introduction. Then we hugged and wished one another good luck.

◆

With nothing more to do in Paris, we found our way to the train station and boarded the train to take us back to Soumoulou. There would be no reason to ever return. And again our luck held. Within days, the Germans would restrict travel between the occupied and unoccupied zones. Then there was the immediate danger of police arrest and Gestapo deportation. And for those who successfully crossed from one side to the other, there was no assurance that one would be allowed to return to their homes.

When we left, we carried little from the apartment – a few of Josef's painting supplies, some clothes, and not much more. In Soumoulou, our needs were simple. Before turning the locks on the apartment door, I went to the bedroom and collected the rounded-arch, mahogany Hofuhrmacher clock. That, I would take.

In Soumoulou, it could sit by my bedside. I needed its companionship and comfort. There we could both watch the pendulum swing and listen to the sound of its chime. America was our destination, and there were reasons to be hopeful. It was time to pick up the brass key. We needed to wind the clock again.

Sixty-Three

W e were not alone. All those trying to leave Europe were aware of the difficult problems one needed to overcome. It was not only a matter of finding a way to an open seaport and booking berths on a ship. Wanting to flee to America did not mean that one was able to go to America. We needed visas. Entry to the United States was not based upon country of origin, citizenship, or passport. It was based upon the country of birth. There were quotas, legal limits on the number of people who could enter in any given year.

These quotas had been set when America's immigration acts were passed in the early 1920s, when certain groups of immigrants were deemed more desirable to America's interests than others. Despite Germany's efforts to force the Jews out of their borders and the life-and-death pleas of those attempting to leave the war in Europe, these laws had not changed. Even President

Roosevelt refused to consider a request for special quotas for those fleeing the Nazi horrors.

Josef and I were subject to the German quota, and the numbers were staggering. We were told that three hundred thousand Germans were trying to leave Europe for the United States. America's German quota only allowed for less than one-tenth of that number, twenty-six thousand in any one calendar year.

In fairness, the United States was not the only country struggling to find the answer to the refugee issue. The entire world had found reasons to limit immigration. I remember when we heard that passengers on the *St. Louis*, the ship that departed from Hamburg, were prevented from disembarking in Cuba and how they were turned away by the United States and Canada. Then they were forced to return to Europe. That was when the Nazi's propaganda boasted that this was all the proof needed. No country in the world wanted the Jews. What were those poor people supposed to do? Can you imagine? To be so close and have to turn around and then be thrown back into this nightmare?

Immigration, allowing people to enter one's borders, was a controversial debate in the United States. It was a divisive topic and subject to the strong opinions of America's politicians and the American public. While there was a compassionate and genuine concern expressed by many who wanted to assist refugees fleeing from Europe, there was a continuing drumbeat of vocal and persistent opposition.

The Great Depression had taken its toll. Many were not prepared to give jobs to immigrants when there were not enough for American citizens. Others were afraid that enemy agents might pose as refugees. Some mistakenly thought that government resources would be needed for our care and feeding. They didn't understand that we were required to have sponsors who would make guarantees for our care. Anti-Semitism remained prevalent, and people were misinformed, too often intentionally. And still others refused to believe or had no interest in caring about what was going on beyond America's shores. Apathy was a terrible curse.

◆

By early fall, we heard the whispers, frightening rumors that the new Vichy government would soon be issuing decrees with regard to the Jews in unoccupied areas. In October, rumor became fact when the Vichy regime issued the Statut des Juifs, laws similar to Germany's Nuremberg decrees, which banned Jews from most aspects of public life. Then, at Germany's urging, the Vichy government began to arrest foreign Jews, particularly Jews like Josef, who had been released from camps during the confusion of the summer months.

I never learned whether this was actually true, but some claimed that those in mixed marriages like ours were excluded from this order. True or not, we were not about to take any unnecessary risks.

That October we traveled to Marseilles to meet the man Moïche recommended to see if he could help us. We had a good excuse to go there and a safe way to do so. Josef's inheritance papers needed to be signed by the American consul based in Marseilles, and the prefecture in Pau had granted us safe conduct passes for our visit.

I am not at all certain that we needed passes because, at that time, it was still pretty safe to travel without papers. However, one needed to be careful because you never knew when you could be stopped and what might result. The Marseille train station had a well-deserved reputation for this practice. The police routinely checked the papers of arriving passengers. Even with our passes, to be extra cautious, when we arrived, we did what others told us to do. We avoided the police checkpoint by leaving through the rear of the station restaurant and following the corridor to the exit door behind the kitchen.

As we left Gare de Marseille Saint-Charles, I remember our amazement. The streets of Marseilles were crowded and busy, an enormous change from the peace and quiet of Soumoulou. It wasn't only refugee families who filled the streets and created the commotion. Trainloads of soldiers were arriving on their way to Southern France and Northern Africa, and there was a continuous flow of people walking in and out of the station doors and parading up and down the boulevards of the Canebiere and Vieux Port.

It was quite a colorful sight. We saw the Senegalese with their turbans, cavalry officers dressed in khaki

tunics and riding breeches, soldiers who had been sta-
tioned along the Maginot Line wearing their gray jump-
ers, French mountain infantrymen in their olive-green
uniforms, wearing large berets that hung over their left
ears, Algerians and Tunisians with broad black sashes
around their waists, Zouaves from North Africa in baggy
Turkish trousers, and the bright red fezzes of the French
Foreign Legion. Everyone was closely packed together –
pushing, shoving, jostling. The restaurants and cafes
were filled.

◆

Moïche had given Josef the address for Varian Fry, a
young Harvard-educated American from New York who
had come to Marseilles as the agent for the Emergency
Rescue Committee, a group assisting Jews trying to flee
the Nazis, especially artists and intellectuals. We met
with Mr. Fry not long after his arrival. He had been in
Marseilles for less than two months and was still getting
organized. His office was in a converted and crowded
hotel room on the fourth floor of the Hotel Splendide on
the Boulevard d' Athens, only a brief walk from the train
station.

When we arrived, papers were scattered everywhere,
and there was hardly any room to sit down. Our meeting
was cordial and brief. It was clear that Mr. Fry was a very
busy young man who had limited funds, a challenging
position, and very specific priorities. I believe that the
personal note from Moïche helped, and there was no

question that Josef's inheritance had become an important factor in our favor.

An assistant even asked to view some of Josef's artwork to see if he was an artist worthy of their assistance. We left with no commitments or promises, but Mr. Fry assured us that he would personally look into our situation and cautioned that it would be some time before we would hear anything more. He wished us well.

Then, after Josef signed the inheritance papers at the American consulate, we returned to Soumoulou to sit and wait. I must say that we were both disappointed. We had hoped for more but were helpless. There was little more that we could do.

◆

Years later, after the war was over, I learned more about the extent of Fry's work. When we met with him, he was still in the early stages of creating an elaborate network, searching for any means possible to circumvent French officials, who were refusing to issue exit visas to Jews.

With the support of a small group of volunteers, refugees who were unable to travel legally and those targeted by the Nazis were often hidden at the Villa Air-Bel, a château on the outskirts of Marseille. There they would avoid detection until they could be smuggled out, either by foot or by boat. Then they were taken across the border to Spain, where they traveled to the safety of neutral Portugal. There were occasions when papers were forged, but mostly this was a process of finding friendly assistance.

Fry worked closely with a senior U.S. State Department official based in Marseilles, a man sympathetic to the situation who was able to issue entry visas to many of those in need. From Marseille, the Emergency Rescue Committee also worked closely with the Unitarian Service Committee in Lisbon, which was able to find berths on ships. And someone else, who remained unknown, was able to secure the necessary transit visas for Spain and Portugal.

Sixty-Four

It wasn't long after we returned to Soumoulou that we learned the Vichy government had started their campaign to arrest foreign Jews and send them to internment camps for deportation. Even in our small village, we waited in fear as patrols drew nearer and nearer. It was very unsettling. Day and night, we always felt threatened. One never knew if the noise on the steps or the sudden knock at the door might be the police coming to arrest Josef.

We had no way of knowing that it would actually be several months before general roundups began. Then they would start in Marseilles, and the arrests of Jews would take place primarily in the larger cities. At first, the small villages and rural areas were largely ignored by Vichy officials.

Having this information would have been helpful, perhaps allowing us to relax in these moments, but we couldn't and always remained wary. There was an additional worry. The police didn't need mass roundups as their excuse to arrest the Jews. There were stories about swindlers and blackmailers who threatened to alert the authorities.

I never learned whether these rumors were true, but we could never ignore them, and fortunately, we were never subjected to such blackmail. I have always felt that French citizens would rather protect us than report us. Most we met were disgusted and repelled by German behavior.

There were alarming moments, moments that left us fearful and uncertain. On more than one occasion, patrols came through Soumoulou and passed by the small house where we were staying. While usually a friendly and caring soul from the village would alert us, at other times, there was no forewarning. Then, when the patrols arrived, we had no idea whether the police were searching for Josef, whether someone had reported his presence, or whether it was simply a chance encounter.

I remember how upsetting and sudden this would be. Taking no risks, Josef would rush me, literally push me, out the rear door. Together we would run through the fields, towards the Limendous Forest, where he had created a place to hide, a shelter hidden in a thicket behind some trees. We had prepared for this possibility and vowed to never become separated again. If we were caught, we would take our own lives. Each of us carried capsules Josef had retrieved from his medical supplies in Paris.

Months went by with little additional word from Mr. Fry or his associates in Marseilles. Occasionally we would hear something, enough to know that they were working on our case, but we had no idea when or how we might depart. And while we continued to largely keep to ourselves, our kind neighbors in Soumoulou helped and looked over us. I will always be grateful. They were concerned for our safety and kept us informed.

That fall the Vichy government severely limited exit visas, a nightmare for fleeing refugees trying to reach the seaport in Lisbon. It was not possible to leave France without these papers. Next it became difficult to obtain transit visas permitting one to enter Portugal. Too many visas had been issued by the sympathetic Portuguese Cônsul General Aristides de Sousa Mendes in Bordeaux, and transit visas could no longer be issued without telegraphed case-by-case approval from Lisbon. Soon Spain issued similar regulations for their transit visas and went a step further when they refused to recognize affidavits in lieu of passports issued by the U.S. consulate in Marseilles.

As it took time for the required approvals to be granted, it became almost impossible to be issued visas valid for the same dates, a problem compounded by needing a ticket or proof of a berth on a ship before Portuguese officials would allow one to enter Lisbon. With proper papers, Spain and Portugal would allow fleeing refugees to pass through, to enter and exit, but neither country was prepared to shoulder the expense of indigent refugees staying within their borders for any length of time.

Finally, in January of 1941, the Vichy government announced a new policy that made it easier to obtain an exit permit. Evidently, the Gestapo and other secret police had completed the task of going over the lists of political and intellectual refugees in France and had decided who must stay and who would be permitted to leave. The irony was that by the time the Vichy authorities eased their restrictions, Spain and Portugal had made their approval procedures even more difficult.

As for the battles and the war, we remained well out of danger. There was no fighting in France. Germany's attention was focused on Yugoslavia, Greece, and the conflict in North Africa. From broadcasts on Spanish radio, we knew that Germany was bombing London and Great Britain's Royal Navy had begun shelling industrial areas and naval ports in Southern Italy. A few months later, we learned that over three million German troops had begun their massive invasion of Russia.

The longer we waited, the more uncertain our situation became. By spring, there was no question. We knew we were in grave danger. In early April, the police became more menacing and stepped up their activities. Jews staying in Marseilles hotels were arrested when Vichy police swept through the city. Controls at the Cerbere-Portbou border, one of the two legal ways to cross into Spain, were tightened. The guards there were rumored to have their own way of conducting business, and the border, when it opened and closed, followed no fixed schedule. Many were stranded for days when it would close in no predictable way.

In late May, the Vichy government began a systematic registration and census of all Jews in the unoccupied area. Josef was required to fill out a long questionnaire, listing bank accounts, securities, and real estate. Then everyone's whereabouts became known, and we all understood that it was only a matter of time. The police knew how to find us. They could do so without warning, whenever they chose.

One day Josef received a brief letter from Moïche. He and Bella had changed their minds. They had decided to leave France. While visiting Marseilles, Moïche had been arrested, and Bella had become frantic. Fortunately, he was quickly released after intervention by Varian Fry and others. They would leave for America as soon as final arrangements could be made. He encouraged us to remain hopeful.

◆

Later we would learn that Moïche and Bella were able to successfully cross into Spain by train and continue their journey to Lisbon, where they boarded a ship to take them to America. However, Spanish authorities were pressured by the Gestapo to hold up the transfer of his paintings. It would be months before the paintings were released and found their way safely across the Atlantic.

Sixty-Five

I t wasn't only the European countries that were making it difficult to leave. Our situation became much bleaker when the United States issued a series of measures designed to tighten their immigration policies even further.

In June, the American consulate in Marseilles received new instructions. Consul generals were directed not to admit anyone, including those in Vichy France, to the United States if there was any doubt about their political reliability. A second regulation forbade the granting of a visa to anyone with close relatives in an Axis-occupied territory. Visas could not be granted except on specific authorization from the U.S. State Department after a security review by various officials.

We had no idea what this might mean for us, if I would be prevented from being approved for a visa if the activities of my brother Karl became known. Josef and I had many tearful conversations. I pleaded and pleaded with him to be prepared to leave without me, but he

329

refused to even consider the possibility. We would wait and remain hopeful that this issue could be avoided. I found this to be a terribly difficult time and worried about what might happen next. There were stories that those held in internment camps were being loaded on trains like cattle and sent to Nazi concentration camps.

Finally, one day in early August of 1941, we received the message from Marseilles we had been waiting for. All the necessary documents were being prepared, and arrangements had been made. Our visas had been approved. We would be sent to Lisbon and could go to America. We should plan to depart for Marseilles as soon as possible. Then, the next day, we received a second message. This time it was frantic. All plans had been canceled. We were told to continue to remain in Soumoulou.

Vichy authorities had been watching Varian Fry's activities for months. He had been detained and questioned by the police, and now the Vichy government had acted. Fry had been ordered to leave France immediately. He would no longer be able to assist us. He had been sent back to America. There was little we could do. We were devastated.

◆

We were never told, but I can only assume that the Vichy authorities were aware that there were other groups based in Marseilles who were continuing the work of the Emergency Rescue Committee. Within days, one sent a message. We should not give up hope. They had been given our file and documents. They would help. You can imagine our relief.

At their request, I traveled to Marseilles. I went on my own. There was no choice. It was far too dangerous for Josef to accompany me. Additional funds were necessary to cover the cost of our berths, and more time would be required to finalize the arrangements, but I returned to Soumoulou convinced that we would leave soon. And this time the plans were not thwarted.

◆

In mid-November of 1941, seventeen months after we arrived in Soumoulou, we received safe conduct passes and left for Marseilles. There we were given the necessary papers and train tickets to take us to Lisbon, where berths on a ship had been booked. I have never learned how these arrangements were made, whether any of our papers were falsified or whether any of their stamps were the work of forgers.

I have no idea whether any officials were bribed or whether there were any misleading statements. And I do not know why or how our U.S. immigration visas were expedited. I have no reason to suspect that anything illicit occurred and have never asked for the answers to any of these questions. I never will. What I do know is that was when we were able to begin our long-awaited journey to America.

Sixty-Six

Others have asked what might have happened had we not been able to leave for the United States when we did. I will never know the answer, but I am convinced of one certainty: our fate would have been out of our control and left in the hands of others.

Months before we left, many of Europe's exits had closed. Already Jewish refugees in Belgium and occupied France were prevented from leaving. And in the final days before we departed, Germany stopped any Jewish migration from other Nazi-occupied countries and began deporting Jews to their concentration camps. That fall, as we were leaving, many Jews in Vichy France held in internment camps, like Gurs and Bassens, were loaded into railroad cars and given this death sentence.

By the middle of 1941, five months before we left France, Germany had begun the first phase of the mass murder of Jews. The Nazis used mobile killing units to extinguish thousands of lives across the occupied eastern territories. And by year's end, the Final Solution,

Germany's mass extermination of Jews, was well underway. Then, across all German-occupied Europe, captured Jews were sent on death trains to concentration camps, where they were murdered.

I suppose, living in Vichy France, in Soumoulou, it is possible that our fate may have been different, that we might have survived, but I will never know. What I know is that we were fortunate. Josef and I never had to learn the answer to that question.

◆

Our journey from Marseilles to Lisbon took a little more than five days by train. The route began by retracing some of our steps, and we were able to have one last look at familiar places. After departing Marseilles, we traveled to Toulouse and then back to Pau, where we changed to the single-track Pau-Canfranc railway.

At the Pau train station, as if by magic, all of our crated possessions shipped from Paris and kept in storage suddenly reappeared. I watched in amazement as the three large crates, including Josef's piano, which had been unassembled for transport, were lifted by crane and loaded onto the train. Somehow, in the rush of those moments, I failed to ask Josef how he had accomplished this feat.

◆

As we left Pau, the train quickly passed by the small train platform in Soumoulou before making a stop at the

Oloron-Sainte-Marie station, near the Gurs internment camp. I will never forget the terribly sad event we witnessed that day.

At Oloron, a group of children on our train pressed their faces against the windows and waved their final goodbyes to family members standing near the tracks at the station. These were prisoners who had been brought from Gurs. They were allowed to stand and see the faces of their children. At least they were given hope that their children would survive.

No one has ever told me the fate of those parents who stood on the Oloron platform that day, but I can only imagine that most never lived to see their children again.

◆

After Oloron, the train crossed the L'Estanguet bridge and climbed the foothills of the Pyrenees and through Sompoert tunnel before reaching the Aragón Valley on the Spanish border, where it entered the immense Canfranc international railway station, the second largest in Europe. There, with France at our back and facing the gateway to Spain, our visas were stamped, first the exit visas allowing us to leave France by Vichy officials and then the transit visas to cross Spain by Spanish border guards. Then we boarded the train that carried us to Zaragoza before going on to Madrid.

A problem with the connection caused a delay and forced us to spend two unplanned days and nights in Madrid. After converting our Vichy France currency to pesetas, we managed to find lodging, and in the midst of all of this commotion, Josef insisted on an afternoon tour of Madrid and a visit to the El Prado museum. Then we caught the train for the final day-long leg of this journey.

Sixty-Seven

For refugees escaping Europe, Lisbon was the last open gate, the last remaining way to leave the continent. Lisbon was the European capital least touched by the horrors of the war, a lively, hardworking port city of a half-million people in an underdeveloped country of six million that had direct access to the Atlantic Ocean.

The war had not come to Portugal. Antonio de Oliveira Salazar, Portugal's heavy-handed prime minister, had managed to maintain a position of neutrality, trying to preserve his regime by successfully staying on the sidelines despite extraordinary pressures exerted by the Allied and Axis powers. Both wanted Portugal's tungsten ore, a major material needed to manufacture the powerful weapons of war.

I am unable to fully recall my mix of emotions when the train passed through Lisbon's surrounding hills. I wish I could remember more as we slowed along the banks of the Tagus River and pulled into the old Santa

Apolónia railway station on the outskirts of Alfama. Before the doors opened, I can only recall the shrill squeal of the train's brakes, the hissing sound when the steam was released, and the slowing of the engine's vibration. I know we were relieved and elated, but my only clear memory is the sense that our long nightmare was finally over, that we had survived this journey.

We were both terribly exhausted, and I was concerned about Josef's health. He had carried the weight of our burden and was very much in need of some restful sleep. We had remained worried and guarded for such a long time. It had been months since we could truly relax.

Our Lisbon stay lasted nearly eight weeks. Although we arrived in late November, our ship, the *Nyassa*, was not scheduled to depart until late January of 1942. We were surprised to learn that most refugees were granted a less-than-thirty-day stay in Lisbon. I have no idea how it was that our documents allowed us to stay longer, but we were certainly grateful. I am not sure what we would have done, where we would have gone, or how we would have fared had we not been granted permission to remain in Lisbon for this extra amount of time.

A room had been booked in a private home in the Baixa district, an area that extends from the banks of the Tejo Estuary in the south up to the Praça Marquês de Pombal in the north and is situated between the two hills of the Alfama and Chiado districts, the historical part of Lisbon bound together by a series of squares. Since our accommodations were quite spartan, with no kitchen facilities, a bath shared with our neighbors, and space for only a writing desk, a chair, and a small bed, much of our time in Lisbon was spent walking the narrow cobblestone streets of the Baixa, resting on park benches, and sitting in one of Lisbon's many modest and small outdoor cafes, where we shared our meals.

We did so in the company of others, trying to make the best of a difficult situation, as that is how most managed to survive those days. These outdoor venues became our daytime homes. They were our living quarters. We saw faces that became familiar.

Whether wealthy or poor, most of us in Lisbon shared a common anxiety and often felt a continuing threat. Perhaps we had expected too much when we had arrived. We had thought our time in Lisbon would be restful and peaceful, a time for our anxieties to lessen. To our disappointment, we both found it difficult to relax, and we remained on edge for nearly all the days we were there.

It seemed there was always an observable undercurrent of activity: silent, secretive, and worrisome, the sense that other eyes were watching. It was clear that there were activities taking place around us, things that we knew little about, things we were not supposed to know.

Many worried that at any time, the Germans might decide to occupy Portugal, that we would be thrown back into the maelstrom of danger. Some days it was as if there was too much news. The newsstands were filled with a vast assortment of newspapers, written in every language and, all too often, with stories that led to contradictory conclusions. Suspicions were frequent, and again, the confusion continued. Rumors were rampant.

We never knew when we might be stopped on the street to have our documents examined. This could happen with little notice, a tap on the shoulder or the nod of a head, and always with a great amount of officialdom. This was not often, but when it did occur, we held our breaths, clenched our fists, and kept our silence.

We shared the fear that unbeknownst to us, our papers would not pass scrutiny for one reason or another. We did not see many, but we did see a few who, for reasons never told, were whisked away from the streets and never seen or heard from again. There was little doubt that among us, there were spies and double agents sympathetic to the Germans, who were well aware of the enemies list of intellectuals, writers, and artists maintained by the Gestapo. They would not hesitate to act when someone on the German list was spotted in Lisbon.

I suppose we both expected Lisbon to be more crowded, that there would be greater numbers who were fleeing. We had heard stories about the massive influx of those trying to leave and the difficulties many faced, particularly those who escaped by hiking over mountains and had found the way to Lisbon without documents. We had been told of the long lines and the scarce accommodations, of the high prices charged by those trying to take advantage of this desperate situation, but it seemed much of this had passed by the time we arrived, that many leaving Europe had already found their way out. We understood that the smaller numbers were a mournful reminder of this terrible situation. The reality was that most of Europe's borders had closed or were closing. Time was running out, and sadly, most who had not found their way to Lisbon by this time would never be given the chance to leave.

Fortunately for us, Josef's paintbrushes and easel were the perfect cure for our worries, a magical way to escape and find a tiny bit of happiness and privacy as we waited to leave this distant foreign place. Lisbon offered a fascinating collection of street scenes, and I spent many afternoons quietly observing as Josef enjoyed this favored pastime. With his brushes, he had an amazing ability to concentrate all of his attention on the smallest of details and remain oblivious to anything around him.

One afternoon we ventured near the covered market along the Praca da Figueira, where everyone feeds the pigeons, a delightful setting to watch the comings and goings of Lisbon. While Josef stood before his easel, silently working, wearing his painter's beret and frock, I sat on a park bench, quietly watching, basking in Lisbon's warm rays of sunshine on that cool late-November day.

I'm not sure what it was, perhaps the voice of a passerby or the cry from a young child, but something caused me to turn and look. In the distance, it appeared that someone was waving, trying to get my attention, and then I realized that I was looking at an older couple quickly walking our way. I suddenly jumped to my feet. I knew these people. Their faces were familiar. They

were smiling. How was this possible? It was the Oulmans, Mamarella and Paul, our old friends from the Pensione Alexandra in Naples. They were in Lisbon, too.

What a tearful, joyous reunion. Our time together
was brief. We learned they were leaving for Cuba the
very next day.

Sixty-Eight

We spent their last evening in Lisbon together, retracing our journeys, voicing our opinions, and trying to make sense of all the world's madness. I was pleased to learn that their children, Emilia, her twin brother Arthur, Alex, and my good friend Lotte were safe in America. They had been there for more than two years and were healthy and busily occupied with their new lives.

After several failed attempts to leave Naples, they had finally said their emotional goodbyes, leaving only days after the outbreak of the war, before Mussolini and Italy chose to act. Their departure had been sudden and chaotic. They had been given less than twenty-four hours' notice, when the port's shipping lanes were briefly reopened and they found berths on one of the last ships to depart Naples.

For Paul and Mamarella, we learned, the situation had become more difficult. They could not join their children. Because both had been born in Germany, they found themselves standing in line, waiting. Like for us, the quota system made their United States immigration visas difficult to obtain. While they waited, they continued to operate the pensione, providing rooms and meals to those in need. Mamarella told us tragic stories about the many refugees who passed through their doors.

Then their situation in Naples became unsettled. When the British began shelling the Naples port and bombing the industrial areas in February, the American consulate closed its doors and moved to Rome. That was when it became necessary to follow, and they gave the keys to the Pensione Alexandra to their landlord.

When they left, they each carried one suitcase, room for a few clothes, and some cooking utensils, only what was necessary. Their memories of nearly a half-century and whatever didn't fit were left behind. There was no choice. They left with little money and could only afford to take what they could carry, and they were forced to rely upon the kindness of others. I had tears in my eyes when Mamarella told me these things. I felt so bad for these very proud and good people.

Mamarella said that in Rome, they were taken in by a kind older woman who owned a small guesthouse and was sympathetic. She allowed them to stay in her tiny attic apartment, and since Mamarella helped with the chores, the rent was set to what they could afford to pay. There they continued their wait. There was little else they could do. They listened to the radio at night, and Paul went to the American consulate each day, where he stood with others, all trying to learn more about their situation. But the waiting list remained lengthy. There were so many trying to leave, and they were given little encouragement from consulate officials. All they were told was to stay safe and wait.

Finally, in the summer, when America's immigration policies were abruptly changed to discourage Jewish refugees, Paul felt that their time was running out. Mamarella had close relatives who had remained in Germany, and they were unsure whether, because of this, their visas would ever be approved. They knew their funds would not last and they could no longer afford to take any more risks. They worried about their safety. What would Mussolini do if the Germans marched into Italy? Would they be sent to concentration camps, too?

When they heard rumors that transit visas were about to be denied and borders across France and Spain to Lisbon were beginning to close, they reluctantly gave up on America and began to search elsewhere. They knew they needed berths on a ship before they could be issued documents allowing them to travel to Lisbon. All they wanted was to be with their children.

That's why they were going to Cuba. They were unsure how long they would be forced to live there, but it appeared to be their only option. Mamarella's first cousin's daughter lived in Havana and had helped arrange their visas. The children had found the money to pay for their tickets. At least, in Cuba, they would be safe. There they could wait until they were granted permission to enter the United States

Josef and I said little. We had our stories, too, but listening was the best thing we could do. I couldn't help but think about our situation, about the crates with all of our belongings that had found their way to Lisbon. I thought about how fortunate we had been with Josef's inheritance and wondered how it was that our visas had been granted. How had we jumped ahead of them in the line for America?

As we cried and said goodbye that evening, I wondered if we would ever see Mamarella and Paul again. We knew that our final destination would be New York City. Josef had exchanged letters with an old associate, someone he had worked with in Paris. If he could pass the exams and be licensed to practice again, he thought there would be a position at a hospital.

There was no way of knowing what might happen to Paul and Elsa or how long they would stay in Cuba. Mamarella told us that if they finally made it to America, they would go to Chicago. That's where Emilia was. Mamarella had an older sister who lived nearby. They would stay with her. She knew they had no money and had offered them a room in her home.

Sixty-Nine

We woke to the noisy commotion on the streets of Baixa. In Lisbon, it was Monday morning, December 8, 1941. We heard people shouting. That's how we first learned that the United States had been attacked. The Japanese navy had conducted a surprise military strike against the naval base at Pearl Harbor in Honolulu in the United States territory of Hawaii.

I remember thinking I knew nothing of these distant places. Josef told me we were nearly thirteen thousand kilometers from Pearl Harbor, halfway across the world. There was little else known that morning. No one seemed to have any idea what this might mean.

We learned more the following day, but even then the reports were confusing. Most thought that a conflict between Japan and the United States in the Pacific would have little to do with the war being fought in Europe and North Africa. A short while later the details began to emerge. By the end of that week, Germany and Italy had joined Japan, and America had responded. Then the entire world was at war.

I can only tell you that Lisbon seemed more abuzz with intrigue after the Japanese bombed Pearl Harbor. Nerves were on edge, particularly for those preparing to board ships. When America entered the war, there were widespread rumors that American relief efforts would be halted and American citizens evacuated. Yet it seemed that this did not happen. Instead, the urgency of these relief efforts to get refugees out of harm's way only appeared to increase.

Everyone was threatened by the war, and we heard many speculate that Portugal was profiting, that the country's hands were deep in the pockets of all sides of the conflict. Mostly we were tired and exhausted by the worry. These feelings refused to stop. We were anxious to depart. All we wanted was to be done with this war, to be somewhere safe and go forward with our lives. And now we wondered about America.

Seventy

We held our breath, monitored news from the war, and counted the days until departure. Our worries continued to increase, again for good reason. After the attack at Pearl Harbor, American Export Lines, a company that operated four passenger ships out of Lisbon, suddenly stopped their service across the Atlantic. They feared that their ships would come under attack by German U-boats.

Spanish and Portuguese ships still carried passengers, but then Spain announced that it would suspend its operations to the U.S. Their ships would carry passengers only to approved ports in Latin America. Every day there was a new announcement, and everything remained uncertain. All we could do was wait and cross our fingers. Our tickets were for berths on a thirty-five-year-old Portuguese ship that had been seized from the Germans and renamed during World War I. Fortunately, the *Nyassa's* service had not been canceled.

At noon on Tuesday, January 28, 1942, we joined the other eight hundred third-class passengers anxiously standing in line, ready to board. We watched the limousines and taxis arrive, carrying the elegantly dressed first- and second-class passengers. There was strict separation. They would travel in comfort.

No one complained. We were grateful to be leaving. Our accommodations were simple but all that we needed: bunks on the lowest deck, meals served in an open mess hall on the first level, and limited outdoor seating available where one could spend the day.

As the ship left Lisbon's dock later that evening, we couldn't help but notice that there were no lights on any other ships near the port. The *Nyassa's* lights were kept lit to let any German U-boats know that the ship belonged to a neutral nation. Two days later we arrived in Casablanca, where we watched a procession of additional war-weary passengers board.

The remainder of the trip was largely uneventful. We all had idle time to reflect. I imagine everyone wondered what would come next. Most were left to their diversions. Many read, some played cards, many slept under blankets in the sun, and others spent their time engaged in conversation.

Josef and I spent most of our afternoons napping on the outdoor deck. We heard some gossip about minor clashes between passengers whose nerves might have been frayed, but most of us were entertained by the notion that we had been fortunate enough to secure our berths. Two weeks after we left Lisbon, the *Nyassa* pulled into port in Hamilton, Bermuda.

◆

There was one tragic episode during our three-week voyage. A six-year-old child died when she slipped under a railing and fell to the lower deck shortly before we docked in Bermuda. This was such a sad and terrible time for the family, who had traveled so far. I don't believe there was a dry eye on the *Nyassa* that afternoon. We all cried as we watched the small coffin being carried off the ship.

◆

Perhaps more than most, I've had the good fortune to encounter a few coincidences in my life, and I believe I have told you the story of each. The first occurred in Berlin when Frau Samson introduced me to Josef, who, years earlier, had been my brother's doctor. The second was in Lisbon, when we were suddenly reunited with our old friends Paul and Mamarella. On the *Nyassa*, there was a third coincidence, one that was equally remarkable and would shape the years that followed.

One afternoon, as we were sitting outside on the deck, Josef struck up a conversation with a charming couple from Germany close to my age. Like everyone on the ship, they had survived a difficult journey. As we conversed, we learned that there was something else we shared in common, a love for Naples. Several years earlier, George and Nina Winkle had traveled there for a wedding and had stayed at a lovely, small pensione overlooking the Bay of Naples, the Pensione Alexandra. You cannot imagine our surprise. They knew the Oulman family.

◆

Three days after we left Bermuda, we began to celebrate as we watched the *Nyassa* approach the dock in Newport News, Virginia. Most of the third-class passengers would continue their journey to Cuba and ports in South America, but this was our destination.

That afternoon, as we excitedly walked arm in arm down the ramp and left the ship to meet with the immigration officials, my only thought was that once again my world was spinning and I had no idea if it was going faster or starting to slow down.

I was thirty-two years old. None of this seemed possible. It had only been nine years since I had left Berlin, but it seemed like a lifetime. Just like when I arrived at Gare de Nord in Paris, everything here would be new. Now my world would be reinvented again: a new language, a new culture, a new way of life. Neither of us could predict what might come next. But that did not matter. Somehow Josef and I had survived this journey and still had one another to cling to.

Seventy-One

Our stay in Newport News was brief. It was only a matter of days before we found our way to New York City. There we rented an apartment on the fourth floor of a recently modernized Beaux-Arts building on Riverside Drive, in the Audubon Terrace neighborhood of Washington Heights, an area populated with mostly European immigrants much like ourselves.

For me, this was an easy decision. As soon as I saw it, I knew, and Josef quickly agreed. The apartment building was on a tree-lined street that reminded us of Paris. The rooms were spacious and bright, and when I opened the front window and peered out, I was greeted by a small park with a bench and the scent of flowers that filled the air from the park's small garden.

It didn't take long to furnish our new home. We had the three crates that followed us from Paris: the art deco tables, settee, chairs, cabinets, glass-fronted bookcases, medical textbooks and literary classics, silver vases, crystal and china, silver tea service, radiola, and gramophone. There were oil paintings, etchings, and watercolors to be hung on the walls and oriental rugs to set about upon the polished wooden parquet floors.

Most had started their journey long before Paris. These were the furnishings Hilda had purchased shortly after she and Josef had married, when she had decorated their Berlin apartment, before the Great War had begun. Many items had traveled further: the wedding gifts and heirlooms from Hilda's family. They had found their way from San Francisco. Some items were even from Japan, like the small black lacquered cabinet, a turn-of-the-century purchase from Yokohama.

We filled the study with Josef's desk and old typewriter and lined the walls with the settee and a few chairs. Josef's cherished baby grand piano nearly overwhelmed the sitting room. A bit worn from the journey and in need of a good tuning, it wasn't long before he was able to resume his morning practices. And as we had done every morning in Paris, I sat close by his side on one of my favorite possessions, the two-person bench. There I watched and carefully turned the pages.

The Hofuhrmacher clock? It survived the journey, too. Now we knew it was finally time to silence the chime. There was no longer a need to hear its sound, but I did use the brass key to faithfully wind the clock every eight days. The ticking swing of the pendulum was a familiar memory, one that helped me sleep each evening. We put it by our bedside. It was finally home and where it belonged.

354 | RALPH WEBSTER

When we unpacked, a few items were missing. One was the small painting Hilda had purchased in Berlin from Moïche Shagalov in 1914, before he had changed his name. We could only assume that it had been confiscated when the crates had passed through one of the border crossings by someone who had recognized its value. Despite our many attempts, the painting was never found.

◆

I've lived long enough to know that certain moments can never be understood. When Josef and I left Lisbon and encountered the Winkles on the *Nyassa*, we found it hard to believe that they also knew Lotte, my friend from the Pensione Alexandra in Naples. She was their childhood friend. They had grown up together in Germany. That's why they had visited Naples in 1937. When Lotte married Mamarella's son, Alex, George and Nina traveled there to help celebrate their marriage.

Not long after we settled in New York, George and Nina telephoned and suggested we meet for dinner. That evening Alex and Lotte joined us. It was a joyous reunion, and we quickly learned that we all shared much in common. We began having dinner together each month, a cherished tradition that ended only when I was the last one left of our small group of six. For five decades, these dinners became our way to share the happiness we had found in America. There were always reasons to celebrate: birthdays, anniversaries, important events in our lives.

I will never forget the reunion parties we had when Mamarella and Paul finally arrived from Cuba and Emilia came to visit or when Alex's nephew and his lovely wife, Ginger, began to join us. These were wonderful, treasured times. We were all so fortunate to be here. America has always treated us well.

◆

For Josef and me, the years in New York passed quickly, too quickly, like Josef once said, "in the blink of an eye." They were filled with friendships and wonderful memories: long walks in Riverside Park along the Hudson River, quiet evenings reading, small dinner parties, visits to museums and galleries, concerts and musical performances, summer vacations in Maine, afternoons with Josef's easel and paints, and mornings in front of the piano. We lived a comfortable and peaceful life, perhaps a little self-indulgent, as we didn't have children or any other family, but one that I have always thought was well deserved, particularly after all that Josef had been through.

In New York, Josef was able to practice medicine again. First it had been Berlin, then Paris, and finally New York. I imagine few can make that claim. After passing New York State Board examinations, he was recertified and appointed to the staff at the New York

City Hospital, where he worked until his seventieth birthday in 1949.

After Josef retired, he began a private practice and opened a small office on Park Avenue. He went there every morning. That was how Josef was, serious about his profession, curious about everything, and always opinionated and set in his ways – like his mother and just as he was in Berlin when I first met him. As for me, I regained the position I always liked best. I became a *hausfrau* and devoted my time and attention to being by Josef's side. That really was all I ever wanted to do.

◆

We returned to Europe on a few occasions, never to Berlin or anywhere in Germany. Neither of us could bear the thought of going there. Those memories were long forgotten. But we did enjoy old, cherished habits in Paris and spent our days walking the streets and joining in the conversations at cafes. And we found our way back to Naples. The Pensione Alexandra was no longer there, but the views of the Bay of Naples were exactly the same.

Wherever we were, Josef donned his beret and painter's frock, the one with the smudge that I always detested. He couldn't resist spending afternoons with his brushes and easel in the Parc Monceau aside the Pavillon de Chartres or by the fountain filled with pigeons at the Villa Comunale in Naples. And I couldn't resist sitting in my favorite place, silently by his side, and observing.

For my fortieth birthday, in 1950, Josef treated me to a trip to France to visit our old friend Moïche. We were always grateful for his help and had stayed in touch over the years. After Bella died, Moïche remarried and returned to Southern France, where he was living in a small medieval town near the French Riviera.

◆

It was early in the spring of 1961, only months before Josef's eighty-second birthday, that I first observed the changes. It began with the little things that often go unnoticed, a small trembling in the hands, a little shortness of breath, words that were forgotten, steps that were slower, and stumbles that occasionally made one fall, those random things that mean little until they are repeated too many times and become cause for concern. I know others noticed as well.

◆

By summer, the piano keys were left untouched, and the bench stayed empty. Then one morning in August, the day after Josef died, I woke up to find myself alone in a silent apartment, left with words that remained unspoken.

◆

It was only after Josef died that I began writing again. I found joy and comfort in doing what he once encouraged me to do. We still had the old leather-bound notebook that his grandmother had given him for his ninth birthday, the one with the gilded pages he had once started to fill.

That was when I penned many of the stories you are reading here. I started slowly, picking up where I had left off in Paris when the war began, when Josef was sent to the internment camp and I sat alone in the back of the neighborhood cafe with my single glass of wine.

Seventy-Two

When I opened the mailbox one morning several weeks after Josef died, I found a letter from our attorney. He requested a meeting in his office – at my earliest convenience. An issue had been brought to his attention, a matter of urgency and importance that required a private and confidential discussion, something that I have kept close to my heart and have chosen never to share with others, not even those closest to me.

◆

Not long after Josef's obituary and death notice were published in the New York newspapers, there was an inquiry from an attorney. His client wished to contest Josef's will and challenge the distribution of his estate. The will had named me as the sole beneficiary, and I was the subject of this dispute. The attorney's client, an eighty-year-old woman residing in New York City, asserted that she was the legally entitled Mrs. Josef Samson. When I was told of this, I was in utter disbelief.

As discussions proceeded, evidence was presented – a marriage certificate and other documents, conclusive proof that this person was *another Mrs. Samson*, Josef's second wife. She married Josef before I met him, in Berlin in 1925, and they remained married as our relationship blossomed - until he suddenly abandoned her and disappeared in March of 1933 without reason or notice. When she returned from a five-day visit to her mother's home in Hamburg, she found nearly all of the possessions from their apartment removed, and despite multiple attempts to locate him, he was never seen or heard from again.

A number of years later, Mrs. Samson left Germany, moved to the United States, and became a resident of New York City. She claimed to have never remarried, and there were no children. When she read Josef's obituary in the newspaper, she was completely surprised as several decades had passed since his disappearance. Prior to seeing this notice, she had had no reason to believe that Josef had survived the war.

◆

When I was confronted with this information and became convinced that the facts were true, I was devastated – financially, as I had no funds of my own and no skills to support myself, and emotionally, as this came as a complete and sudden surprise to me, too. I was shocked. I had no idea. How could this have been possible? How could I not have known? How could Josef have deceived me? With time, the financial aspects of this dispute were settled and resolved. There is no need to include any of those details here. They are no longer important.

My emotions are a different matter. They will always remain clouded and confused. What I do want to say to anyone who may read this now is that despite my lingering questions, life has taught me that love is not always perfect but it is worth enjoying.

◆

Today I understand that I am *The Other Mrs. Samson*, the wife of a man who was still married. This was never my plan, not my intention. Do I wish my life would have been different? I cannot say – only that I chose the life that I have lived.

Others can ask whether I was the cause, whether I could have been part of this secret and never known, whether I was too young to notice and might have been taken advantage of, whether Josef told me and I chose not to listen, or whether I did always suspect but refused to care and simply closed my eyes.

Now there are times when I talk to myself and ask, if Mutti had lived, would she have suspected? What would she have told me? Would she have asked? Would she have allowed this to happen? These questions continue. The answers, I will never know.

And when I think of Josef, my heart still aches, and I long to have his arms around me. That will never change. I wonder how unhappy he must have been to have done this, how difficult it must have been to keep this hidden for so many years. Was this woman the enemy who had once been his friend, the secret he could never tell me? And why had she not found him? I know there were ways. How hard did she try? How much had she loved him?

Today I can only judge the man I knew and loved, not the man I did not know. I have chosen to forgive and forget. I can only hope that Mrs. Samson did the same.

◆

It is true that when Josef died, he left me with many un-answered questions. Was he selfish? Was he dishonest? Was he good, or was he bad? I have struggled with these questions. And someday soon the answers will no longer matter. Then others will be left to decide.

As for me? Now that I have finished writing these pages, I will put them where they belong – into that little box hidden in a secret place that will always be forgotten. Then I will do what Papa always chose to do. I will prefer to be content. "Why should I spend my time worrying about these things when there are so many better things to do?" For the days that are left, I would rather spend my time remembering the wonderful life Josef and I spent together.

Epilogue

The first time we entered Katie's apartment, Ginger and I were struck with the sensation that time had stood still. That was in 1995 – the day she moved to the study and remade the bed. She even left us some chocolates on our pillows. At that point, we did not know that these stories existed.

It had been more than thirty years since Josef had died, and it was apparent that Katie had changed little in the apartment, not even the black rotary dial telephone that sat on the desk and that she still leased for a few dollars each month from the phone company. Perhaps the only items added were a transistor radio on the kitchen table, the small black and white television sitting on a metal stand in a corner of the bedroom, the one with the rabbit ears antenna, and the framed photo of Josef that sat next to her bed.

As we opened the front door, the polished Shreve and Company silver tea service was there to greet us. It sat atop an art deco table in the hallway. A beret and painter's frock hung from the coat stand. A silver mono-grammed vase with fresh flowers sat on the small table in the kitchen, and an old manual typewriter rested on the desk in the study. Josef's medical bag was in the closet, and the Hofuhrmacher mantel clock sat on a small stand near her bed.

Everything appeared as it must have always been: the pictures on the wall, the books in the glass cabinets, the oriental rugs on the floor, the Ritmüller & Sohn baby grand piano, and even the two-person piano bench. The good china and wine glasses were still being used, but there were no longer twenty-four of each. Time had taken its toll, and their numbers had dwindled.

One day Katie showed us a collection of photos of Josef's apartment in Berlin, wonderful photos that Hilda had arranged to be taken after decorating their rooms in 1914. Copies were to be sent to her mother in San Francisco. The similarity was startling, the same objects, the same furniture, the same arrangements. And I imagine that if we had been given a photo of the Paris apartment, it, too, would have appeared much the same. Some things tend not to change.

We have always thought that Katie was grateful that she and Hilda shared a connection, that they shared the same husband, and that she was able to complete the life Hilda had started. Like she said, she felt a certain kinship. Katie was quite content in this role. She wasn't bothered that she had added little – not much more than her clothes, a clock, and a two-person piano bench. Katie was happy to be the caretaker. Her love story is certain. We know that all she really cared about was Josef.

◆

When Katie died, she had lived in the New York apartment on Riverside Drive for sixty-three years, from when she was thirty-two to when she was just over ninety-five years of age. Josef had been with her there for the first nineteen years, but for the forty-four years that followed, Katie had lived alone. She had had this time to wrestle with her memories, the stories written on her pages, and the secret she kept buried until the end.

We think there was one time when she tried to tell us, when she said a few words about another Mrs. Samson, an incomplete sentence that ended with more questions than answers. That day, much like the day after Lotte died, when we sat at the Cloisters, her words caught us by surprise and appeared suddenly out of thin air. They were not part of any conversation. We assumed she was talking about Hilda.

Ginger and I were quite surprised and shocked to discover Katie's secret. Only then did we begin to ask ourselves whether we had been confused. Perhaps she was referring to Josef's second wife that day. Now, years later, we believe that Katie did want to tell us more, to explain, to teach us something about life and love. Why else did she leave these papers for us to find? Had she forgotten about them, or did she truly want us to know one day? We will never know the answers to these questions. What we do know is that talking about herself was never her nature. Like she once said, "Don't waste your time. I don't know why anybody would be interested in my old stories. I'll leave it to you to decide."

◆

Katie's stories were complicated and sad, but somehow she managed to adopt the trait for happiness that she always admired in her father. She didn't worry about those things when there were so many better things to do. That's how she was. She didn't dwell on things much, at least, not when we were with her. And when she did, like her Papa, she remembered the good times and found ways to forget the bad ones.

Hilda had a much different story, one with a tragic and premature end that was never expected. And while we only were able to know her through her letters, we're pretty certain that when it came to how she lived her life, she would have always been given some very good advice. Oma's words would have been her guide.

◆

Not long after Josef died in 1961, the Hofuhrmacher clock stopped, as if it knew to do this by its own free will. It wasn't the first time. It had stopped by itself before, in 1947 and again in 1959. The first two times, Katie had chosen to have it repaired and left notations written inside its door. After Josef died, Katie never used the brass key to wind it again. We will never be certain about her reason, but she did once remark, "Memories can only be remembered. They can never be repaired."

◆

Today the Hofuhrmacher mantel clock Katie's father gave her on the day she was born sits silently on a shelf in our great room. The pendulum does not swing, and the brass key remains untouched. There is no need for repair. We think the clock is perfect just as it is. The seven-piece silver tea service Hilda and Josef received as a wedding gift from San Francisco rests in the dining room. As it often begs to be polished, it is not quite as perfect. We have never used it to serve tea but are reminded of these stories.

As for the lacquered Japanese cabinet, its journey has not ended. Now the cabinet is in Baltimore. Our granddaughter Ryan keeps it in her bedroom. Sometimes I wonder if we should tell her about the secret compartment. Someday it will be Ryan's turn to look. Then she can be surprised to discover what we might have left inside. I can assure you that it is not empty. We all have our secrets.

I will never be certain whether I actually found the secret place Katie referred to when she wrote her stories or whether this was the same hidden box Josef referred to when he saved Hilda's letters. I can only say that the cabinet does exist and the box I found was full of clues.

The day when I climbed into the attic to look for furnace filters and stumbled upon the cabinet, I never expected to begin a treasure hunt, certainly not one like this. But now that the story is complete, I am quite satisfied with the notion that the treasure may have found me. And while I have no way of knowing whether there really is a little box hidden in a secret place that has long been forgotten, I cherish the idea and often wonder whether most of us might be happier believing that such a place actually exists.

Acknowledgments

A book like this cannot be written without real-life characters. Hilda, Josef, Katie, and the others gave me the literary freedom to write these pages. Without them, there would be no story to tell. Of course, anytime one tries to recount the past, there are gaps to be filled. Then I was left to my imagination. And, wishing no harm or misrepresentation, I altered names whenever it seemed appropriate.

There are many others, not characters in the story, but real people in my life today who helped with this project. They all must be thanked because their contributions were extraordinary. My grandson, Brady Patterson, read the first chapters in their earliest form and was always a source of encouragement. Reviewers of various drafts included my talented friend of fifty years and old work colleague, Barbara Ifshin; my friends John Ramsay, Dave Connaughton, Fritzi Redgrave, and Steve Kenney; and my sister Joan Webster-Vore and cousin Ruth Mendelson. My cousin Manfred Sprung and his daughter

Nadine helped translate old letters. My neighbor Dr. Scott Starsman, who, in addition to being a history buff, demonstrated an amazing ability to find details that don't quite comport, and his wife, Stacey, taught me about the complications of pregnancy in the early 1900s. Rachel Bryant at the Camden County library spent a great deal of time with the manuscript and offered a wealth of insights. Romi Lindenberg, the talented Israeli artist, designed the cover, and Jefferson, from First Editing, once again proved that he has the patience to find and correct all things I have missed. To Nina Price, the Audible narrator, a very special thanks. You have the remarkable ability to bring to life what is written on paper.

The toughest critic was my wife, Ginger. There is no one more deserving of my gratitude. Not only is she my collaborator, best friend, and lifelong partner, but she is also my biggest cheerleader. Throughout she was dedicated, devoted, and giving of her time. Perhaps written in invisible ink, her fingerprints are on every page. I know that she is happy to have our conversations move on to different topics. While she was unrelenting with her support and encouragement, she was patient with my unrelenting chatter.

The final thank you is reserved for you, the readers. You allow me to share the story, and that makes it all worthwhile. I will forever be grateful.

R.W. 2020

Book Club Discussion

- Parents and grandparents played an important role in the lives of Hilda and Katie. Which relatives most significantly changed the course of Hilda's and Katie's lives?

- Hilda is first introduced as a pampered and spoiled little girl. How did her character change over time, and what events shaped her personality?

- Did you learn anything new about American immigration in the mid-1800s and lifestyle/cultural changes that took place in San Francisco into the early 1900s?

- How did Hilda's and Joseph's lives change in Berlin during WWI? Were you surprised that she chose to stay? How did the war affect young Katie and her family?

- Did you like the relationship between Joseph and his mother? Between his mother and Katie?

- With a thirty-one-year age difference, is it believable that Katie and Joseph could be so in love?

- What did you think of Joseph's character? Do you think he was involved in some kind of underground movement of German Jews? Can you justify his secrecy and dishonesty?

- There were many difficulties for refugees escaping Europe during WWII: different and frequently changing rules depending on country of birth, logistical nightmares, and dangerous undercurrents. Joseph and Katie's pathway was quite different from Paul and Mamarella's. Are there parallels in today's world?

- A Hofuhrmacher mantel clock features prominently in the book. Discuss its importance to Katie.

- Was the ending a surprise? Were you surprised that Katie had never disclosed this "secret" to others?

- Could there be a little box hidden in your attic?

ABOUT THE AUTHOR

 Award-winning author Ralph Webster received worldwide acclaim when his first book, *A Smile in One Eye: A Tear in the Other* was voted by readers as a Goodreads 2016 Choice Awards Nominee for Best Memoir/Autobiography. His books, *A Smile in One Eye, One More Moon,* and now this third book, *The Other Mrs. Samson,* are proven book club selections for thought-provoking and engaging discussions.

Whether in person or online, Ralph welcomes his exchanges with readers and makes every effort to participate in conversations about his books. Now retired, he lives with his wife, Ginger, on the Outer Banks of North Carolina. In addition to writing, he enjoys his time with family, playing tennis, hiking, and traveling the world. Ralph can be reached through his website.

www.ralphwebster-author.com

Made in the USA
Columbia, SC
17 February 2021